THE PRINCESS

 OF

THORNWOOD DRIVE

THE PRINCESS

OF

THORNWOOD DRIVE

KHALIA MOREAU

FOREVER

NEW YORK   BOSTON

Forever
Hachette Book Group
1290 Avenue of the Americas, New York, NY 10104
read-forever.com
twitter.com/readforeverpub

First Edition: November 2023

Forever is an imprint of Grand Central Publishing. The Forever name and logo are trademarks of Hachette Book Group, Inc.

The publisher is not responsible for websites (or their content) that are not owned by the publisher.

The Hachette Speakers Bureau provides a wide range of authors for speaking events. To find out more, go to hachettespeakersbureau.com or email HachetteSpeakers@hbgusa.com.

Forever books may be purchased in bulk for business, educational, or promotional use. For information, please contact your local bookseller or the Hachette Book Group Special Markets Department at special.markets@hbgusa.com.

Print interior design by Taylor Navis

Library of Congress Cataloging-in-Publication Data

Names: Moreau, Khalia, author.
Title: The princess of Thornwood Drive / Khalia Moreau.
Description: First edition. | New York : Forever, 2023.
Identifiers: LCCN 2023026356 | ISBN 9781538725269 (trade paperback) | ISBN 9781538725276 (ebook)
Subjects: LCGFT: Fantasy fiction. | Novels.
Classification: LCC PS3613.O717257 P75 2023 | DDC 813/.6--dc23/eng/20230609
LC record available at https://lccn.loc.gov/2023026356

ISBNs: 9781538725269 (trade paperback), 9781538725276 (ebook)

Printed in the United States of America

LSC-C

Printing 1, 2023

To those who sometimes feel like they're struggling to survive
in a world that is oftentimes not so kind.

THE PRINCESS

OF

THORNWOOD DRIVE

PART 1

LAKE FOREST'S HOME FOR CHANGELS

CHAPTER
1

LAINE

Every morning my sister's screams ring through the hallways of our old Victorian home like the echoes of a banshee. Most times, I'm already dressed and halfway to her room as it starts. When it comes to caring for her, if I don't stick to a schedule like the social worker suggested, things can get dangerously out of hand. But this morning, I'm spitting out my toothpaste when she wakes.

Shit. Flossing is gonna have to wait till tonight. Till whenever. We can't be late. Not today.

I scramble into a shirt and some jeans, and march down the wooden stairs of our house like a soldier on a mission. The air is tinged with the scent of burnt eggs, stale coffee, and broken dreams. Today, there's also the earthy smell of rain.

The downpour starts as soon I'm on the house's ground level, as if desperate to throw a wrench in my plans. But I won't let it. Just like I do anytime panic wants to set in, I silently hum "Ode to Joy." It's one of the songs our dad used to play on the baby grand piano in the living room every morning.

Oftentimes, my sister and I played along with him while Mom watched.

But all that was before the accident…before the family was reduced to one daughter who can no longer speak intelligibly or walk properly, and one daughter buckled under the weight of knowing she's the reason things went to shit.

The reason things went to shit—my psychiatrist says that idea can't stay in my head forever, but I'm certain she's wrong.

When I enter the living room, my foot catches on some books piled on the floor, and I fall hard to my knees on the hardwood. Bracing myself against the pain, I rise to my feet and pick up *Lynchburd's Principles of Animal Nutrition*—one of several books I should have sold the moment I decided not to go back to college, but I can't bear to part with it. I put it on top of the piano.

The living room used to be a disco of laughter, storytelling, and good vibes. Now it's just a cacophony of dust and sorrows.

Refusing to let the thought settle, I focus on the pain in my knees, bending up and down a few times to work out the kinks. Sharp pains zip up and down my legs, and I stifle a groan. I'm twenty-two, but I swear my joints scream I'm at least fifty.

Once the kinks feel worked out, I continue with my mission, heading through the narrow hallway that leads to the only bedroom on the first floor—Alyssa's room. The cold metal of the doorknob sends a jitter up my spine, but I keep my hand firmly on the knob.

"Remember, be steadfast, Laine," I tell myself softly, taking a deep breath. "It doesn't matter how much she cries or screams today. You can't let her have her way." Like my mother, who'd whisper motivational words to herself in trying times, I murmur those words aloud until I feel hardwired and, on the count of three, open the door.

The scent of iodine, alcohol, and muscle rub hits me like a brick wall. I sneeze as I turn on the light and find the home-care hospital bed in the center of the room empty. Alyssa is in the corner of the room closest to the curtained window, rocking back and forth, hitting her head with her hands, her fingers stiff and splayed.

I grab the large black comb off the dressing table near the door. "Come on, Lissa. Just bear with me today, huh? I know you're not a fan of the process, but I need to comb your hair and get you ready."

Alyssa's hazel eyes focus on me, if only for a second. "King! Queen! In the forest! King! Queen!"

My chest gets tight.

Since Alyssa roused from a two-month coma a year ago, the only discernible thing she's said is "King. Queen. In the forest."

The first neurologist said her speaking at all was a miracle and wanted to write all these articles for medical journals about her case. The second neurologist, who I got when Alyssa started to seem more like a show pony than a patient, was slightly less impressed and simply insisted I start physical therapy sessions. As for the third neurologist, who was assigned to her when we switched to a cheaper health insurance a few months back? She says I shouldn't read too much into anything Lissa says. Repetition of meaningless words isn't uncommon in cases like these.

There's no money for a fourth opinion. No money for a lot of things.

Get it together, Laine. We can't be late.

I move some of Alyssa's curls over her shoulder and stroke

her cheek gently. "No hitting or biting today, okay? We need to detangle that hair. If we don't, we're gonna have to cut it."

As soon as the words leave my mouth, I glance at the picture of our parents on Alyssa's wall. Dad's blond hair curls slightly at the edge of his jaw. Our mother's hair—dark and glistening, much like her skin—is coiled into a dozen Bantu knots. Somehow, even though they smile, their eyes sear into me, and I lash out. I always lash out.

"You can't blame me, can you? Grease. Moisturizers. Combs. They're expensive. And let's not forget all the detanglers I have to buy because she won't let me comb it half the time!" I yell at the picture as if my parents might answer. Thankfully, they don't. I'm already on Xanax for anxiety since I lost them. I don't need to add more meds to the list, not when I'm already struggling to afford Alyssa's.

Muttering something I can't make out, Alyssa pulls her hands up to her face. I clasp her hands in my own and steady her to her feet. Her lack of coordination makes walking long distances practically impossible, but she can go for short distances with someone to help.

At first, I think she's rather agreeable today; she lets me guide her to a cushioned chair next to the bed. But as soon as the comb touches her scalp, she's screaming at the top of her lungs and trying to hobble back to the corner. I keep her grounded by putting a little pressure—maybe more than I'd care to use—on her shoulders. "I'm sorry, Lissa, but we're gonna have to comb it, especially today."

I don't wait for a response or whatever hints at understanding. I part her hair into sections, then start to detangle each bundle, working my way upward. After a few minutes, Alyssa's thrashing ceases, but she doesn't stop moaning. No, her moans persist until her curls are knot-free and braided into eight large plaits—the same style our mother enforced when we were children.

I rub her right hand gently. On her wrist is a black-beaded bracelet that consists of a small red and white charm shaped like Trinidad. Mom, originally from the Caribbean islands, bought the bracelets for us eight years ago when we visited to see her last surviving relative. She had been a little wary purchasing them, insistent we'd probably lose them upon our return home, but we begged until she buckled. After all, Dad always boasted how she got him one not long after they met. We wanted bracelets, too. Does Alyssa remember? I hope she does...hope she thinks of Mom and feels a little comfort.

With a ten-minute break post-hair combing factored into the schedule, I center Alyssa in the chair and turn on the television, flipping through the channels until I find one playing a Harry Potter movie. I'm not sure which one. I was never a die-hard fan like Alyssa. "You're going to a new day center today. They'll be able to help you, help us. But you know what Mom always said, first impressions matter. I don't want them thinking I'm totally unable to take care of you. If they think that, they might call the social worker and you'll end up—" I can't say the words. Alyssa might not fully understand what I'm saying, but I do. And while my sister very well sucks me dry, she's also the only thing keeping me together. If I lose her, I might lose myself.

So, like a sinner walking away from the pews, I make my way toward the kitchen. The sink is full of dishes, and the wooden floors are covered in an abstract pattern of muck. I ignore it, homing all my attention in on the mail.

All out of coffee grinds, I gulp down the cup I left out on the table the night before and begin sifting through the letters. Most are petty bills I can probably manage with a little more budgeting, but the large manila envelope from R. Maine Credit Collection Bureau and the letter from my uncle make my breath hitch.

Chest tight, I rip open the envelope from the collection bureau and skip to the last page once I've slid out the packet.

Shit. The six-figure sum at the bottom hasn't changed from any of the other notices they've sent. Light-headed, I shove the packet under a pile of magazines and open the envelope from my uncle, choosing to shoulder the negativities in one go.

The words *ridiculous, no, joke,* and *refuse* register before anything else in his letter, and I lower it with trembling hands. We might be blood, but he's made it clear: He couldn't care less about us, his brother's daughters. All he's interested in is our house.

I crumple up the letter. Numb—that's how Freidmore's words make me feel. I swallow hard, tasting the sour dregs of coffee.

I could feel worse. I certainly had when Freidmore showed up to my parents' funeral in his Versace suit, briefcase under one arm. I remember wondering why on earth he'd come then when he hadn't been to any birthdays or family parties before. But once I got the first letter from R. Maine Credit Collection Bureau, it made sense. One of Dad's business ventures had gone wrong, and he had put the house up as collateral. Unless Freidmore was willing to help his family, I'd have to find a way to pay back the bank.

Family. The word gives way to a surge of anger that hot-wires me like a dangerous circuit, and I throw my empty cup at the wall. I wish I could say sweet release washes over me as the ceramic shatters into pieces, but I can't. Because what really annoys me isn't the fact that Freidmore doesn't want to help us.

No, what gets me is the fact that I had to ask for help. The fact that I can't swallow my pride and leave our childhood home. But how could I leave it all behind? Dad's ashtray is still on the table, the pine tree Mom planted in the yard growing tall. Their stuff is still in their room, too. And I don't have any intention of moving it.

Fighting back tears, I do a little sweep of the area, then dump the shards in the bin. A part of me, a part I despise, starts thinking about different ways to garner pity...Freidmore's pity.

Maybe, if I write again and explain my situation in more detail, he'll change his mind. I'll tell him I'm struggling to buy soap and toothpaste...tampons. Throwing in the fact that I'm drinking stale coffee because I can't afford to just buy more should also pull on his heartstrings...right? It's all true.

Fooling myself into believing that my plan just might work, I wipe the tears welling in my eyes and focus on the only thing I can at the moment—Alyssa.

CHAPTER
2

ALYSSA

Rain conjures a dangerous vision upon the castle's walls, crystal ball–like droplets desperate to reveal bleak futures.

I ignore it, always try to ignore it. But I fail. For, in the rain, I see it—not my future but memories, ones that bring tears to my eyes and wails deep from my belly.

I try to force out the images, but they remain clear as day, taunting me.

I bite down on my tongue. Father's advisors stated it'd be dangerous to leave the castle to visit Laine at Tergo Academy with our uncle trying to seize control of the kingdom, but Father didn't care. Back then, I didn't care either. Laine, four years my elder, always got to experience things sooner than I. And one thing I wanted to experience was Tergo's fairy taverns—where the drinks are served in goblets and the boys are as strong as giants.

If only we knew it would lead to this—Father and Mother kidnapped, me cursed, and Laine doing her best not to fall apart at the seams.

Laine enters my chamber, shoulders hunched, black half circles under her brown eyes. More importantly, wearing a silver crown.

My insides swell with hope. The crown of a firstborn only ever turns gold when the life leaves the body of the current ruler of Mirendal, or that person chooses to relinquish power.

In other words, I have daily confirmation that Father and Mother are still alive.

Laine grabs a large comb from my wardrobe. She takes quick steps toward me today. "Please, Alyssa. Just bear with me. You're the second princess of Mirendal. I have to comb your hair."

Hair? I want to say. *You're worried about my hair when the king and queen are still out there? Are you still scouring the forest paths where our carriage was attacked? Still searching for a way to interrogate Uncle? You know he's likely behind this.* However, only *king* and *queen* and *forest* manage to escape my lips.

I let out the only thing I can unhindered—a wailing cry that echoes throughout my bedchamber.

Laine tightens her grip on the comb while calling upon Mirendal's guardian deity, Terra, for strength. "I have to detangle your hair, Alyssa. Terra knows the last thing I want to do is cut it."

As soon as the words *cut it* spill from her lips, she looks at the portrait of our mother and father.

So do I.

Unlike Father, Mother isn't originally from Mirendal but a land where people's skin is seemingly burned in bronze and coal. Her hair twists in on itself, the strands in a constant game of chase. She's beautiful. So beautiful Father thought to marry her despite the elders' objections, despite it almost costing him his crown.

Laine plants me in a chair and parts my hair into eight sections. She starts at the ends, working her way up until she reaches my roots. The comb catches dozens of knots, several beyond the point of detangling. And each time she tugs, I'm assaulted with a stabbing pain that runs across my scalp. Nevertheless, I do my best to comply.

For Laine cutting my hair…well, it's an act that won't break me, but I fear just might break her—the only person who truly empathized with my struggle of valuing my *otherness* growing up.

Once she's done, Laine taps on the crystal slab mounted on the wall, but I don't watch the moving images it casts. I focus on her. Only her.

"You're going to a new temple for changels today. If they deem you too untidy or unkempt, they might perform another inquest into your care. If that happens—" Laine shakes her head. "I'll be back soon to give you a bath. Till then, try not to think about the king and queen too much, okay? Let me worry about that, sister. Please."

I don't bother trying to respond. I can't, and I can't do as she asks. As soon as she leaves my chambers, I pore over every detail from that day one year ago. How the oracle had predicted an uneventful journey to Tergo, Laine's place of study. How Father decided to relieve several of the guards set to accompany us.

It was a mistake on his part. Our coachman had just brought the horses to a trot in a little clearing when something rammed into the side of our carriage, flipping it.

When I came to, Father and Mother were gone and I was alone in the forest. And the air? It was still ripe with dark magic. The kind I'm certain my uncle, who's been vying for Father's throne the last several decades, must have cast.

Laine reenters my chamber. "Ready for your bath?"

She doesn't wait for me to attempt to respond. She props me up and helps me into a wooden chair with a cushioned seat. Made of an enchanted bark found in a dragon's lair, the chair levitates slightly above the ground. It glides forward as Laine pushes its handles through the dimly lit west wing of the castle. There are no servants meandering through the hallways, no laughter. There are only tall pillars that whisper nothing but silence.

Laine slows the chair once we get to a cerulean-painted door, and as soon as she opens it, my eyes scour the bath chamber. One servant—her name was Merna—was always posted next to the pool. I almost expect to see her every time I come here, but I never do. Laine couldn't be sure how she'd react to me. After all, according to Mirendalian myth, changels—unfortunate humans cursed by dark magic—bring bad luck.

Archaic views, of course, much like the views some villagers have about our mixed lineage. But that doesn't change the fact that being shielded like this cuts deep. Too deep.

Once I'm done in the bath, Laine dries my skin and rubs me down in healing oils. She dresses me in commoner clothing—a long-sleeved dress with plain brown shoes. She lets me wear the bracelet from our mother's homeland. The beads aren't as expensive as most Mirendalian jewels and probably won't fetch more than one gold coin on the market. Still, just to be safe, Laine also presses her fingertips to the bracelet.

"A facie veterascet," she whispers.

The bracelet fades out of view twice before reappearing, much like a dying flame that reignites, and Laine smiles. Now, no one aside from the two of us will be able to see the bracelet.

It's an added precaution to ensure no one identifies me once I leave the castle, much like the fact that all the temples I've frequented aren't in Mirendal but the neighboring villages of our sister kingdom, Remwater.

Outside the castle, the sun hides behind thick gray clouds, and lightning illuminates the sky with a stunning display as rain pours down. Laine moves quickly, helping me out of my dragon chair and into the carriage. She then takes a step away from my chair and holds out her hand before whispering, "Parvus."

Within seconds, the chair begins to fold in on itself, shrinking in size to unfathomable proportions. It's another simple display of magic...a low-tier spell all Mirendalians learn from the moment they start spell-caster classes. But watching Laine perform it leaves a bitter taste in my mouth. Magic is also one of the things I lost when I was cursed, and I miss it. Who wouldn't?

Tight-lipped, Laine straightens her black cloak before sitting atop the carriage to steer four large brown horses. As always, the horses thunder through the less-traveled paths of our kingdom, their breaths coming heavy only until they stop at our destination—Lake Forest's Home for Changels.

Through the carriage window, I see Laine pull a small brown object from the inner pocket of her cloak and rest it on the ground. She takes a step back, whispering, "Creserce."

Like a seed rapidly blossoming into a flower, my dragon chair grows in size. It rises off the ground once it has fully morphed, and Laine helps me into it. "Lake Forest is not as bright as Remwater's Prestige Home for Changel Girls, but it isn't too bad," she says.

If I could voice an opinion, I would disagree. Mountainous oak trees surround Lake Forest's four-story structure, and its windows reflect little of the light that has begun to peek through the dissipating storm clouds. The scent of damp earth and fallen leaves might seem a redeeming quality. I've always loved the smell of the earth. However, the smell of something rotten also assaults my nostrils. A large woodland creature must have died somewhere nearby.

Laine readjusts the hood of her cloak before guiding me to the front door of the temple. She doesn't need to knock. A straight-faced woman with eyes as clear as winter frost opens the door. Her robe, like her hair, is a dark shade of red, indicating she's a regent—a white robe's helper. She shakes Laine's hand. "You must be Lamina High?"

"Yes," Laine says. Fake names are another precaution we take to ensure no one realizes that I'm a changel now.

The regent leads us inside, and the rotten smell grows stronger, stinging my eyes. I look at Laine, her breathing steady. Does she not smell it?

"Before a changel can join the others, the head of the temple usually needs to meet with a changel's guardian. But he's running quite late today," the regent says. "As such, we'll make an exception and allow your sister to watch the morning play."

Laine nods. "And what about the parchments I need to sign?"

"Once we take her to the hall, we'll head up to my chambers to deal with such matters," says the regent, and she gestures for us to keep moving.

I try to keep track of all the turns as she leads us down a winding hallway, but the green walls have no markers—no distinct paths to what begins to feel more and more like a murky swamp. By the time we stop, I'm completely disoriented, no way of knowing how to get back to the outside.

The regent pushes on a door, and we enter a large hall. Silent, she gestures for Laine to situate my chair next to a cluster of changels sitting in a straight line. Most of them, dressed in commoner clothing like my own, stare at an empty stage a few feet away.

Laine squeezes my hand gently. "I'll see you before the sun sets, okay?"

I want to reassure her that I'll be fine. I know she only sends me to these temples because she can't always tend to my needs and handle the kingdom's affairs at the same time. However, the smell of something dead is even more pungent in this room, and that makes my stomach churn hot bile.

Do you smell that? I try to ask. *Something smells dead.* However, "that…that…" is the only thing that leaves my mouth.

"Is she going to be okay?" the regent asks.

Laine nods slowly. "She'll feel a little better once she gets settled."

The regent nods and directs Laine to follow her out of the hall. As their backs fade from view, my uneasiness grows like a brewing storm. I try to focus on the positives. At least I can communicate with other changels. Not by speaking, but by a mental connection we can choose to establish.

I turn my head to the right to face a yellow-haired changel girl with a wide smile that appears almost unnatural. *"What's your name?"* I ask. *"Also, do you smell that?"*

"I'm Veranda, and I do smell that," the girl responds. Her grin remains relatively static. *"What's your name?"*

"Ferra," I say. It's the name I used at my previous temple for changels. Unlike Lake Forest, its bowels didn't reek of something foul.

The girl chuckles, but when she stops, her inner voice is raspy. *"You should have picked a better name."*

Wait, don't tell me . . . no. There's absolutely no way she could know. *"Excuse me?"*

She holds my gaze. *"My father was from Mirendal and a big supporter of your family, Princess. He used to clean the castle grounds. Sometimes, he'd bring me to work with him. A few springs ago I saw you playing in the courtyard. I would know your face anywhere."*

I inhale deeply, hands shaking. She—she knows my true identity. What will she do with that information? Does she work for my uncle? Better yet, is she even a real changel?

"You're scared?" Veranda asks.

Mother always said breaking someone's gaze is a sign that one is telling untruth, so I make sure to hold hers as I lie. *"No."*

But Veranda continues smiling. Smiling even though her voice in my head is a shrill cry. *"Well, I'm sorry to say this, Princess, but you should be."*

CHAPTER
3

LAINE

I breathe in the scent of French roast as I run to the register, eyeing the chain of customers that snakes all the way to the door.

"One small vanilla latte," says a girl decked out in Vineyard Vines apparel. She tucks a strand of hair behind her ear before turning to talk to her friend. "Do you think Landen is gonna be there?" she asks. "I have to look good if he's gonna be there."

I clear my throat. "It's gonna be $6.95."

The customer's eyes remain fixated on her friend. "Crop top with leggings or romper?"

Who the hell cares? "Excuse me, that will be $6.95."

The girl looks at me, confusion twisting her features. "I'm sorry, what?"

Looks like you have not a care in the world. "It's $6.95."

It takes a few seconds for things to click, but when they do, she fumbles through her bag. "OMG, I'm so sorry! I can't believe I forgot to pay. Like how, even?" She hands me a crisp twenty-dollar bill.

I give a small smile, but I won't lie. I'm bitter. Despite the girl's auburn hair and fine features, I see myself when I look at her. Not the Laine who's fixing her coffee, but the Laine who partied it up at college and pulled all-nighters in the library with her sorority sisters. "*Work hard, play hard*" was one of her mottos, and she didn't have any room for her family. If only she had been a little more accommodating, maybe the accident wouldn't have happened.

I step to the side so all the customers can get a good look at me. "I'm sorry about the delay, everyone. We're a little short-staffed today, but if you're patient, I'll do my best to get everyone's orders."

Short-staffed is one hell of an understatement. One of my coworkers already called in sick, and my other coworker, Jason, should have been here by now.

There are several peeved expressions, but I try not to lose any cool over it. If there's one thing taking care of Alyssa and the house has taught me, it's how to multitask.

I bounce between the register and the coffee machines, working my way through everyone's orders. My other coworkers would consider this a hassle, something to complain about. But not me. Aside from the fact that Glenn's Coffee Supreme offers pay considerably above minimum wage, it's located near Serca Grace Hospital and Serca College. In other words, it's almost always busy, and I like busy. Busy gets my mind off my uncle, the debt I can't pay . . . my sister.

I've made about twenty-eight lattes and thirteen hot chocolates when the shop finally clears out. The last customer takes with her some semblance of my peace. As soon as her foot is out the door, the only thing filling the silence is the classical music I blast over the speakers.

Desperate for a distraction, I try calling Jason to see why he's not here yet. I'm sent straight to voicemail, and I sigh. I haven't exactly been the most friendly since the accident, nor do I care to be. Being friendly, caring for someone other than my sister, requires energy I don't have. But strangely, today the anxiety that has cursed me since the accident, the anxiety I've done well to control, sits on my shoulder like a little devil. Or, as my mother would say, a jumbie. The red-eyed demon fiddles with my emotions, making me hypersensitive to things I usually don't bat an eyelid at.

Refusing to yield to her today, I count backward from one hundred, just like my psychiatrist taught me whenever my thoughts threaten to unravel.

100. Maybe Jason is sick?
99. Perhaps he overslept?
98. Oversleeping is the most reasonable explanation, right?
97. Yeah, it most definitely is. Jason has overslept several times before.
96. I don't oversleep often.
95. Alyssa makes that a little hard to do.
94. I wonder how things are going for her at Lake Forest.
93. Does she like it?
92. Maybe Jason is dead like my parents.
91. Maybe—Screw counting!

I phone my boss, Glenn. I do my best not to call him when my coworkers are late or fail to show up. I'd like to think it's because I'm cool, that person who isn't a snitch. However, the truth is I'm racking up favors. I never know when I might be unable to come to work. And while Glenn wouldn't necessarily throw a fit, I don't want anything to compromise my job. Not when he pays so well.

I run my hands through my hair, tugging at my curls when Glenn doesn't answer.

The jumbie nibbles on my ear, whispering, *What if Jason got into a car accident on his way to work? What if Glenn found out about it and is so distraught he isn't answering his phone? What if he's too busy playing those Facebook games to even care? You know he has an addiction, Laine.*

Sweating, I get up and shove a chocolate croissant in the microwave. Hopefully, the pastry will be enough to stop me from panicking over what is likely nothing. After all, Jason isn't my mom. He's not hanging upside down in a flipped car, his head smashed in, his limbs broken in several places. Nor is he my dad—his face barely recognizable from all the glass and debris that came flying at them on impact.

I take the croissant out of the microwave and try to focus on the pastry. But as I break it in two and molten chocolate oozes out of the center, my heart begins to thrum in my chest. *Is that how the blood flowed out of Mom's skull? Is that how—* My phone buzzes with a text. It's like a little touch from heaven, snapping me out of my reverie.

I rest the croissant on the wooden countertop behind the register and whip out my phone, breathing easier when I see Jason's name.

I don't need to swipe on the green bar to expand the message. He's only sent three short sentences, and they read: *I quit yesterday. I'm moving to Minnesota. Take care.*

Staring at the screen, I try to dig deep for a sense of anger, sadness, or shock. Jason didn't get into a car accident. He quit. He quit and didn't tell me. Did the times I covered for him before mean absolutely nothing? He could have at least told me he was leaving. Right? But then again, why would he? We weren't friends. No, if we were friends, I might have told him about the accident.

Before my thoughts can start to spiral again, I hear footsteps and sigh in relief. An angel has come to distract me.

Actually, *angel* might be the wrong word. When I step out, I see a man well over six feet, yet his height is not nearly as intimidating as his eyes—the same sheeny black as his messy hair. He keeps one hand around the strap of a laptop bag, the other in the pocket of his royal-blue scrubs.

I clear my throat. "Hi, what can I get for you today?"

"An iced coffee with a double shot of espresso," he says, voice just as crisp as his looks.

"Sure. That will be, um, $4.50."

He hands me a ten-dollar bill as his phone begins to ring. I pause for a moment with his change, providing him with a moment to answer his phone, but he doesn't move in the slightest.

Must not be important. I hand him his money and start making his drink, unable to help noticing his phone immediately starts ringing again. Is it the same person? Something urgent?

Doesn't matter. It's not my business, but it bothers me—him not so much as looking at the phone to see who it is. It might be someone calling to tell him his whole world is about to unravel.

I hand him his order with a forced smile. "Enjoy."

He rests the coffee on the counter, straight-faced. "I asked for an *iced* coffee."

I stare at the paper cup, steam emanating from the small opening. *Shit.* "Oh no! I'm super sorry about that. My head's... it's been a bit in the clouds. I'll get you——"

He leans forward to glimpse my name tag, and my entire body stills when our eyes meet. "I'm short on time. So, please, try not to mess it up this time, will you, Laine?"

I've worked in the service industry long enough to know the customer is always right, especially when you actually do mess up their order. So, I beg my jumbie, who's just itching for a fight, to settle herself before flashing my best professional smile. But she manages to get the better of me——not by much, but enough. I lean forward, glimpsing the ID clipped to the man's breast pocket, just like he did mine. "Just a moment... Dr. Jeon."

Well aware the doctor is watching intently now and his phone is going off yet again, I shovel some ice into a plastic cup and add the two shots of espresso before adding the cold brew. It's a perfect cup of iced coffee, no reason for him to find fault. However, as I hand him his order, I say something before I can stop myself. "You should probably answer that. It might be important."

Dr. Jeon sets the coffee down, lips curling upward into a smile that doesn't travel to his eyes. "I'm sorry, but what business is it of yours?"

Embarrassed, I fidget with my apron, but my jumbie... she's unrelenting. "It's not my business, but you should still check to see who it is. It might be important." *It might be someone calling to tell you the unthinkable just happened.*

"Look, I came here for the coffee, not a lecture, okay?"

"Well, if that's the case, why not silence your phone? I mean, let's be real. Not answering it the first or second time is one thing, but not answering the third? Letting it ring for everyone to hear? Some would consider it a nuisance." I point to the speakers overhead, playing Symphony no. 40 in G Minor. "Mozart sure would."

He laughs at that, and for a second I think maybe he's about to tell me he sees my point. But then his face goes deadpan. "Are you always this obstinate?"

"Only when I care," I snap.

Dr. Jeon freezes, as do I. That...it came out not at all how I intended it, and I brace myself for a barrage of retorts, but his phone comes to my rescue, going off yet again.

Either because he sees my point or wants to prove the call is not important, he whips his phone out. Only, when he stares at the screen, his eyes widen. He answers quickly. "Mom? I'm sorry for not picking up. I thought you were that asshole trying to palm off his patients. How was your day?" He sighs, and when he speaks again, it's in Korean.

I'm expecting a thank-you at the very least. But he stares daggers at me before grabbing his coffee and heading toward the door.

I watch his back as he leaves. God, if he exists, never intended to provide me with a moment's reprieve, did he?

No, because this doctor is finally picking up his phone to speak to his mother of all people? A very much alive mother? It sends me careening back to the hole I was desperately trying to climb out of before he entered the coffee shop, making my breaths come quick and my hands shake.

Shit!

I walk to my bag in the back and grab my bottle of Xanax. I don't cry as I down one tablet and slump to the floor. Instead, I try to focus on the only good thing to happen today so far— Lake Forest's acceptance of Alyssa.

It wasn't going to happen at first. Lake Forest has a long wait list. However, the social worker must have felt slightly obligated to help. She's the one who made it clear after I had a nervous breakdown three months ago and couldn't care for Alyssa for a few days—*you can't afford to slip up again.*

So she discussed with the health insurance company and Lake Forest until they agreed to keep Alyssa five days a week from seven a.m. to five p.m., free of charge. And the luck doesn't stop there.

All the money I'd have used to pay Alyssa's previous day center? It can now be used to pay off the debt we owe.

All of it's a blessing, really, one I didn't expect to get. And I can feel my lips curl into a smile as the minutes pass and that panic eating me up dissipates. We might just make it yet.

CHAPTER 4

ALYSSA

I haven't spoken many words aloud, but my mouth feels dry. *"What do you mean?"*

"Evil runs rampant here. Most of us who come never leave," Veranda says matter-of-factly.

I shift in my chair, hoping to attain just a little sense of comfort, a little sense of ease. *"I don't understand. This is a temple blessed by the gods themselves."*

Veranda has better control over her hands than I do over mine. She readjusts herself in her chair and smooths her dress before glancing at the stage. It's illuminated by a white orb that floats high in the air. *"This place is evil at its core, but you can have a full life if you're lucky. How about we watch the play and I'll fill you in later?"*

Watch the play? If I had full control over my body, I'd be out of my chair running to Laine. No, I'd get up on the stage and demand an explanation from the vorn perched on a stool in the corner of the hall. A lower-tiered white robe helper, he should have some idea of what Veranda is referring to. But alas, my legs are like lead. I can't move without much help. I can't speak and demand anything. So maybe Veranda is right. Perhaps I should just sit and watch the play while silently basking in the fear she's incited.

"I'm sorry, but this is one of the few things we have to look forward to during the day," Veranda says. *"I'd hate to miss it."*

Before I can express my disdain at her nonchalance, a sharp pain zips up and down my scalp, dizzying me. Veranda winces, letting out a murmur. *"Sam is trying to break our mental connection."*

"Sam?"

"Yes. I'm gonna let him in," she says.

My eyes scour the hall for a few seconds before settling on an older man sitting in a chair a few feet away. His hair is the same shade of gray as his eyes, his face a map of wrinkles. *"Who is the newcomer?"* he asks.

"It doesn't matter. I'd like to watch the play," Veranda says.

"Oh, come on, Veranda! Surely, after being forced to watch the same play every day for the past year, you can agree it's a curse rather than a gift."

The edges of Veranda's mouth twitch. I'm almost certain now that her never-fading smile isn't natural. *"Ferra, meet Sam. He's been here longer than any other changel."*

I let my gaze linger on Veranda before turning to Sam. I'm thankful she's chosen not to reveal my royal status. The fewer people who know my true identity the better. But does she hope to gain anything by it? *"Nice to meet you, Sam. I'm Ferra."*

"I'd entertain lengthy introductions, but I don't care about your back-story. If you are going to survive, then we should get right to it," Sam says. He inspects the room with sharp eyes before reverting his attention to me. *"Here at Lake Forest, the only certain thing is that most of us are different, even from each other. Some say 'cursed,' but I'd*

say that just fuels the scorn we're already so desperate to escape. Scorn that Lake Forest is supposed to help us with but just worsens."

I try to remain calm, take deep breaths. However, Sam's words bounce around the caverns of my mind.

Temples for changels have the sole purpose of helping us regain a sense of fulfillment. But does Lake Forest really have the opposite mission, fueling made-up legends against us? If my parents were aware of such…I don't bother to finish my train of thought. If they knew, they'd do something, but they are missing. Laine would have to deal with this problem. Even then, it would involve negotiations with Remwater's king. Lake Forest is in his territory.

My mental voice cracks. *"Have any of you tried exposing them?"*

Sam's bitter laugh resounds throughout my head. *"Most of us can't speak properly except to one another via our mental connection. Even then, a lot of the changels have developed an every-man-for-himself attitude. Most don't bother to try to communicate mentally. The few who do mask their conversations from the others."* Sam slumps a little farther into his chair. *"The only reason Veranda was so willing to let me interrupt your mental connection is because she's a little more weak-hearted and naive than the others."*

Veranda doesn't make a retort, and I take it as a sign that Sam isn't too far off.

Breaths raspy, I glance at the vorn, now standing next to another near the right side of the stage. *"Why haven't the vorns or regents helped?"*

"Their pockets are lined with gold," Sam says.

"What about your families?" I ask. *"Have they no clue?"*

"This temple also functions as a forever home for many of us," Sam says, bitterness coating his words. *"Our families visit us no more*

*than seven days per season. The few you might consider lucky because
they get to go home when the sun sets might as well take their chances
contending with the demons at Lake Forest. Really, is that so hard to
comprehend, girl?"*

Veranda gives me a knowing look, and I look away. It is hard
to comprehend. Yes, things have been different in the castle
since the attack. I'm no longer treated as Alyssa, the girl who
bested most students in her class in magic and debate. I'm broken Alyssa, who is unable to do anything for herself. Still,
despite my afflictions, Laine has tried to retain my dignity. She
does her best to make sure I'm comfortable, even though she
has the fate of the kingdom weighing on her shoulders. If only
I could relay to her what I've heard. Maybe she can make sense
of it all.

A man dressed in a vomit-green costume stands center stage.
I don't listen to anything he says after his introduction. Much
like I do when I'm in the castle, I fall into a vortex of questions
and worries. Who is behind the atrocities Sam and Veranda
speak of? Do I even trust them to believe there are atrocities?
And how do I tell Laine? I close my eyes and offer prayers to
Terra. Those prayers stop once the play ends.

"That's it. The performance is over," says one of the vorns.
His wide-mouthed grin reveals two crooked front teeth. "Now
several of you have to take a morning bath. One at a time, you'll
go. Shall we start with Harold?"

I follow Veranda's gaze. It settles on a red-haired man no
more than thirty, sitting in a wooden chair not far from Sam.
His back is hunched, several of his fingers stubbed. The fingers
that aren't stubbed are covered in white bandages seeping blood
in several areas.

"Apparently he was born compelled to eat his own flesh," Veranda says. *"None of the changels knows why. Just one of Terra's many mysteries, we guess."*

My eyes remained fixed on Harold. He knows not what it's like to be able to run unbound by constraints...to speak and have people listen. However, you can't miss something you've never had, right?

Maybe he loves his life, aside from Lake Forest's role in it, for what it is. Maybe I will one day as well. Maybe...

The vorn pushes Harold's chair with so much force, Harold shrieks.

"Quiet down, Harold," the vorn demands, but Harold shrieks again, only this time he also begins chewing at his bandages.

I shift in my seat uncomfortably as the vorn pins Harold's hands to his sides.

"Good boy! Good boy! Good boy!" Harold screams aloud.

The vorn whispers something in Harold's ear. When he releases him, Harold's hands are pinned to his sides by something that cannot be seen.

My breath hitches. I've been to three other temples for changels since the attack. The vorns in those temples only ever used magic on changels if they posed an imminent threat to those around them or themselves. Even then, magic was the last resort.

"Why isn't anyone helping him?" I ask. *"The vorn is a little heavy-handed with his magic."*

"That's Balding Bennett for ya. And did you not hear a single word we told you a moment ago?" Sam scoffs. *"There's nothing we can do for Harold. If we tried, we'd end up in the same situation, if not worse."*

I glance around the hall. All the changels stare at the floor or the ceiling. Is this how they cope with the indignities here? By pretending they don't exist? I look back at Harold.

"Don't hold eye contact with him for too long," Veranda advises. *"You'll just end up—"* Her words are drowned out by another voice. Judging from the shaky intonation, it's Harold's.

His mental voice booms through my head. *"Help. Good boy. Harold is a good boy."*

"Ignore him, Ferra. There's nothing you can do. You'll just make yourself a target," Veranda says.

"You're already fresh meat," Sam adds. *"Don't make things worse for yourself."*

But it's too late. *Leave him alone*, I try to say. *He has done nothing wrong.* However, only "hi…him…hi…" comes out of my mouth. Even though it makes little sense, I scream it again and again and wriggle about in my chair. I might be a changel, but that doesn't mean I'll just sit back and do nothing. Princess or not, changel or not, Harold needs help.

The vorn's eyes snap in my direction, and I cease all my fussing as he walks up to me. I'm not sure if it's his magic or the sheer look in his eyes that has petrified me. But when he refocuses his attention on Harold, Veranda lets out a mental sigh of relief. *"You're lucky. I thought for sure Balding Bennett was going to send you to one of the dark chambers."*

"Dark chambers?" I ask, and the rest of changels in the hall echo a chant.

> *Dark chambers. Dark chambers.*
> *A short time there and your sleep will be light.*

Just enough and sweet dreams all night.
But beware, oh child, for too long is smite.
And those who've been smitten will sleep forever night.

"What does that—that mean?" I ask.

Sam is all too eager to give me an explanation. *"The dark chambers are where they've harnessed Terra's power to cast their spells. If you stay for a short period in one, you end up in a walking slumber. A little longer, a deep sleep. Too long and the power will overwhelm you completely. Not all the vorns and regents who work here put changels in them, just a few. But unfortunately, those few are of higher rank. Not to mention discreet, especially when it comes to dealing with changels who they deem troublesome."*

"You mean changels like Harold?" I ask.

Sam nods. *"Yes, Ferra. And changels who I get a feeling are much like yourself. Now, do your best to fit in, will you?"*

I don't want to fit in. I can't. What the vorn did to Harold just now was wrong.

"I see that look in your eyes," Sam says. *"You have fight. And that's good. But think about the bigger picture. What do you stand to gain by racking up bad favor with the vorns? Do you have no home you want to return to? No family that will miss you?"*

I do have a family that will miss me. I have Laine. And, even though they're not with me right now, I have my parents. Parents who need my help. So I make up my mind to take Sam's advice for the day. I'll follow his rules. And when Laine comes to retrieve me in a few hours, I'll tell her of what is happening. How I'm not sure, but she'll find a way to put an end to the injustices here. Just like she'll find a way to find the king and queen.

CHAPTER
5

LAINE

I can't believe he left without any explanation." Glenn wipes a snotty nose on the cuff of his blue shirt, the buttons of which strain against his gut. "I just don't get it. I thought I pay you guys well for your work?"

I hand the fifty-two-year-old a napkin, and he blows his nose.

"Am I a good boss?" he asks.

"You are," I say, and I mean it. Aside from his gaming addiction, and the countless invites he's sent me to play with him online, Glenn is pretty kind. He wouldn't hurt a fly. Literally. He once saw me try to swat a fly and insisted I find a way to shoo it out of the shop unharmed.

I pat him on the back like my mother would do for me whenever I was in a funk. "I'm sure Jason didn't mean anything by leaving. Maybe he just needed a change of scenery."

Glenn sighs. "But—"

"No buts, Glenn. Customers are starting to file in. I don't want the evening shift to be slammed from the start. So, if the boss doesn't mind putting on an apron, what do you say we knock out these customers?"

A whimper, followed by a sob, resounds throughout the shop. Glenn grabs an apron from the back, and even though it takes a couple of minutes, he eventually loses himself in work.

Busy, snippy customers anxious for their dose of caffeine— they're blessings in disguise.

By the time I'm leaving, Glenn's laughing with the next shift. The topic is some show I don't have time to watch. I wave goodbye.

Virginian springs don't exactly transition seamlessly into summers, but the weather has been extra temperamental as of late. The cool rain this morning has been followed by a treacherous sun. I blast the AC in the SUV, hoping to offset the heat. However, I'm still a sweaty bundle of nerves by the time I arrive at Lake Forest. Can't help it. My body and mind are on overdrive, and I imagine they'll stay that way until I find out how Alyssa's first day was...if she liked Lake Forest...if they liked her.

I hustle up the steps and through the door, my mind continuing to whirl as I meet eyes with Reena, the day center's personal nurse who greeted me this morning.

"You're late, Ms. Highland."

Late? I glance at my phone. It's 4:56 p.m. "Isn't pickup time five? I'm four minutes early, actually."

Reena's face remains iced over as if to hide all emotion. "You filed through the social worker for your sister to come to Lake Forest three months ago, right? We had a different schedule back then. Pickup time is now four."

I'm tempted to avoid Reena's gaze, much like a child being

scolded. But I keep my eyes fixed on her. "Well, I'm sorry about that. I hadn't been made aware of the changes. I'll be on time tomorrow."

Reena's tone remains steely. "I expect nothing less."

I nod, even though I want to snap back. When I asked Reena this morning about anything I should know, she never mentioned pickup time was four. To be honest, though, she might not have gotten a chance to say much. I bombarded her with questions: Could Alyssa get care from their visiting physician? What would she be fed? Would they clean the J-tube after? Would the residents only get to watch cartoons and children's movies? *Peter Pan* was playing, and while I have nothing against the boy who never grew older, it's important to me Alyssa has variety.

After all, Alyssa's previous day center was stellar when it came to that but expensive. From what I know about Lake Forest, and I don't know too much considering reviews online were few, care is also good and only a fraction of the price of other day centers because of some grants or something. That said, when it all boils down to it, all I really care about is that my sister's being taken care of properly.

Reena offers to take me to Alyssa but then demands I wait while she answers an "important" call. Not exactly sure I have a choice in the matter, I look at the large display on the wall near the entrance while she's on the phone. Most pictures are of residents doing arts and crafts, watching television, and interacting with staff. They put me at ease . . . these pictures. Alyssa won't be staring at four walls, no one talking to her unless it's time to use the bathroom or eat a meal.

Reena taps the top of the display, drawing my attention to the "Please don't touch" sign, even though I clearly wasn't touching anything. I hold my tongue. I don't want to get off on the wrong foot on Alyssa's first day. "Sure. Let's go."

In silence, she leads me to Alyssa. I peep into a few empty rooms along the way and get a disconcerting feeling. Most of the nonresidents and day center's caretakers must have already left. Reena and I are the only ones meandering through the corridors.

She stops at the entrance of the hall. I do, too. And I watch, stunned.

Alyssa sits in her wheelchair, her legs covered with a thick blanket. Sitting in a chair across from her is a man with a book in his hands. The cover, dog-eared and coffee-stained, has a black horse with a white star on its head.

In a low voice, the man reads to Alyssa, his face a picture of serenity.

Reena clears her throat. "That's Dr. Remson. He's the associate director here at Lake Forest. We don't like to leave our guests alone for very long. Since half the staff left already, he's been keeping an eye on your sister."

At first, Reena's words don't register, at least not in the way that they should. I'm too busy observing the way the director interacts with Alyssa, how calm she is, the way her head cocks in his direction.

One of Alyssa's favorite books was Anna Sewell's *Black Beauty*. I wonder if she understands Dr. Remson's words? If they connect to some part deep within her? A part unscathed by the accident?

"Tomorrow, pickup time will be at four p.m., okay?" Reena's patronizing voice redirects my train of thought.

I run my hands through my hair, my mood starting to spiral.

The idea of the director taking personal time to read to Alyssa no longer seems to be a good thing.

Maybe he's waiting to give me an earful about showing up late. Maybe—

I shake my head and make my way toward him and Alyssa. I won't let myself get worked up any more than I need to. I don't need to take another Xanax, especially not in front of him or Reena.

"Hey, Alyssa. I've come to take you home," I say.

Dr. Remson's blue eyes meet mine, and I almost forget to breathe. His blond hair is slicked back neatly, his stubbled jaw so sharp it just might cut something. Tucking the book under his arm, he gets up and stretches out a hand. "Nice to meet you. I'm Dr. Remson, the associate director here at Lake Forest."

I wipe my hands on my jeans before shaking his hand, suddenly hyper-aware that I smell like coffee beans. "I'm Laine Highland, Alyssa's older sister."

Dr. Remson gestures at Alyssa. "Lovely sister you have. Right, Reena?"

"Yes," Reena says flatly.

I glance at her before looking back at the director. I get the feeling Reena doesn't like me, but as long as she likes Alyssa, that's okay.

I brush my fingers against Alyssa's cheek. "I was a little worried about dropping her off this morning. She can be feisty at times."

"Really? She seems to be fitting right in." Dr. Remson gives Reena his book. "I'll help get Alyssa to Ms. Highland's car. When I'm done, I'll take a look at Veranda. Her mother wanted an update, also wants to know if we can host a Peter Pan–themed birthday party for her next month."

Reena's expression doesn't change, showing no hint of emotion. She simply nods and heads toward the exit.

I watch her back as she leaves. She should take a page out of Dr. Remson's book when it comes to hospitality. Shit, she should take several, I think, as he helps me buckle Alyssa into the back seat of the SUV. He closes the wheelchair and places it in the trunk.

"Thanks again," I say.

"No problem at all. I like to make sure our guests are comfortable, you know?"

I try to smooth my hair even though it's beyond neatening. "That's really respectable of you."

He closes the trunk. "I'm glad you think so, Ms. Highland."

I get it's a formality. Still, Ms. Highland coming from him—he's probably no older than thirty-five—makes me feel twenty years older. I hold up a hand. "Please, call me Laine."

"Laine. Unusual name. Can I ask you the origin?"

"It's Estonian," I say, and I brace myself.

Brave people—it doesn't matter their race—sometimes like to voice their curiosity, showering me with statements such as, "You don't really look Estonian. Are you? Wait, what are you?" The questions never really bothered me until I started undergrad. A guy named Jeremy—I had the biggest crush on him—told me he wasn't into black girls but would make an exception for me because I was mixed. Oh, and how could I forget—my name was cool; pronounced "lane" as in car lane, it had an element of badassery to it. My sorority sisters Jenna and Avila had to comfort me with popcorn and repeat episodes of *Grey's Anatomy* after that one.

Dr. Remson's smile doesn't falter. "If you don't mind me asking, what does it mean?"

No microaggressive statements covered in stereotypes—well, that's a plus. "It means 'wave.'"

"That's pretty cool. Definitely cooler than Robert."

"Robert is a pretty cool name, too."

Dr. Remson lets out a throaty laugh that makes my stomach do a backflip. "No need to lie. Then again, Roberts do seem to get some hype. Like that Robert who was in *Twilight*. I think he was in the new Batman movie, too."

"Ahh, you mean Robert Pattinson. If I'm being honest, I never really got the hype. Besides, you're way more handsome," I say, and as soon as the words leave my mouth, I regret it.

I lower my head in a pitiful attempt to avoid Dr. Remson's gaze. Like I seriously couldn't think before speaking?

Dr. Remson just looks at me. No smile. No laughter.

I wobble back and forth on the balls of my feet. I must seem desperate to him. Thirsty. To be honest, I am. It's been a long time since I've been with anyone. Still, those words should have never left my mouth.

As the silence between us persists, the butterflies in my stomach are snuffed out by waves of self-loathing. My voice is barely a whisper when I decide to speak. "Uh…thanks again for everything. I should head home."

Dr. Remson rubs the back of his head. "I'm sorry. I've always been bad at taking compliments." His eyes, ocean blue in the sun, are tinged with something I can't quite characterize. Attraction, maybe? A glint of humor?

I almost laugh at the thought. Pity is more likely.

Nerves on fire, I fumble with the car keys, desperate to

escape. "I should go. Alyssa needs her evening bath, and I have some mail to go through."

Dr. Remson taps the hood of the SUV, and it's quick, maybe even imagined, but I'm sure a little smile crosses his face.

I lower my head in shame. Girls hitting on him must happen often. Shit, and I didn't even mean to hit on him.

I'm a mess.

Waving a quick goodbye, I hop into the driver's seat and pull off.

It isn't until I'm on the highway, a mile out from Lake Forest, that I manage to stop my mind from mulling over Lake Forest's hot associate director and the way I embarrassed myself.

I glance at Alyssa in the mirror. She stares at nothing in particular while muttering something indiscernible. What I'd give for her to focus on me the way she did Dr. Remson. What's his secret?

CHAPTER
6

ALYSSA

It's only when we get home that the pernicious magic dulling my senses dissipates.

Laine draws me a bath, and I savor the feeling of the warm water against my skin.

"You're quite calm. What did I do to earn such a blessing tonight?" she asks.

I take a deep breath. I take another.

Not long after Harold was taken away, they fed us a meal. Things after that fell into a monotonous sort of routine, much like I was accustomed to at the other homes for changels. But when all the forever guests were taken to their rooms and I was in the hall, things went dark, much like a moonless night in our castle's garden.

The darkness didn't last too long. Seconds later a wall of flame stood in front of me. It made my stomach churn and skin sting, my vision haze and ears ache. But I was unable to move a muscle, unable to utter a word.

When it disappeared and the magic overpowering my senses

lifted, I was being helped out of the carriage by Laine, our castle welcoming us home.

She fondles the ends of my hair once we're back in my room and I'm in my nightgown. "Thankfully, your hair is still neat from this morning. That said, it is still a little dry." Without further explanation, she exits my room and returns holding a jar of wax. Based on the green color and minty smell, it's wax from my mother's homeland, imported to Mirendal.

Laine sits me in a chair, dipping her fingers in the jar. She then runs her fingers along my scalp, focusing particularly on any dry areas.

"Before the attack, you always liked me tending to your scalp. Do you remember?"

Of course I do. When I was younger, Laine and I would fight to have our mother grease our hair, ensure the moisture from whatever magic her ancestors infused into the waxes would make our hair grow. When Laine got older, not long before leaving for Tergo, she'd offer to do it for me. I imagine it was her way of bonding with me, spending time together before she left to perfect her magic skills.

It's something that only takes place rarely now. Because rarely can I sit still for her to do such an activity when we should be looking for the king and queen. But she always opts for these activities, hiding details of her search for our parents, never discussing any clues as to their whereabouts. I'm not sure if it's to protect me or because she simply deems the information useless in my hands.

"So how was your day?" she asks.

Lake Forest is evil. I can't go back. "Ev . . . Ev . . ."

"Ev as in your friend Evangeline?" Laine asks, and my stomach lurches.

Oh, Terra. Please, tonight let her understand me. Let her pull my thoughts from my mind!

Scalp tending complete, Laine helps me to bed. "Watching your favorite plays hasn't gotten much of a reaction from you. But maybe reading will." She crosses the room to my bookshelf and selects a volume. Smiling, she returns to my side and begins reading a story she's read to me since we were children—a story about a dragon's journey in the realms. The struggles he faces as he's shuffled from kingdom to kingdom, struggling to find his way back to a young boy. It's always been one of my favorite tales, not simply because I love dragons. Rather, because Laine lights up while telling it, the same way she'd always light up while riding.

Oh, how I wish for her to be able to ride as freely as she did before...entrance all those watching her. However, that is a privilege she—I—can't afford. Not when there is a truth she must know.

Lake Forest is evil, sister! You must rescue me from there! If you don't, I will not be able to reunite with the king and queen. We will not be able to make our family whole again.

I bite back my frustration. *King* and *queen* are the only words that come out of my mouth.

I need to find a way to get her to understand me. That's the only way I'll survive Lake Forest. But how?

"Just what am I doing wrong?" Laine's voice cracks and her hands shake. "You were so calm for them earlier, but now..."

Calm? How can I be calm when the king and queen are still

out there? When Lake Forest just might prevent me from finding them, if I'm not careful?

Wriggling around in my chair, I hope to express just a sliver of my frustration with the temple. However, Laine's breaths start to come quickly.

"Please, Alyssa. I—I have to tend to matters in our stables tomorrow, ensure the stable hands have everything they need. I also have to speak with the kingdom's economic advisors at the Green Mount. So, please, just tonight, relax for me. Will you?"

The desperation in her voice is almost palpable, so much so that, for a second, I deliberate granting her request. But the idea of Lake Forest, what the vorn, Balding Bennett, did to Harold, what he might do to me, is all-consuming.

Lake Forest is evil, I try to say once more. And this time I channel all my strength into my hands. Vorns using magic against changels? Father and Mother would never allow such treacheries to exist!

I'm only trying to point to the portrait of our parents, but my control over my limbs is limited. Laine doesn't dodge in time, and my hand collides with her jaw.

A dangerous silence creeps over us as she backs away from me.

"Why would you do that?" she asks while cradling her face.

I didn't mean to hit her. I just wanted to point to the picture of our parents. However, Laine's hands begin to shake more violently, and tears spill from her eyes. Her hand moves from her jaw to her throat, almost as if she's fighting for air. She tries to say something, but she can't breathe or speak. Seconds later, she rushes out of my chamber.

I can feel tears well in my eyes as my heart breaks. I've seen her experience this before—a panic spell. She started getting them after the attack. The only thing that relieves her suffering is a potion provided to her by a white robe.

A dozen questions whisk through my mind while I'm alone.

Is Laine alright? Did she get her hands on her potion in time? Will she return? Is her jaw hurting? How can I tell her what's happening at Lake Forest? Am I going to die there? Die before I can meet my parents? I'm useless, aren't I?

I'm not sure how much time has passed when Laine returns. One hour? Two hours, maybe? But when she enters my room, her face is a mask of serenity with a few shards of bitterness peeking through. I don't try to apologize. I can't. And even though I'm laden with regret for hitting my dearest elder sister, part of me thinks she deserves it. I'm cursed, yes. I can't communicate properly, yes. But she's the first princess of Mirendal. She was born to rule the kingdom. She should be able to tap into my mind and see what exactly is troubling me so. She should be stronger. She should be braver. She should be better. She should be more.

I should be more.

Laine doesn't try reading to me again. After providing me with a meal, she covers me with a fur blanket. "Good night, Alyssa."

I call out to her in a pitiful attempt to ask her not to leave me. But in Laine's eyes I see one thing—despondency, the kind that eats a mortal from the inside out.

She doesn't look at me as she blows out the candle and exits my bedchamber.

CHAPTER
7

LAINE

Ve need to practice keeping your legs tucked firmly against the saddle. It stops you from bouncing. Still, great job overall. You're picking things up quickly." I give Danny, an eight-year-old boy whose helmet hair reminds me of Jimmy Neutron, a high five. He beams as I take him to his mother, who waits in the parking lot next to the stables. She barely says two words to me, scrolling through her phone until Danny tugs on the hem of her blouse.

"How was your lesson this morning, honey?"

"It was good. Laine said next time we'll learn the two-point position. I'm gonna be a jumper in no time," Danny says.

His mother gives him a sheepish smile and directs him to get into the car before handing me a check for eight hundred dollars. "These are for the next ten lessons. I'd like to stick to the same times. Tuesday and Thursdays, nine to ten a.m. I'd also like to throw in Friday mornings now that your schedule has opened up."

"Yes, Ms. Wright." I fold the check and slip it into my

pocket, leading an older quarter horse named Dice into the stables once I wave Danny off. I give him a sugar cube I pull from my pocket. "Ready to get cleaned up?" Only once he's finished with his cube do I unbuckle his girth with a sigh.

Danny should be here with me, engaging in this process. A rider is not a rider if they don't know how to properly untack their horse and get them settled in their stall. However, Ms. Wright can be so impatient at times that I almost always let him go to the car. Not to mention, she helps pay my bills.

Dice whinnies as Ana, the stout owner of the stables, bustles through the walkway with a clipboard in hand. She peeps into each stall and pats down a few of the horses before stopping outside Dice's stall. "How was Danny's lesson?"

"It was good. He's developing a nice seat." I hand her the check. "Ms. Wright paid for the next ten lessons."

Ana raises a brow. "And why are you handing me this?"

"Because it's yours," I say.

"You teach the lessons, Laine. You've only had Danny six times and he's already a little pro in the making."

I wipe a bead of sweat off my face as I begin picking Dice's hooves. I'm careful to avoid any sensitive areas. "Danny is a natural."

Ana shrugs. "Even then, he loves you. All the kids love you. Even the few adults who take lessons here. They all want you. I'm not sure why you just don't work for me full-time."

"You know why," I say, slightly annoyed. Can't help it, given we've gone over this at least a dozen times already. Since Ana's the boss, people tend to be nicer to her than they are to me, even the ones who claim they love me. One guy, for example, kept pulling too hard on the reins of his horse to bring her to halt. I told him once, twice, three times. When the horse bucked him, he blamed me, yelling a few choice words in my face. It's one thing to deal with rude customers at the coffee shop, but I can't abide seeing anyone take it out on the horses.

He apologized once he gathered himself, but I've had more of those experiences than I'd care to admit. Not to mention, Glenn offers me a stability Ana can't. Even if the world were burning to the ground, the local college kids wouldn't miss their daily dose of caffeine. People coming to Ana's stables for their lessons, on the other hand? There are a few regulars, but quite a few have a habit of canceling at the last minute.

"How's Alyssa?" Ana asks. "She likes the new place?"

"I think this place is gonna do her well," I say. "She doesn't really focus on much. You know she's trapped in her head. But you should have seen her yesterday, Ana. It seemed as if she was focusing." Focusing on Robert that is, considering when I took her home and tried to read to her as he did, she flipped out on me, hit me dead in the jaw. Thankfully, it didn't leave a bruise, but it still hurt like a bitch. And even though it wasn't my proudest moment, I stormed out on her, a wave of panic, dread, and anger washing over me.

I returned to feed her after a couple of hours, but I still felt like a real asshole.

Ana shoves one of the sugar cubes meant for the horses in her mouth. "That girl would have gone on to make it big in the horse world, you know?"

I finish picking Dice's last hoof. "That she would have."

"There's only one other girl who could have bested her. A shame she's wasting her talents." Ana smiles slyly as she hands me a brush.

"I'm not nearly as good as I used to be," I say.

"You were always a natural, Laine. You just need to get back in the saddle."

"I don't have the time."

Ana huffs. "Don't give me that. You started shying away from riding long before the accident. Even your father said it. After Sprinkler died, your relationship with riding wasn't the same."

I take a deep breath, imagining the eight-year-old black Friesian my father bought when I was thirteen. She was technically a family horse. Everyone rode her, including Alyssa. However, in my heart she was mine. I competed on her, would practically beg Dad to spend nights in the stables to be close to her, would talk to her as if she was a person. When she died, I thought to myself I'd never again be able to experience such an insurmountable pain, the kind that made me want to crop anything that involved her out of my life.

I was wrong, of course, but it doesn't change the fact that her death messed me up enough that my psychiatrist brings her up along with my parents when we discuss loss.

"We shouldn't have let you sit out of the saddle for so long. We should have got you riding again. You would have gone far," Ana muses.

"Yeah, but my horse died. Then my parents died, too." Dad always said Ana had a heart of gold, but when it came to making a name for her stables, her passion bordered on obsession. Still, certain my words sting, I try to soften their blow. "I know you offered to front the cost to get me back into riding. Did I ever say thank you?"

Ana almost drops her clipboard. "Since when?"

I force a smile. "After I got the first letter from the collection bureau, things started to click. Dad always promised Alyssa he'd get her her own horse for her sixteenth birthday, but that never happened. Boarding Sprinkler, much less buying and boarding another horse for Alyssa, would have been too much. And the biggest sign? When you came to Dad a month later, talking about a two-year-old gelding Alyssa and I should see. How you'd split the cost with him."

"Bullet—that was his name. He was quite a show-off, much like Sprinkler." Ana's eyes glaze over with a forlorn look. "In hindsight, I was wrong to talk to you and your sister about that gelding. I overstepped boundaries. I offered to front the cost without thinking about how it would make your father feel." Ana sighs. "I couldn't help it, though. It was nice to see riders of color taking the world by storm."

Nice that those riders came from her stables, I'm sure. There are so few of us that winning a prestigious competition would have garnered the stables some hefty attention.

I grab Dice's saddle and plant it on the wall rack in the tack room. "I know," I holler. "And I'm grateful. One day, hopefully, I'll get back into riding."

Ana presses her lips together as she nods. We both know it's a lie. I don't see myself doing anything other than teaching lessons. After all, riding when Alyssa's no longer able to feels wrong somehow.

My psychiatrist and I are still tackling that.

I hand Ana the check once again, but she gestures silently for me to have it. I don't argue this time, shoving the slip of paper into my pocket. "Thanks. I'll put it to good use." I'd love to be like my father, not taking handouts. However, I need this money. If I want to keep the house, I need to pay off the debt.

Once I finish up with Dice, I drive downtown to the bank. Thirty minutes early for my appointment, I kill time in the bathroom of a nearby coffee shop, one much more congested and cramped than Glenn's.

"It's okay, Laine. Just explain the situation carefully," I mutter. "You just need more time."

Time. I'm not sure how much I need exactly, but I know it's a lot. After the accident, most of my parents' life insurance policy went to Alyssa's hospital fees; her health insurance could only cover so much of it. Coupled with what I work for, what remained has helped me pay for food, meds, bills, and, most importantly, the private day centers. But now there's no more money from the life insurance policy. The only cushion I have now is being able to funnel the money I don't have to pay Lake Forest to the debt.

I splash some water on my face, letting the coolness invigorate me with a sense of hope and confidence; however, as soon as I'm in the bank, my shoulders are hunched and I'm fidgeting my fingers, already anticipating bad news.

A woman—her name tag reads Janet—rattles off a whole lot of something about the weather as she looks for an available clerk. I'm not really listening. I don't care about the weather. She ushers me into a room and I freeze.

"Britney?"

Blue eyes semi-covered by auburn bangs look up from a desk. "Laine?"

All the blood must have drained from my head, because I feel dizzy.

I want to turn around, run out of the bank and back to the safety of my car. But this can't wait. I can't wait.

Feet dragging against the floor like they're lead, I close the door behind me and sit in the chair.

Britney rests both hands flat on the desk—a neutral position that would make me feel comfortable if her eyebrows didn't practically kiss each other. "What can I do for you today, Ms. Highland?"

So she's gonna pretend we don't know each other? Let our history in undergrad be bygones?

There's a fly buzzing around the space. My eyes toggle between it and Britney, my sorority sister—or more like sorority enemy.

We used to be quite close actually. We both enjoyed watching *Grey's*, consuming wine and popcorn on Thursdays, and partying it up on the weekends. No doubt, she was a true ride or die, and when I found out she was graduating a year early, I was bummed.

My reverie stops as she clears her throat.

I shift in my chair, uncomfortable. "Well, I'm hoping for an extension on the mortgage." The words spill out of my mouth, and papers—bank statements and costs of previous day centers I pulled together—fly across the table.

Britney James shuffles through the papers.

I perk up in my chair. Is she actually reading them? The last time I brought papers to ask for an extension, no one looked over them.

She nods a couple of times, staring at the pamphlet of Lake Forest. "I read your file already. And just so we can make this less painful for the both of us, I'm just gonna come right out and say it. We can't approve your extension, Laine."

"Are you serious? But—"

She drums her fingers against the table, a small smile snaking its way across her face.

I pray my voice comes out steady, but it doesn't. "Are you not approving my request because you're following the rules or because you hate me?"

Her jaw drops, and she rests a hand on her chest, clearly feigning hurt. "Excuse me? I keep my work and personal lives very much separate, thank you very much. Besides, you sleeping with Ishan Khan?" She doesn't blink. "Not a big deal."

Fucking Ishan Khan.

Britney had worshipped the ground he walked on. I had, too, secretly. But it was an unspoken rule among me and my sisters. If two of us liked the same guy, we'd yield to the girl who declared their love first. And even if a sister was shot down, no other sister would approach him.

I thought it was a silly idea back then. I liked Ishan, too, for crying out loud. I did from the moment he clapped back at our math professor for expressing disbelief that he was struggling with some of the equations.

Britney had thought it made Ishan *badass, a rebel.* But there was more to it. He didn't want to be labeled a stereotype. It was something I knew all too well. And when I went to his frat's party, and we got to talking, one thing led to another.

In hindsight, I regret sleeping with him. Not just because Britney found out. Not just because I lost her as a friend. But because I was with him when . . . I force down the memory.

"Look. Britney. I know you're still mad at me, but please. I'm begging here."

The little horned jumbie on my shoulder whispers in my ear—*Yes, Laine. Beg her like you beg Freidmore.* "I'm in a bind. I know I'm behind on payments, but if I can just get an extension, possibly work together to come up with an affordable payment plan, I'll be out of your hair. You won't have to see me again."

Britney chuckles.

She fucking chuckles while I'm borderline in tears. And even though I should keep my shit together, I lose it. "Do you have to be such a bitch?"

"Don't make me call security," she snaps.

I laugh. Of course. Call security. They won't hear me out. Why would they? She's the pretty brunette dressed in a suit. I'm the half-black girl with buzzed-down hair and a figure some might deem lean but others might say is boyish.

Surely, security will be all too happy to escort me out, and I right myself, well aware that I need to get my act together.

"I want to make this clear before you leave, but this isn't payback for you sleeping with Ishan," says Britney.

There it is. The final words needed to tip me over. My descent into the abyss of panic comes slowly at first. The tremor running up my arms is so fine that Britney doesn't even seem to notice it. But it's there. "You don't need to pay me back for shit, Britney. I already got that from God."

"You never even apologized to me when I found out about Ishan. No messages. Nothing. Not even when I found you two together at the party. You just ran out of the house." She runs a hand through her auburn locks. "I waited by your room, you know. For hours the next day. But you never came back. Never responded to any emails. Never responded to any texts. I was worried, thought you were dead or something. But the school told us you were alive. And that they'd deliver your stuff to you because you'd not be returning." Britney gathers up my papers and hands it to me. "I imagine it was the shame, huh?"

My sobs rumble in my chest, and my head bobs up and down with the pulsations of my heart. "It was. If I had just gone home that weekend. If I hadn't said I was sick, they wouldn't have come to see me. They wouldn't have . . ."

"What are you talking about?" Britney asks, but I can see it in her eyes. The pieces of a nasty puzzle fitting together. That day I was with Ishan at the dardy—daytime party—was the day before my birthday. My parents thought I was sick, that that's why I couldn't spend time with them. But I was partying it up.

"I didn't realize it was then," Britney mutters, and her face hues red, her embarrassment palpable, but not nearly as palpable as the panic that has started coursing through my veins. I sink to the floor, my throat feeling as if it's closing. My eyes tear up as I gasp for breaths.

My tremors morph into violent shakes. I try to still myself, fight the panic, as I dump out the contents of my bag. I grab my bottle of Xanax and down a pill with a cup of water Britney hands me. And I sit there, rocking myself back and forth, listening to my inner jumbie tell me how horrible I am until she finally stops talking, and I don't feel like I'm dying.

CHAPTER
8

ALYSSA

Like a predator on the prowl—that's how the crooked-tooth vorn, Bennett, paces the hall today. He eyes each changel for several seconds, frowning at some, smiling at others.

He smiles at me and somehow I'm certain that's worse than a frown. Nerves coiling up like wire, I hold on to the arms of my dragon chair, breaths all backed up because I can't exhale. Not until another changel begins to yell and Bennett tears his gaze away.

"Again. Again," Harold says in reference to the play that finished a few minutes prior. I still don't know what it's about. How can I when the walls of Lake Forest are burnished in blood and tears of changels?

"That's it," says Bennett. He's the only vorn in the hall today. "It's time to get your bandages changed, Harold."

"Don't want to go," Harold says, but Bennett pokes his head out of the hall. He says something, I'm not sure what, and two people enter the hall shortly after. "You two keep an eye on them. I'm going to get Harold's bandages changed."

"Harold doesn't wanna go," Harold says, and Bennett shoots him a gaze that makes every changel in the room, even me, recoil in their seat.

"Harold doesn't wanna—"

Bennett's voice comes out like a clap of thunder. "Quiet!"

One of the vorns, a rosy cheeked girl with raven-colored hair, stares at Bennett with wide eyes. "Is that completely necessary?"

I think I'm the only changel who perks up in their seat. I look at Veranda, then at Sam. *"Someone to help us."*

"Don't get your hopes up," says Sam.

But I do. The woman crosses her arms. "They might be changels but—"

Bennett holds up a hand, silencing her. He leans close and whispers something. And I can see it, the muscles in her face pulling into a frown. She says something, a retort I take it, and she looks at the other vorn in the room—a lanky man with scruffy red hair. He avoids her gaze, and Bennett smiles.

Seconds later, the woman storms out of the hall. No one seems surprised. Not the other vorn, not any of the changels, and Bennett sets his eyes on Harold once more. "Where were we?"

I don't have time to wrap my head around the woman abandoning us. My blood curdles in my veins as I watch Bennett make his way to Harold. I need to do something to help my fellow changel. My parents would expect me to, wouldn't they?

I suck in a breath and yell, "Get away from him." Nothing remotely close comes out of my mouth, but I scream it again and again.

Bennett's eyes settle on me, but I don't stop.

"Calm yourself, Ferra," Sam says, but I can't. I won't.

Bennett snaps his fingers at the other vorn. "Anders, change Harold's bandages. I think this one might need to go for a little walk. Who knows? Maybe Reena can make her more agreeable."

Anders nods, and Bennett grabs on to my chair.

"Agreeable? What's he talking about?" I ask.

Veranda's mental voice comes out like a whisper, almost as if she's afraid the vorns can hear our thoughts. *"He's talking about the dark chambers."* She lets out a whimper as Bennett leads me out of the hall. *"Don't act out again, Ferra. It won't do you well."*

No longer in the same space, our mental connection breaks. However, my connection with Harold, who is led behind me by Anders, is still present. *"Thank. Thank. Thank,"* he says incessantly.

I should be angry at him. His thanks will not keep me safe. It will not keep me alive long enough to help find my parents. However, it makes my actions—which I've deemed the most dull-witted thing I've done since I tried playing with a wild baby dragon (its mother was nearby and extremely protective)—seem a little bit more worth it.

Once we come to the end of a narrow hallway, Harold is taken right, and I'm taken left. I focus on the bare green walls, searching for ways to navigate the maze, but there are none. We stop outside a small bedchamber, where the regent who first welcomed me to the temple waits.

"What's the matter?" she asks.

"She won't listen, Reena," Bennett says.

"They're changels, Bennett. Most of them don't listen."

"But…"

Reena narrows her eyes. "Are you sure this wasn't a reason to get me alone?"

At first, Bennett says nothing. He just stares at Reena, his eyes wide. Then he narrows the distance between them. "I just want to see you again. And I don't mean behind these walls. When can I?"

Reena swats away Bennett's hand. "Things are hectic right now."

Bennett's face contorts in a hellish way. "You know, your attachment to him reminds me of a caged bird. One caged so long it doesn't fly away, even though the owner no longer cares to hear it sing."

Reena takes a step closer to Bennett. She's shorter than him, but he hunches down, her gaze seemingly chipping away at his height. "I might be a caged bird, but you are nothing but an easily fooled pauper he gave a touch of class. You'll never be on his level, no matter how much he pretends to enjoy your company. No matter how much power he gives you the impression of having. The sooner you realize that, the safer you'll be."

Eyes still burrowing into Bennett like he's an ant at her mercy, Reena gestures at me. "Now shall you take this changel back to the hall? The magic of the dark chambers should only be used sparingly."

"Understood, Regent Harken," Bennett grumbles.

Tight-lipped, Reena turns on her heels to walk away, but Bennett calls out after her. "Ah! Before I forget, how are you faring with the transgressions against Mirendal? Makes no sense using the king and queen to barter for terrain if the first princess isn't even doing a great job looking for them."

Reena spins around like a top, eyes like shards of glass ready to cut Bennett down to size. "We've come this far, haven't we? Besides, Mirendal isn't the kingdom it used to be. Word has it the princess's uncle has been trying to seize control of the king-dom. It'll fall by their own hand, if not ours. Until that happens, the king and queen will remain in the Dark Forest. Now, do you have any more questions for me, Bennett?"

Reena's words are like venom, stopping my heart once I've processed them.

I take a deep breath. I take another.

I always thought Uncle orchestrated the attack on my parents, but I was wrong. Very wrong.

Remain calm—that's what the situation demands of me. I'm helpless without Laine. But nothing can assuage the anger building inside me.

Using all the energy I have, I begin to wriggle about in my chair.

"What's wrong with her?" Reena asks.

"I'm not sure. She's just been a pain in my ass," Bennett says, leaning closer to me.

I'm weak and my control is limited, but I throw a right fist at Bennett. He dodges the fist but underestimates me, failing to dodge when I swing my left hand. The entire thing lacks coordination but as my left fist connects with Bennett's jaw, jolts of pain shoot up my arm.

Eyes hazy with aggression rivaling my own, Bennett opens the door to the chamber and shoves me inside. "It's a pity this had to happen so soon," he says. "Separatio."

As he closes the door, I can feel it—the magic that seeps from the earth and rolls off the four green walls. Its power has been used to bend changels to the will of others, and much like things did after our carriage was flipped a year ago, everything goes dark.

My hands brush against my sides as I rise to my feet. They finger something satiny, and I look down. No longer am I wearing the commoner clothing Laine dressed me in this morning but a white dress that kisses flowers beneath me. Their buds, the size of my fist, permeate the air with a smell I love, the smell of earth. And there's something else—something sweet that makes my senses tingle, my eyes tear.

I pick one of the buds, jumping back when the petals unravel. A fairy, no larger than the size of a monarch butterfly, emerges. Her wings are like glass, the sun's rays beaming through them to cast little shadows on the earth below as she takes flight.

Her eyes, green like the lush forests untouched by mortals, burrow through my soul, paralyzing me.

"I'm—I'm sorry," I say. "I didn't mean to wake you."

The fairy shakes her head, a smile igniting her fine features.

I've only seen a fairy once before, when I was seven, playing in the castle's garden with my mother. She had forbidden me from communicating with him. Fairies, though they do communicate with mortals here and there, usually avoid us.

The fairy's voice is like a sweet whisper on the wind, audible honey.

I shake my head as she continues to speak. "I'm sorry, but I don't understand you. I was supposed to take a class on the different tongues spoken by your kind, but an attack—"

There it is—the word needed to shatter the little shred of serenity keeping me sane. My breathing quickens as Veranda's warning about the dark chambers echoes in my mind. What if I stay too long? My hands begin to tremble, and I tuck them under my arms in an attempt to keep them still.

Matter of fact, how am I standing? How am I speaking? What about the other changels? These questions whirl around my mind, stifling me, until several of the buds begin to unravel. Fairies, dressed in garments as white as the clouds racing across the sky, begin to take flight.

I do my best to keep my voice pleasant, even though the fact that I've roused them adds to the fear, anxiety, and anger that already sit heavy on my chest. "I'm sorry. I don't mean to wake you all. I'm just—a—a little out of sorts. Do you know where I am exactly? Is this—" The words stall in my throat. It's a question I don't want to ask because there's no taking it back. "Am I dead?"

Some fairies, more than I'd care to admit, keel over with laughter. Some even land on the ground so they can roll about in the grass, their mirth seemingly too much to contain.

I smile awkwardly, tension rolling off my frame. If I were dead, they wouldn't laugh at me, right?

After their giggles subside, the fairy who tried talking to me earlier gestures for me to follow her. She might not be able to provide me clarity, but I listen. I have no other option.

Aside from the vast expanse of white jasmine flowers, there's no notable feature to this place. No crossroads, no signs. The thought should be enough to make me panic, resign myself to a dozen gut-wrenching possibilities. But the more I walk, the more I'm taken by the way my right foot comes out in front of my left. I don't veer off to the side. Pain doesn't radiate from the tips of my toes up to my calves. I do a little hop, relishing that I can balance, relishing that I have control over my limbs. The only thing that steals my attention from my regained ability is the field's transition from jasmine to lavender.

Elation fights against uncertainty, flooding my veins as the fairies' white outfits shift to purple.

The fairy leading the troupe—I've coined her Emerald—spins around in place before gesturing for me to do the same. I do as told, smiling the first time since the attack, as the color purple races across my dress like a flame desperate to ravage a field of white.

I'm so engaged in the display of magic that I don't hear him approach.

"I haven't seen you in this plane before."

I stop and turn to my right. Standing a few feet away is a young man who appears to be around my age, maybe a few years older. His black hair shines obsidian in the light, his eyes nearly as green as Emerald's.

"Who are you?" he asks.

"Alyssa Highland. Second—" I fall silent, preferring to think it's the magic from the chamber that steals my wit and not the man's beauty. Laine would scold me for such a slipup. I force down a pang of self-loathing.

The man's brows shoot up. "Alyssa Highland, as in Second Princess Alyssa Highland?"

I nod slowly. It's too late to take back my words. And, even though I'd never admit it aloud, it feels good to hear him say my name, my birthright. "And you are?"

He stretches out a hand. "Wren. It's nice to meet you." A smile flits across his face, a lopsided grin. It's coupled with a twinkle in his eyes, one that reminds me of the pranksters I occasionally encountered in my spell-caster classes.

"So they've put you in one of the dark chambers, huh, Princess? Performed a separatio spell."

I can feel the muscles in my face tighten as my anxiety mounts. "I thought it led to a walking slumber or death. But..."

"Too much time in the dark chambers can be detrimental." Wren begins spinning around in a circle with wide arms, his head tilted up to the sky. "But they fail to realize that the power seeping into the bedchambers has a strange effect. It transports strong-minded changels here—a place that belongs to neither the living nor the dead." Wren feigns a yawn. "To everyone in the other plane, we are in a walking slumber." He taps a finger against his head. "Mentally, however, we are here, able to move and talk freely."

"So, what did you in?" he asks. "Angry outburst? You pulled a white robe's hair? Were you like me and bit one of their regents?"

"I hit the vorn in the jaw," I say. "He and the regent didn't take it too well."

Wren keels over with laughter, but I spare not a second to share his enthusiasm. "Look, I need to get out of here. I need to speak to my sister. Can you help me?"

Wren's laughter morphs into a deep sigh, his smile into a frown. "Unfortunately, that's something we have little control over, Princess. We can only leave once the spell wears off, and that takes time. Even after you're removed from the chamber, you'll experience lingering effects of the magic cast on you."

"Wears off? I need to leave now." My words grate against my throat, my vision blurring as tears well in my eyes. "I need to get back to Lake Forest. I need to warn Laine. Our kingdom is under attack!"

Wren rests a brawny hand on my shoulder. "Relax. You can actually use this place to your advantage."

My voice cracks. "How so?"

"I'm assuming the problem now also has something to do with the attack on the king and queen of Mirendal last spring? They suspected they were taken into the Dark Forest, no?"

I put distance between Wren and me. Was that ever made public knowledge? Even if it was, Wren is most likely from Remwater. How did he get word of such? Does he have contacts in Mirendal?

Wren chuckles. "I have no foul intentions, Princess."

My blood runs cold, like the icy river that borders Mirendal to the west. "I never said you did."

Wren widens his eyes and opens his mouth, pretending to be scared. "Your face says otherwise."

I can feel the heat creeping up my neck as something other than fear, other than anger, struggles to breach the surface. Laughter, maybe? I clear my throat. "You seem to know a lot about me. It's only fair you share something about yourself."

"It is reasonable," Wren says. "But how about we discuss my background while we walk? There's something I'd like to show you."

I remain grounded in place. "And what's that?"

"It's a surprise," Wren says, sighing again. "And don't worry. I won't trick you. The fairies won't allow it. They keep the peace here."

I meet eyes with Emerald. She smiles at me before gesturing for me to follow Wren. Options limited, I follow like a skittish dog.

He walks with hands behind his back, much like my mother

would do when taking an evening stroll in our garden. I shove the thought out of my head, the comparison threatening to spiral into thoughts of my parents, thoughts of them in the Dark Forest, suffering.

"I was born in Remwater into a family of traders," Wren says. "That's why I know so much about Mirendal. Word of your parents' kidnapping spread like wildfire after the attack. You being cursed, however, not quite. I heard that you were physically injured after the encounter in the forest but not spelled. But I guess that makes sense. If your people caught wind that you were a changel, it would be the final dagger needed to bury your family. Your lineage is already a point of contention."

"I don't need a history lesson on myself, Wren. How did you end up a changel?"

Wren doesn't seem fazed by my snappishness, my question even eliciting a smile.

"I was racing wild dragons with my friend, when I became a little too eager. I tried showing off by flying up toward the sun and diving down toward our finish line. I'd done it before on my own mount. However, it didn't work out so well on a wild male dragon. He threw me off as we started to ascend, and I fell to the earth below. I was lucky the trees broke my fall. I was unlucky in that a boy I thought was my friend cursed me to ensure I wouldn't ride again."

Wren's words are like rope, tethering us, two strangers, together. I might be a princess, and he might belong to a family of traders, but we're the same—unlucky. We had little physical constraints before becoming changels, and now we're bound by several of them.

I clear my throat, aware my guard has lowered. Just slightly, but lowered nonetheless.

"We're almost there," Wren says.

I stick to him like molasses now, the fairies falling back as the lavender starts fighting a losing battle against fairy weed. "Are the fairies not coming?"

"No." Wren keeps staring frontward. "They don't venture past the field of lavender."

"Why? Where exactly are we headed?"

"You'll see. Till then, I must ask, where did you get that bracelet? It's unusual, something I've never seen in this land."

I stop, pulling my hand to my chest. My guard is once again up and operating at maximum capacity. "You can see it? I'm certain my sister spelled it this morning."

"All spells cast in the other plane are nullified when you come to this realm, at least for the duration that you're here," Wren says. "We traders have a keen eye for things that are special. May I ask you where you acquired such an item?"

I fondle the bracelet; its obsidian beads connect to others the colors of snow and fire. "My mother isn't from Mirendal but from a kingdom far across the sea. Women in her family are gifted with special items at the time of their birth. For some, it's a necklace. For others, it might be a rose spelled never to wilt. Either way, when they're of age, they relinquish it to the man or woman of their choice as a sign of love."

"Sounds very intimate," Wren says.

I let my hand fall to my side. "It is."

Before I can say anything else, Wren points straight ahead. The field of fairy weed has come to an end, yielding to a forest. Tall, dark trees shelter a thick fog. Echoes of nothing in particular bounce off bark. Dark shadows frolic along to a sporadic tempo.

"It can't be," I mutter. I don't need to step any closer to know I'm looking at the Dark Forest, and I don't wait for Wren to offer any advice on how to proceed, hurrying toward it like there is a fire on my trail.

Wren yanks me back just before the sulfur-ridden smog can singe my lungs and engulf me. "We can see the forest and hear its calls. However, in this plane, one cannot escape once they enter."

I stare at him with wide, teary eyes. I shouldn't cry in front of him, let him see my tears. He gifted me the key to my family's salvation, only to tell me I can't use it. "I'm so close to finding them. I have to find them!"

"To enter the Dark Forest from this plane is to bind yourself to certain death, Princess."

As the word *death* slips off his tongue, something shifts in my periphery. I take a step back as a chain of creatures rise from the ground. They are the size of little children, their feet turned backward and faces devoid of any mouths, eyes, or noses. They wear large circular hats of palm leaves on their heads. I gasp, hot bile threatening to rise up my throat.

When Laine and I were growing up, my mother would tell us stories of the magical creatures distinct to her homeland. Most of the creatures I would have loved to meet, to best in battle or outwit. However, one type of creature left me completely shaken. The douen.

Not exactly jumbies, or what my mother would call ghosts, they are the spirits of children who died before their christening, and they are destined to roam the earth forever.

"What is it? What do you see?" Wren asks.

I point to the chain of douens. "You don't see them? The faceless children?"

Wren shakes his head. "No. I see a woman."

I almost choke on the word. "A woman?"

Wren pulls me closer to him, his eyes still glued to the Dark Forest. "What guards this wretched place is different for each of us. For me, it's a large woman, almost as tall as a tree. She has a deformed face and long snaky fingers. She lives in a house with chicken legs and she rides in a mortar. Her tongue hangs low as she rasps one word."

I force myself to voice the question aloud. "What's that?"

"Hungry," Wren whispers.

Through gritted teeth, hoping my voice doesn't reveal I'm scared, I say, "I need to find my parents. Guarded or not, they're somewhere in the Dark Forest. Alive."

"I can't let you go, Princess. I already told you, you'll die. But there is a way. It just required you to see this."

"What way?"

I don't ever hear Wren's answer. Before he can say anything, everything around me begins to blur. I reach for him, his body morphing into swirls of colored air. My limbs start to feel like weights; my head begins to ache. When the world stops spinning, and things come into focus, I let out a sob, a shrill cry that echoes.

I'm back in the dark chamber of Lake Forest.

CHAPTER
9

LAINE

If there's one thing good about having a panic attack in front of someone who hates you it's that it might, just might, move them to pity. I pull up at Lake Forest thinking about the look on Britney's face as she handed me that glass of water. She didn't say much, not that she's sorry, not that she didn't know my life had gone to shit to such an extreme. She just promised to get me an extension on the payments. Thank God.

If only tears had worked on Freidmore.

I'm so wrapped up in the thought of him, of Britney, that the sound of a hand against the bumper of the SUV doesn't register, not until the second time.

I hit the brakes. Thoughts of Britney and debt fly out of my head when I see who I've almost hit.

Shit.

Dr. Remson gives me a wry grin. I turn off the ignition and hop out, feeling the heat skyrocket to my head. "I'm so sorry. I've been a little out of it."

I half expect him to chew me out, kind of like the bitchy

doctor did yesterday at the coffee shop. But Dr. Remson just gives a half-smile. "Is everything okay?"

"I'm fine," I mutter. "Just here for Alyssa."

Dr. Remson arches a brow. "Are you sure? You don't seem okay, Laine."

I'm not okay. I might have dealt with the bank, but that doesn't mean I'm out of the woods just yet. And suddenly I feel like crying again.

"You know, if you want to talk about it..."

I don't want to talk about it. The only reason I talk about it with my psychiatrist is that she prescribes me my Xanax. Somehow the thought of her, the thought of everything, hits me like a brick wall. I grind my teeth. "I'm not the patient."

Silence—that's what follows. And much like when we were in the parking lot yesterday, I'm back to wishing I thought before I spoke.

I wobble back and forth on the balls of my feet, feeling nauseated. I just snapped at him, and all he was doing was being nice.

I clear my throat. "I'm sorry...I didn't mean to..."

"No, I'm sorry for prying. Also, for making you feel like you're a patient," Dr. Remson says.

I sigh. "You did nothing wrong. I just had a bad day. And I lashed out at you," I say quickly.

Dr. Remson's lips curl upward into a smile. "I don't think you lashing out was as bad as you almost hitting me with your car."

His tone is familiar, but I can't quite put my finger on it. An open invitation to flirt, maybe? I'm not sure, and I tread carefully. "I'm so sorry, Dr. Remson. Really."

Dr. Remson laughs. Loud. "Please call me Robert. And there could be worse things than meeting my end at the hands of a pretty woman."

"Pretty woman?" I ask, and I feel both of my brows rising.

Dr. Remson's—I mean, Robert's—grin falls flat, and he looks down at the clipboard in hand, then to the doors of Lake Forest. I look at them, too.

He was flirting, wasn't he? I can feel it—the butterflies in my stomach stretching their wings, eager to take flight. But I stifle them with a deep breath. He can tell I'm having a rough time, so he's probably just being nice.

I don't exactly hate it. I miss having a boyfriend...being intimate. But I'd do nothing but get hurt flirting with a man who's not actually into me.

"Uh...so do you need help getting Alyssa?" he asks.

I speed off, hollering, "No. I've got it."

Thankfully, Reena isn't around today. A staff member takes me straight to my sister, in the hall, watching the Tinkerbell movie. Or rather the Tinkerbell movie watching her.

I squeeze her shoulders gently, and Alyssa gives a murmur. It isn't as loud as her usual murmurs, and I brush a lock of hair out of her face.

She must be tired. I don't blame her. I've had enough of Lake Forest for the day...or rather enough of me embarrassing myself in front of Lake Forest's associate director.

Sighing, I wave goodbye to a few of the staff members and hurry out of Lake Forest with Alyssa.

The doorbell wakes me up the next morning. I've gotten used to sleeping in the living room for quick access to Alyssa, so it doesn't take me long to trudge my way to the door and open it.

"Laine, is that you?"

I recognize the voice before I recognize the wrinkled face fringed with graying bangs. "Marcella?!"

The older woman tightens her arms around me, and I press my face against hers. The warmth of her skin is like an overdue medication, one that doses me with fond memories. I breathe her in deeply, savoring the scent of oranges. The smell of cigarettes isn't there. She must have quit.

"It's been a while," she says.

I keep my arms wrapped tight around her.

Two years ago, before they moved back to Ireland, Marcella and her husband lived a few houses down from us. When I was much younger, I'd go to their house after school and ask Marcella to read my fortune. It probably didn't change overnight, but she would always read it anyway. Tarot card reading was one of her favorite pastimes.

"You cut your hair," she says "Also looks like you lost a lot of weight. Is your mother not feeding you?"

All the warmth in the air dissipates. I avoid her question as I break our embrace. "Um, how was Ireland? Is Mr. Kelly doing better?"

The sadness in Marcella's eyes gives me fair warning. "He passed away seven months ago. I kept calling your mother to tell her, but she hasn't been answering me. Is she home?"

Sounds become muffled. It's like I've been submerged in a pool of water, and the water is so cold my limbs begin to feel numb.

"Did your mother change her number?" Marcella asks.

I don't answer. After the move, Marcella and Mom would chat over the phone occasionally about the progression of Mr. Kelly's cancer, but obviously those chats stopped after the accident. I should have reached out to Marcella, but honestly it didn't cross my mind. I had tunnel vision, homing in on only two things—Alyssa and the debt we were saddled with.

Marcella doesn't hide her mounting confusion.

My voice cracks, but I don't break down into a sob. Thankfully.

I direct Marcella inside the house. "There's something you need to know."

CHAPTER
10

ALYSSA

I should be filled with joy to see Marcella. I haven't seen her since before the attack. But I'm still wrapping my head around the magic in the dark chamber, the way it transported me to another realm.

I take a deep breath, my nerves threatening to overwhelm me.

When I had returned to Lake Forest, everything was a blur and I felt weak. I couldn't make out many voices, couldn't see much either. But after a night's rest, the magic has worked its way out of my system.

"How is my favorite princess faring?" Marcella asks.

I want to say I'm not faring well, that my stomach is wrenching, my heart beating out of my chest. But I say nothing. Even if I could, I wouldn't.

The Dark Forest is vast and full of vile creatures that pray on mortal fears. The Mirendalian army won't willingly scour the entire thing, at least not to the best of their ability. They need more information, and until I can get that information, I will remain at Lake Forest. That means no attempts to relay to anyone the injustices that roam rampant at the temple. So I try to say I'm doing well. As expected, nothing remotely close comes out of my mouth.

Marcella cries out, her eyes bulging out their sockets. "Bountiful Terra, please no! She had the whole realm to explore. Please, don't let this be!"

Laine looks on with a grim expression as Marcella's cries shatter the air. She walks up to Laine and pulls her into an embrace. "I'm sorry about the king and queen. I'm sorry about the second princess. I had no idea."

Laine does not say anything, but her arms remain wrapped tightly around Marcella for what feels like hours. When they finally break apart, Marcella wipes her tears with the hem of her dress, the ruffled sleeves white like her shoes. She helps Laine get me out of my bed. "You had a dragon chair made for her?"

Laine nods. "She can walk a few steps on her own with guidance, but long distances are much harder. The chair helps me get her from place to place." A transient smile plays on Laine's lips. "Not to mention, Alyssa loved dragon riding. She is— was—the best rider in our kingdom. It might only be a few inches, but I'm sure she appreciates getting to hover above the ground like this."

Laine doesn't praise herself nearly enough. Father was the first to teach me how to mount a dragon, ease up on its reins, feel the scales beneath me to sense my dragon's needs. However, the only reason I wanted to climb a dragon in the first place was that I saw Laine in the sky with her mount. I wanted to be like her—graceful and skilled. I'd say the attack made Laine lose her love of riding, but she lost it much earlier than that, when Sprinkler died from dragon fever.

Laine guides the levitating chair through the castle, and Marcella follows close behind. She takes me to the great hall in the west wing. A year ago it was the heart of our home. If laughter was not echoing off the warm cerulean walls, music was. Now it's nothing but a skeleton, desperate to have what was stolen returned.

Laine situates my chair next to a cushioned seat and gestures for Marcella to sit. "Do you mind entertaining Alyssa for a bit? I shall go fetch you a drink."

"That's not needed," Marcella says.

"I insist. Besides, I'm sure Alyssa would love it if you stayed for a while." Laine does not wait for a response before bustling out of the hall.

Once we're alone, Marcella holds my hands in her own. "The kingdom must have suffered greatly after the attack. I'm sorry, Alyssa. I promise I will do my best to help you two in any way possible."

I do not doubt Marcella's intentions. This is the first time since the attack that someone I know has been allowed to see me in my current state. If Laine thought Marcella would notify the villagers that I'm a changel, she'd have had the guards remove her immediately.

Laine returns with a cup, a golden ribbon, and a glass jar of honey. She presents the cup to Marcella. "It's the same kind of tea Mother would make, the one with a hint of lemon."

Marcella frowns. "You shouldn't have."

"I should, and I did," Laine says while tying one end of the ribbon around the jar. She ropes the other end around my stomach.

"She's incapable of eating on her own?" Marcella asks.

Laine does a final inspection of her knots. "Her curse stole much of her control over her limbs and voice. She can walk a few steps with help, pick up objects now and again. But most times her grip is weak, and balance is poor. Sitting, hunched in the corner of her chambers, is how I find her most mornings."

I can still think for myself, and that will have to suffice when I'm at Lake Forest in the next few hours.

Laine's deep breath is audible. She rests her fingers on the ribbon. "Fame et abierunt."

The ribbon shimmers, illuminating the cerulean walls with an incandescent yellow. Once Laine falls silent, the light fades, the warm glow of magic making my skin tingle.

Laine holds up an empty jar, and Marcella gasps.

"A non-famem spell is hard to master. Who taught you?" she asks.

"Alyssa's curse was strongest following the attack. To prevent her from starving, twice a day, the white robes would use magic to rid her of hunger," Laine says. "I asked the white robe in charge of her care to teach me."

I'm thankful Laine learned the spell. Consuming anything other than bland soups and fruit sauces is hard, so the spell ensures I get sufficient energy. However, it doesn't allow me to savor the saltfish and bakes my mother taught the servants to cook, the cassava and pigtail. My hunger is simply there one minute and gone the next.

"And what about her mind?" Marcella asks.

Laine presses a gentle hand against my forehead. "She doesn't listen to me even though everything I do is for her own good, always bringing up the king and queen. But I can't afford to assuage Alyssa's worries all the time. We're between a rock and a hard place, and Uncle isn't exactly helping."

Marcella slams her cup of tea down on a small pedestal next to her chair. "So I take it Freidmore is still a mean old goblin?"

If anyone hates my uncle more than my immediate family, it's Marcella. She hails from a land where her people were once rounded up and persecuted for being different. Coming to Mirendal with her husband to partake in trade when she was younger, she was shaken to learn that several of the villagers very well wanted to do the same to their own royal family. She was even more angered that the person fronting the aggression was the king's very own brother.

"Don't insult the goblins," Laine says. "In my experience, they're little tricksters but not as foul as my uncle. Not to mention, the goblins love the king and queen. They would never commit treason."

I force myself to remain calm. Uncle is a horrible person, but he's not behind the attack. Terra knows I want to tell Laine. For now, however, it's best that she believes Uncle is the one who attacked our parents. If she thought otherwise and stopped feuding with Uncle, it might make Reena suspicious.

Once the bowl is empty, Laine gets comfortable in her chair.

"It's been a year since the attack, right?" Marcella asks.

Laine nods.

"And you've been managing the kingdom's affairs all alone? Have you not had time to eat properly? You've shrunk. You need to put some meat back on your bones. What man will try to court you if you don't?" Marcella chuckles for the first time since she's entered the castle. "Speaking of men, have there been any of interest?"

Laine runs a hand through her short curls. "None."

Marcella's brows furrow. "I doubt that. You're the first

princess of Mirendal. You're beautiful and strong. There must be at least one who has caught your eye."

For the first time in a long time, Laine's laughter echoes throughout the castle. "None, Marcella."

Smiling slyly, Marcella pulls a deck of blank cards from her bag. "How about we ask the cards?"

A look of unease flits across Laine's face. Marcella's great-grandmother was a seer. Marcella always claimed she's not as gifted, but when she lived in Mirendal, she'd have peculiar senses about things yet to unfold.

"I don't know if that's such a good idea," Laine says.

Marcella pouts. She has lived more than fifty moons, but I can't help but think of her as a child in this instant. "Come on! It will be fun, just like old times. Besides, don't you want to know if any lovers are headed your way?"

Laine hovers her hand above Marcella's, her face twisting as she deliberates. She lets her hand sink into the older woman's after a few seconds.

Marcella doesn't hesitate. She extends her hand that holds the deck of cards. Eyes glazing over, she whispers something I can't quite hear. Suddenly the cards fly out of her hand and whisk around her and Laine like a small hurricane. When the vortex of wind dies, only three blank cards remain in the air. The rest pile themselves onto the table neatly.

Marcella scours the three cards, seeing Terra knows what, before putting them in the deck.

"What did you learn?" Laine asks.

"There are two mortals of interest who have walked into your life. One set your heart bitter, unhinged you. The other is a scholar with much power."

Judging by the way Laine's eyes widen, Marcella is onto something. "What else?" she asks. "What else did you learn?"

"You will love both in time, but you must be very careful. One of them is a wolf. He will try to destroy you."

Destroy her? I think back to Bennett and Reena's conversation. What if they have something to do with this?

"Well," Laine says, "I did meet two men recently. One threatened to steal my heart. The other...I pray to Terra I never see him again."

Marcella and Laine's cacophony of laughter bounces off the walls, but I'm not laughing. Just who is this man who threatens to steal Laine's heart?

Another problem added to my list.

When Marcella leaves, Laine gets me ready to go to Lake Forest. I'm a bundle of nerves, anxious muscles that won't listen. Yet, when we enter the temple, all my twitching stops, the foul smell strong enough to paralyze me.

Laine lingers in the hall for a while after we arrive. Her presence doesn't go unnoticed. "May I help you with something?" Reena asks.

Laine speaks through pursed lips. "I'm just ensuring my sister is settled before leaving. You did say she was a little uneasy yesterday, no?"

Reena does not blink. She does not smile. Her face is a mask that holds little emotion. "I did. Please take your time."

Laine smiles, but her gaze is unblinking. She matches Reena's tone. "Thank you for your understanding, Reena."

Don't thank her, I want to say. *She was involved in the attack against the king and queen one year ago.* However, I remain silent, my blood boiling.

Once Laine is sure I'm settled, she leaves me. I inhale deeply, reminding myself to remain calm. I have a mission to fulfill, and it requires that I return to the other plane. Hopefully, I will meet Wren again, and he will help me figure out how to navigate the Dark Forest from the other side.

"It's nice to see that you're well," Veranda says. Her everlasting smile looks like it causes her pain today. The edges of her lips twitch sporadically.

"Sam said time in one of the dark chambers would put one into a walking slumber. He didn't tell me anything about another plane," I say.

"I shouldn't have to. The other plane is dangerous." Sam cocks his head in our direction. *"We might be able to run and cast magic while there, but it's a blessing as much as it is a curse. Too many changels have lost their minds by pushing the vorns and regents to unwittingly send them to the next plane."*

"But Wren said—"

"Wren says a lot of things," Sam cuts in. *"He practically lives in that plane. And he's well on his way to losing his mind, if you ask me. I mean, take a look around. He's not here in the hall."*

I glance left, then right. Sam's correct. Wren is nowhere to be found. *"Where is he?"*

"He's prone to fevers, so they keep him away from everyone else, under strict supervision. Thing is, they keep him in a chamber a little too close to one of the dark chambers. And while Wren's mind is certainly strong enough to fight the lingering magic, he has a tendency to let it whisk him away day after day."

Sam glances at Veranda. *"I'm not saying that getting used to our way of life comes easy, especially with Lake Forest in the picture. But there are wonders one can experience in* this *plane, as a changel. Wren refuses to see such. And he'll die because of it."*

The way Wren spun around in the next plane, arms outstretched—indeed, it reminded me of all the times I'd prance around in our castle's garden. Before the attack, it was my favorite place.

But it doesn't matter whether Wren is a changel desperate to regain abilities taken from him. He must—will—help me find a way to navigate the Dark Forest.

"Ferra, Sam can be a little blunt, but he's right. You'll be taking a big risk each time." Veranda's words are like the whisper of a child who is afraid she might be reprimanded. I shield our connection from Sam for only a few seconds.

"I know you like watching the play, Veranda, but it's now or never. I need to get to the other plane."

"What if you die?" Veranda asks. *"Do you think your sister would be happy?"*

Veranda's words weigh heavy on my chest, dredging up fears and gruesome possibilities. What if I'm put in one of the dark chambers today but die in the process? What if I never make it to the realm and acquire the information I need to save the king and queen? What if Laine is left all alone? What if Remwater wins? What if she falls in love with someone set to destroy her?

I try not to let the thoughts settle, jerking my head forward. This place is evil, I try to say, but "Ev. Ev. Ev," is the only thing that leaves my mouth. I scream it again and again while attempting to get out of my chair. Bennett doesn't advise the actors to put their performance on hold.

He points a long finger at me. "Settle down!"

"Are you crazy?" Sam asks.

"I am," I say. *"I need to go to the other plane."*

"I already told you it's not a good idea," Sam barks. *"You—"*

"I need to go back to the other plane, Sam. My family's fate depends on it."

Sam gives me a curious look, but I say no more on the matter, focusing on Bennett and continuing to rock in my chair as hard as I can.

"You guys need to keep the newcomer in check," says another changel. *"She'll get us all in trouble."*

I frown. *"Excuse me?"*

"You heard him," one girl says. *"Why don't you just listen to the vorn?"*

The mental chitter-chatter extinguishes as Bennett comes up beside me. He glances at the other changels. "I want this to be a reminder to the rest of you that misbehavior won't be tolerated."

"Ferra, please, just sit still," Veranda pleads.

But I refuse.

Cussing under his breath, Bennett drags me through the halls, waving at a few wary-eyed vorns until he isn't waving at all. "Two days in row…you're building a reputation. But you know what they say, right? Fool me once, shame on you. Fool me twice, shame on me. I wonder what happens if you act up a third time?"

Bennett pauses, brows raised as if he's expecting an answer. When one doesn't come, he opens the door to the chamber, the mere air wafting over us making me feel weak.

As soon as the door closes behind Bennett and I'm facing those four walls, darkness envelops me.

Wren's green eyes are the first thing I see. I sit up even though he's leaning over me, and we butt heads.

"Owwww!" he hisses while massaging his forehead, a bruise quickly forming.

I don't indulge him or the pain. I rise to my feet and look around. Like the last time I came, I'm in a field of jasmine. I'm wearing the same white gown, and my bracelet jingles on my hand. "We need to go to the Dark Forest," I say.

Wren sprawls out on his side like he has not a care in the world. "I've already told you, you can't enter the Dark Forest. You'll die."

"But I need to."

Wren props his head up with a fist. "No buts. You can't enter."

"I need to find out where my parents are being held. You said being here could be used to my advantage, did you not?" I stare at him with pleading eyes, my heart threatening to break in my chest with each passing second. Was he lying before?

Wren dusts off his sandy-colored trousers as he rises to his feet. "I did say that, and I mean it. However, entering the Dark Forest is off-limits."

"But—"

Wren holds up a hand. "Let me finish, won't you?"

I hold my tongue.

"We can't enter the Dark Forest to find your mother and father, but we can speak to someone who can tell you what you need to know. It will require a bit of a journey, though."

I'm practically jumping in place, my legs ready to run but unsure of where to go. "Please take me to them!"

"I will help you, but on one condition," Wren says.

"What?" I ask, warily.

"You have to trust me."

I'm not sure if it's the look in his eyes or the bass in his voice, but his request makes my heart beat a little quicker. I take a moment to gather my thoughts. "I will."

Wren claps his hands together. "Great. Do you like horses?"

"Truth be told, the only thing I love more is dragons."

Wren whistles, and a whinny resounds throughout the air.

I spin around, marveling as a horse gallops through the field of jasmine. She's like a bolt of obsidian in a blanket of white, her breaths like little gusts of wind. She rears several times once she's next to Wren, stomping her front hooves until he reaches out to pet her. "This is Nerra. She will take us where we must go."

Like an acrobat performing a trick for the umpteenth time, Wren hops onto Nerra's back effortlessly. He reaches a hand out to me, and I climb on. He places my hands around his waist, and I swallow hard.

"Hold on tight. You're in for a treat," he says.

On the count of three, he kicks Nerra into a gallop. The horse is like a dragon bound to the earth. Her gait is smooth, her gallop so strong it practically feels like she's trying to take flight with each stride. I hold on tightly to Wren.

We head north. Dressed in bright garments that appear to be dipped in a ray of sunlight, Emerald flitters around as we enter a field of daisies.

"Hi," Wren says. "We're on our way to see Omniscius."

Emerald gives a graceful nod, following behind Nerra with several other fairies. Much to my delight, as we exit the field of daisies and encroach on a field of red roses, the fairies' beautiful yellow garments turn red. Wren's shirt and my dress do the same.

Wren slows Nerra once we've cleared the field of roses and come to an expanse of water.

Emerald perches on my shoulder, saying something. I stare at her, confused. Her words make no sense to me.

Wren must notice. He translates, "She says this is as far as she'll go, but she hopes to see you again soon."

I wave goodbye to Emerald, watching her race one of the other fairies inland. "You're lucky to speak her tongue."

"To be honest, I'm shocked that you can't. Most adults can," Wren says.

His words make me feel a little more inadequate than they should. "I was supposed to study it this year, but with the attack…"

"I'm sorry," Wren says quickly. "I didn't mean anything by it."

"It's okay." I look left to right, scoping out the barren beach. "Do you have a boat? I don't see any."

Wren seems happy to change the subject. "We don't need one. We'll ride Nerra across."

"But—"

"No more buts. We're not changels here. The magic we're no longer able to use in the other plane, we can use here." Wren turns his head so he can hold my gaze. "Would you—can you—do the honors, Princess?"

Even though it's been a long time since I've performed a spell, the mere idea sends blissful adrenaline coursing through my veins. "I shall." I don't have to think long on what spell to cast. I plant a gentle hand on Nerra's hind. "Tuum erit vobis. Supernatet."

Wren claps. "Nicely done, Princess. However, I must say I would have done it with a little more poise."

"No one likes a humble braggart, Wren," I say while nudging him in his side, and we both burst out into laughter. That laughter echoes like a harmonic hum as Nerra gallops across the lake. Her hooves kick up foamy spray, her body spelled so it doesn't sink below the surface. The noise must still cause a commotion below. A mermaid breaches the surface. Her curly hair, much like her skin, is the color of umber, her eyes the color of mahogany.

I can feel twinges of both pain and happiness shoot across my chest. The mermaid looks like my mother, so much so that I'm disappointed once Wren halts Nerra on a beach.

"Thanks for the company, Freah," Wren hollers, and the mermaid delves back deep below the surface of the lake.

I raise a brow. "You know all the creatures here, don't you?"

Wren helps me dismount, eyes narrowing slightly. "Is that a bad thing?"

"No," I say. Wren's tone defensive, I don't say anything else on the matter, but I can't help but wonder what he's thinking... if there's some truth to what Sam said and he might be here a little more than he should be.

The island itself is not that big, home to only a single tree. However, the tree reaches high into the sky, almost as if it is trying to kiss Terra's hand. Its branches, abundant with leaves, allow not a single ray of sunlight to penetrate to the earth below. As we trek farther inland, I feel like I'm on a midnight stroll, hundreds of fireflies providing the only source of light. There are crickets and cicadas, too, and their soft buzz gets louder and louder, their song reaching its climax when we arrive at the tree's gargantuan trunk.

I stand absolutely still, engrossed. Wren does not interrupt me, letting me bask in the beauty until the ground begins to pulse like a beating heart, cracking in several places. Wren gestures to a crack closer to the tree's trunk. A small green head emerges.

I step closer. "It's a goblin."

Wren nods. "His name is Glior. He's the guardian of Omniscius."

Once he fully emerges from the earth, Glior stands no more than three feet, his skin green and patchy. His black eyes, round and beady, skim me up and down.

Wren whispers in my ear, "It's time to introduce yourself."

I stoop low so Glior and I are face-to-face. "Hello, Glior. My name is Alyssa Highland, and I'm the second princess of Mirendal. I need to speak to Omniscius about the king and queen."

Glior points to the tree.

I look at Wren, confused. "Do I climb it?"

Wren bites back a chuckle. "No. You ask it your question. The tree, Alyssa, is Omniscius."

I look back at the tree, brown but of so many different shades it reminds me of a mermaid's scales. I take a step forward. "Hello, Great Omniscius. My name is Alyssa, and I've come to ask for help in finding the king and queen of Mirendal."

Dozens of leaves begin falling to the ground, showering me with whispers. Those whispers come from men, women, and children. They boggle me until they synchronize to say clearly, "One more must die for all to live. When such comes to pass, you will be reunited with the king and queen."

"I don't get it. What do you mean?" I ask. However, they repeat the same words until the leaves stop falling. Glior does not stick around. Once Omniscius loses no more leaves, he sinks back into the earth, leaving Wren and me alone.

"What did it say?" Wren asks.

"*One more must die for all to live. When such comes to pass, you will be reunited with the king and queen.* But I don't get it. Who is the one who must die?"

Wren idles a finger by his chin. "I was born in Remwater, but I hope it's the prince. He's rotten to the core."

"The prince? You've met him?"

Wren nods. "Haven't you?"

"I met Reena and Bennett. The vorns and other changels. I don't remember meeting a prince. No."

"Strange. He frequents Lake Forest. There we are his to do with as he pleases." Wren stares at me with reservation. "Are you sure you didn't meet him?"

I think back, my mind sifting through everything that happened since I arrived at Lake Forest. A darkness envelops me when my thoughts settle on my experience in the bedchamber. I didn't see anyone, but someone was there, no? Was it the prince?

"I did encounter a strange presence," I say. "I didn't see the person's face, but I sensed them. It was not long after I returned from this plane the first time."

"It's quite possible it was him," Wren says.

We begin trekking back to the lake. "I didn't even realize the prince was at Lake Forest. None of the other changels said anything."

"Most of them never encounter him," Wren says. "Only those he deems truly special."

"Special?"

Wren looks up at the canopy of leaves. "When I was younger, I always wanted to be different, but at Lake Forest I'd have wished to be nothing but ordinary." He grabs my hand as we breach the forest. "He doesn't differentiate between men and women, Alyssa. All he cares about is your soul. And yours is so bright. I fear that he will come for you, take what you hold most dear."

In Wren's grip I can feel his warmth, his pain, his happiness, his ambitions, his worries. My heart hammers in my chest. "I'm happy you're concerned for me, but I'll be fine. Even if the prince tries something, as long as he leaves Laine be, it'll be okay."

Wren raises a brow. "Your sister?"

I think back to her discussion with Marcella. "She said she met two men recently. One she hated, but the other, who threatens to steal her heart, is a scholar. He isn't a prince, which means I have time to figure out this riddle."

Wren shakes his head. "I always believed only Terra has the ability to pass true judgment on the living. Taking up her role is an act of disrespect. But, Alyssa, I do hope for your sake that if—when—you encounter whoever it is Omniscius refers to, you're able to put aside that faith. For Terra..."

I don't like this pause, the heaviness it carries. "For Terra what?"

"She didn't come to rescue me or any of the other changels when we cried for her. You should worry about your sister less and more about yourself."

CHAPTER
11

LAINE

When I get home, I take a quick shower, washing away the musty scent of the stables. I brush my curls smooth, slip on my most durable pair of blue jeans, and head to Glenn's coffee shop.

I smile at a few familiar customers as I make my way behind the counter, where I'm met with big blue eyes framed by platinum curls.

"Hi! My name is Caroline," says a girl who looks no more than eighteen. "I'm new here. I'm also Glenn's niece!"

Glenn stands behind her. "Isn't she adorable?"

I don't see the need to provide affirmation, but I do so anyway. "She is." I shake her hand. "I'm Laine. Nice to meet you."

Introductions complete, I head to the back to put on my apron.

Glenn bustles behind me. "Thanks for coming in today. Jenny had a little emergency come up. She should be back to cover the rest of her shift at three thirty."

I wash my hands in the back sink. "No problem. So what's the plan? Afternoon rush is gonna start any minute."

"Well, Caroline has worked in a coffee shop before, so there's no need to explain a whole lot. I've covered mostly everything. So just think of it as a regular shift," he says.

"Sounds good." I walk out to the front.

"One small caramel macchiato," Caroline yells in a high-pitched voice, and one thought rattles in my head. *I miss Jason. He wasn't this loud.*

Sighing, I get started on the macchiato, wishing shortly after that I took a moment to grab something to eat earlier. The orders are called out like notes of a never-ending sonata, and my stomach rumbles in response. Even when Caroline joins me to make orders and Glenn holds down the register, we fall behind. And somehow, despite all the hustle and bustle, Caroline initiates small talk.

"So how did you meet Glenn?" she asks.

I set a large iced coffee on the countertop. I answer only because it's polite. I'm polite mostly because she's Glenn's niece. "I saw an opening for a barista online, and the rate was better than most desk jobs. I came in for an interview and got the job. What about you? What brought you to your uncle's coffee shop?"

Caroline beams, her smile making her look even more doll-like. "I just started school at the local college. I'm hoping to make some extra hard-earned money."

"Cool. What are you studying?"

"The classics with a focus on Latin language," she says.

I wince a smile. When Alyssa was in high school, she studied Latin. I remember advising her to take something else. What was the point of studying a dead language? Surely, she'd be better served by something like Chinese or Spanish. Alyssa didn't care. To her, Latin had a magical sound to it, and oftentimes she'd use random words in conversation just to get under my skin.

"What about you? Glenn said you went to Virginia Tech? What did you study?"

I wonder if he told her I dropped out? "I studied animal nutrition. I was hoping to apply to their vet program."

"Animals are so awesome! Why did you drop out?"

So I guess Glenn did tell her. I also guess she's nosy. I speak through pursed lips, unable to hide my irritation. "I was hoping working with horses for school would help me rekindle my passion for riding, but that plan fell through after my parents died."

Caroline straightens up like a pin, her face reddening so much she looks like an overripe cherry. It serves her right. She shouldn't pry. Then again, what else should I have expected? She's Glenn's niece, and Glenn swears he and his staff are best friends. Part of being best friends is knowing everything about one another.

Caroline's voice is barely a whisper. "I'm sorry."

"Don't be." It's not my intention, but the words come out of my mouth like venom from a viper.

Caroline doesn't ask many more questions. She heads to the register to relieve Glenn, who needs to take a call. For the next thirty minutes, she leaves me to my own devices and I leave her to hers, even though the shop has cleared out. She's like a jack-in-the-box whenever a customer walks in, sparking conversation with each one. Most of them indulge her, some even relishing the exchange. Well, that is until one customer enters the coffee shop.

"What can I get for you today?" Caroline asks.

"A large iced coffee with two shots of espresso."

I recognize the voice immediately. Dr. Jeon is standing at the register, his hands in his pockets.

Caroline strikes up a conversation while I work on the doctor's order. "Enjoying the nice weather outside?"

"It's okay," Dr. Jeon says.

"Busy shift at the hospital?"

Before Dr. Jeon can answer, his phone rings. He answers the call, his face paling. "I understand, but I was just following protocol." He says nothing else for quite some time. When he does speak again, his voice is several octaves lower. "I'm sorry for the needless workup, Dr. Thomas. In and out. I get it."

I'm so shocked at the change in his tone of voice that I don't realize I'm staring at him until he asks, "Can I help you?"

Lucky for me, I have his coffee in my hand. "Here you go. Have a nice day."

Our fingers brush together slightly as he takes the cup from me, and a spark of static electricity has both of us hissing.

"Geez, be careful, will you?" he snaps.

Caroline's eyes shift back and forth between Dr. Jeon and me. If I didn't know any better, I'd swear she was about to step in between us with a white flag.

I try to be the bigger person, especially given I have an audience. "I'm sorry. I'll make sure to…" Screw it. I can't stand his attitude. "I'll be sure to keep my electric powers under control next time. Please do take care, sir."

Caroline does a piss-poor job of biting back laughter.

I brace myself for the retort that would cause her to stop laughing and get a rush of secondhand embarrassment, but Dr. Jeon's irate stare melts into a sheepish smile. "Touché. I opened myself up for that one. I have a habit of—"

"Redirecting your aggression to those around you?"

"Like you have a habit of interrupting, Laine?"

I hold his gaze, not exactly horribly annoyed with the way my name rolls off his tongue. "You remembered my name?"

"How could I forget after your big spiel on answering my phone?"

I roll my eyes. "It wasn't that big."

"It wasn't that small either."

I shrug. "Agree to disagree."

Thankfully, before there can be any more back-and-forth, he gets some urgent call and darts out of the shop. I have to admit, I'm secretly pleased I got in the last word.

Caroline joins me in the back once he's out of sight. "Shit. You really let him have it."

I sit on a short stool and lean against the wall, not bothering to look up at her. "Are you gonna tell your uncle?"

"Do I seem like the type?"

I take a bite of one of the stale strawberry tarts Glenn retired to the staff area. "Honestly?"

"Honestly."

"You do. You also seem like the type to work here for a few weeks before deciding it's hard work and that you'd rather just suck up your pride and ask your parents for help."

Caroline collapses on the stool beside me while making a buzzing sound. "And you are incorrect."

"Incorrect?"

"Yup! You see, you're not the only orphan in the shop. My parents died, too, although not at the same time. My mother died in childbirth. Father a few months ago from cancer. Oh, and since we're sharing, the real reason I'm here is because Glenn hyped you up…said he had a feeling we'd get along well." She takes my tart and inspects it before taking a bite, way too chipper considering what she just said. "Can't say we're off to a great start, though. You're, and I say this nicely, kind of an ass."

I rub sweaty palms against my apron. I was out of line. No, more than out of line. I was a total bitch, and I apologize to Caroline profusely.

She tells me it's alright, but I don't feel any less shitty. I judged her, and even though she seems okay about it, there's no doubt in my mind that my words have thrown salt on deep, painful wounds. How could they not?

I pinch the bridge of my nose. "I'd totally get it if you want me gone from the shop, but please, just let me stay for a few more months? Just until I can find something else."

Caroline waves her hands back and forth. "Slow your roll! I have no plans of telling Glenn anything about this."

I stare at her wide-eyed. "Really?"

She bobs her head aggressively. "Of course! But only because of the way you didn't take any of that, might I add hot, doctor's shit. My uncle…he needs people like you in the shop. Lets people walk all over him, I swear."

Relief washes over me. "Well, I appreciate it."

"I'm glad! Although, if we do wanna stay cool, you're def gonna have to be down with me blasting my music playlist. Think a mash-up of every genre possible."

Needless to say, I indulge Caroline in conversation for the rest of the shift, discussing hair, foods, and even her newfound obsession—the doctor and me, together.

"That man was drop-dead gorgeous and you know it," she says while ringing someone up at the register.

I chuckle as I hand a customer a croissant. "Doesn't make up for the bad attitude."

"But that makes him so much hotter, no?"

I stare at her like she's just spoken another language.

Pale cheeks flushing, she starts explaining before I can say anything. "I know it sounds toxic, but you two were giving serious enemies-to-lovers vibes. Besides, you weren't exactly Friendly Betty during the convo. Rather, Flirty Shirley?"

I gasp. "I was not flirting!"

She rolls her eyes. "Uh-huh, and neither was he."

Before I can protest any further, my coworker comes to relieve me. I run to the back to take off my apron before waving goodbye to Caroline.

Our conversation having put me in good spirits, I hum along to a song on the radio I haven't turned on in months on my way to Lake Forest, certain my mood can't peak any further. But I'm wrong. It skyrockets when I see Robert in the parking lot. His blond hair shines like a halo under the sun as he approaches me.

"I'm glad I caught you here," he says.

I close the door to the SUV. "You are?" Worry immediately kicks in. "Did something happen to Alyssa?"

"No. Your sister is fine. I actually wanted to talk to you about the comments I made yesterday."

And cue my mood nosediving. "It's okay. I get it. You were just being nice." Yeah, better to make this conversation as painless as possible.

Robert slows his gait and, almost instinctively, I do too. "Laine, I don't think you understand. I did mean something by it. That's why I'm here, outside, trying to get what I have to say off my chest."

"And what's that?"

"I know your sister is a guest here, so this might be a little weird. The last thing I want is to make you uncomfortable. I also don't want you thinking this will affect my work when it comes to your sister in any way."

Robert and I are at the doorstep at this point. I tuck my hands under my arms so he can't see how his words make me quiver.

"Would you care to grab a drink with me this week? To be honest, if I didn't ask, I'd never forgive myself. I only met you a few days ago, but I can't get your face out of my head."

"You can't get me out of your head?" The words come out of my mouth like a whisper on the wind.

He smiles.

I smile, too, but not for long. My jumbie rears her head, and she asks several questions. *What if he's used to this—asking a woman out not long after he meets her? She says yes, they sleep together, and he moves on? Look at him. He's beautiful. They probably flock to him. What if you do get drinks with him? Then what? What happens when he finds out about your struggles? The bills and debt you have to pay? It will never work. Also is this really appropriate?*

I try to drown her out, not ruin what might be a good thing. But my jumbie is relentless. She cackles as I say the words "I'm not so sure, Robert. Don't get me wrong. You're an attractive guy, and I appreciate that you're asking me out, but... I just don't know."

Before Robert can reply, the door to Lake Forest opens, and Reena comes out. She pauses for a second, her eyes darting back and forth between Robert and me. "Wren is running a fever. I suggest we take him to the ER."

Robert's eyes linger on me for a few more seconds, the

disappointment in them making my stomach wrench. "Thanks for letting me know, Reena. I'll contact his family and get the paperwork ready."

"Is there any way I can be of assistance? Any documents you want me to get started on?" Reena asks, and while the question is clearly meant for Robert, she deadlocks us in a stare that screams of jealousy.

I don't say anything to her or Robert. I follow them into Lake Forest and make my way to the hall where Alyssa sits calmly along with several others.

As I wheel Alyssa out, I can't help but wonder whether I made the right decision about Robert's offer.

CHAPTER 12

ALYSSA

Laine enters the hall, her black cloak sweeping the floor. She lets out a big breath as she approaches me. Something is wrong.

I remind myself to relax. Just a little longer and I'll ensure she won't bear that pained expression again.

By the time we arrive at the castle, Marcella is waiting for us outside the west wing. Laine escorts her inside and directs her to have a seat next to me in the main hall. She leaves to fetch a cup of tea for Marcella.

Marcella takes a sip of her tea once Laine sits. "How was dealing with kingdom affairs today?"

"It started off surprisingly pleasant," Laine says. "I upbraided that no-good white robe. But I'm worried I may have ruined a relationship."

Marcella's brows snap upward. "What do you mean?"

"The scholar initiated a courtship." Laine turns her attention to the soup, blowing several times before pressing the spoon to my lips. "I turned him down."

Marcella almost chokes on her tea. "What? Why?"

I use what little energy I have left to lean forward in my chair. I, too, am shocked.

Laine wipes my mouth with a small washcloth. "With everything that is happening, I won't be able to truly commit to a courtship. I have too many obligations."

Marcella takes another sip of tea before speaking. "The king and queen wouldn't have wanted for you to burden yourself like this."

Laine takes off her crown, still shimmering silver. She stares at it as if it holds secrets only she is privy to. "Still...what kind of daughter would I be if I entertained a courtship right now?"

Marcella folds her plump arms across her chest, her eyes narrowing. "You will be doing your duty to the kingdom. Think about it. Your uncle is practically enjoying the way everything has been sucking you dry. You handle the kingdom's affairs, yes. However, I heard some of the villagers talking today. You need to change your outlook on things."

"What did they say?" Laine asks.

Marcella whispers her words, almost as if she can lessen their blow by doing so. "They believe you do not have a handle on the kingdom. They have also started referring to you as a shut-in."

Laine practically rises out of her chair. "How dare they?! I—"

"The villagers are right, Laine. It doesn't matter what you do for the kingdom if they believe you're barely managing. You need to give the appearance that you are thriving."

"And how am I supposed to do that?" Laine nearly barks the words.

Marcella does not seem to take offense. "Simple. Start partaking in activities any princess with free time on her hands would."

Laine stares at Marcella for several seconds before nodding slowly. "I want to say it is a bad idea, but it does make sense."

Marcella winks at me. "I'm sure Alyssa would agree it would send your uncle into a frenzy. What a nice added benefit."

Laine looks at me, almost as if seeking approval. I want to tell her it is okay. She should enjoy being courted. However, there are too many things that are more important. It would have to be left up to Laine. She is the one able to wield a sword and cast spells.

I stare at her.

"My heart was practically dancing in my chest," she says. "I wanted to say yes so badly, but I could not help but be wary. I come with so much baggage. Why would he be interested?"

Laine is right. She does come with baggage…she comes with me. The princess who can't help herself. A princess once strong now weak…a princess who is no longer a princess. A girl who—

Marcella claps her hands together, pulling me from my thoughts. "So you will indulge him? I would be happy to keep Alyssa company at any time while I am still in Mirendal. I will also do my best to ensure her changel status remains a secret."

Laine looks at me, her smile withering. The sight of it fading makes my heart break, mostly because I feel as if I am the one stealing her happiness. She should enjoy herself for now. There is nothing she can do until I figure out where our parents are. Once I do that, she can put whatever romantic affairs she has on hold. Till then, however, I should play my part, and that part is returning to Lake Forest tomorrow. To go to the next plane.

This in mind, I try to say, *Go meet the scholar.* Only *go* comes out of my mouth, but for the first time in a long time, the one word to escape my lips is enough to relay my thoughts.

Laine looks at me with wide eyes, as does Marcella. After they seem to snap out of their daze, Laine tries to coax me to say more.

"Go? Really, Alyssa? Try saying something else," she says. However, "go" doesn't leave my mouth again. I can see Laine's disappointment as she sinks back in her chair, but I am happy. It was enough for her to understand me. After performing a non-famen spell to round out my meal, Laine looks at both me and Marcella with big brown eyes that haze almost gold under the light. "Let the courting begin then."

When I get to Lake Forest the next day, my eyes are practically closing in on themselves. Despite the dulling of my senses, I notice Laine seems to be looking for someone. She must not find them; disappointment radiates from her face like the glow of a candle.

As she turns and strides for the exit, I strike up a conversation with Veranda, sitting in the same place, in the same chair as the previous day. *"I need to go back to the other plane."*

"You don't listen, do you? You'd think your little encounter with Bennett the other day would be enough to set you straight, yet you keep pushing, drawing unwanted attention."

"You don't get it. If I can take down Reena, I can take down Lake Forest!"

Sam stares at me like I've uttered pure silliness. *"Reena? She's just another one of his brainwashed followers. He'll replace her with the snap of his finger."*

"Who?" I ask.

Sam huffs. *"The one overseeing this hellish place."*

"But I thought—"

Sam cuts me off. *"No, Ferra. You didn't think."* Sam's sudden hostility sends a chill up my spine. His eyes dart back and forth, and he shifts in his chair, his face paling. He is afraid. It's enough to make me afraid, too.

"Who is he? Have you met him?" I ask Sam. When he doesn't answer, I turn my attention to Veranda.

She shakes her head. *"I do not remember much of our encounter except that once it ended, I couldn't see or hear well for days. Changels, all of us, have resigned ourselves to not speak of him."*

"Who?"

Veranda's mental voice quivers. *"We call him the prince of Lake Forest."*

The look in her eyes makes my blood run cold.

"Did he do something to or take something from Sam?" I ask.

"No," Veranda says. *"However, he took something from a girl he practically considered a daughter."*

"Where is she?"

Sam is the one to respond. *"Dead, Ferra. She's dead."*

My breaths rumble in my chest and my palms get sweatier by the second. *"What did he do to her?"*

Sam does not answer.

I direct my questioning expression to Veranda. She looks as

if she is fighting her utmost to turn her smile into a true display of her emotions. *"After her encounter with the prince—she had several—she got sick. At least that is what those who aren't changels were led to believe. To us, the truth was clear. He inflicted a curse upon her, one that would lead to her death."*

"He silenced her," Sam says.

My inner voice comes out raspy. *"How in control of her words was she?"*

Sam gazes up at the ceiling. *"She could speak, though her words were slightly convoluted at times. She told her mother what happened. When her mother moved her from here, I was certain people would start looking into this place. But . . ."*

Sam's words fade out.

"But what?" I need to know what happened.

"But he gave her mother the right amount of gold to keep her quiet."

The blood pulsing in my veins grows hot, my vision hazing red. How could a mother stand for such injustice? How could anyone? We changels might not be able to walk, talk, or cast spells like other humans. But we deserve respect just like they do.

The seconds pass slowly in silence until Balding Bennett enters the hall. His eyes scan his surroundings for several seconds before settling on me.

Sam's voice is shaky. *"The play is still ongoing. There's no reason for them to take you."*

My tone matches his. *"Then why?"*

"The only reason they'll tear you away from the rest of us so suddenly is if he's ready for you," Sam says.

I ask the question even though I know the answer. *"Who?"*

Sam isn't the only one who speaks an answer. All the

changels, even those who don't look at me, whisper in a disjointed rhythm, *"The prince."*

When I open my eyes, I'm practically reeling. I take a deep breath, digging my palms into the earth beneath me. The last thing I remember was the vorn taking me to a chamber, but this one was different. It wasn't four slabs of clay boxing me in, but a vast room, warm even. There was a bed in the center, a canopy of rose petals above silky sheets. After the vorn put me on the bed, Reena entered shortly after, a potion in her hand.

"I'm trying to make this easier for you," she said, "The magic is weaker in this chamber. This potion will help you enter your sleep quicker, and quicker you must."

I shouldn't have fought. I wanted to go to the next plane, but Reena's intention of giving me the potion made me act out.

The last thing I made out before slipping into the darkness was the regent, looking around the room frantically before exiting.

"What's wrong, Princess? You look worried about something," Wren says.

His chipper voice should be a comfort, but anger and urgency cord around my neck like a noose.

"I need to go see Omniscius," I say.

Wren walks a slow circle around me as I rise to my feet. I shift back and forth, getting comfortable with using my legs.

"He won't tell you more than he has about the king and queen," he says.

"What do you mean he won't tell me anything else? Maybe if I explain how imperative it is, he'll tell me what I really need to know."

Wren's entire face lights up as he laughs, much like the flicker of a light in a dark hole. He's beautiful. He really is. However, I want to wipe the smile off his face. Now is not the time for his antics.

"Try not to get so worked up. That's just how it is," he says. "You can ask him about anything but the riddle."

I fold my arms. "And how can you be so sure? He might not have told you anything else about whatever you asked, but he might tell me. My situation is dire."

Wren's smug grin withers. He takes one step toward me. "Are you saying my situation wasn't?"

I avoid his gaze. Wren isn't smiling anymore. I thought it would make me happy, but it only adds to the sadness and anger ravaging me from the inside out. I fidget with the hem of my dress. "You seem so carefree sometimes that it's hard to take you seriously, Wren."

Wren's gaze softens, but he says nothing. We stand together in silence for several minutes. Once he's finished deliberating Terra knows what, he directs me to follow him. He leads me through the meadow of jasmine, then into the one of daisies. We head south once we encroach on the field of roses, the soft petals brushing against my skin. We only stop once we get to a large hill.

"It's a little bit of a trek up. Think you can manage with those brittle-looking legs of yours?"

"I bet I can get to the top with these brittle-looking legs faster than you."

"I don't think so, Princess. My father always told me I was the fastest mortal alive."

I wave a finger about teasingly. "Funny, my father told me—and my sister—the same thing."

"So is it a race?" Wren asks.

I don't reply, sprinting up the hill as fast as I can. I can feel the blood pumping in my legs, coursing through my veins. My breaths come quicker, and my knees burn. It's been a long time since I've run, and while my body screams at the intensity, it also revels in it.

I have no doubts that Wren lets me win. When we're halfway up the hill, he lingers for a few seconds, watching me, the hint of a certain kind of urgency in his eyes. It doesn't last long, flittering away as soon as he starts running again.

I collapse at the top of the hill, which looks like it might almost kiss the plane's sun.

Wren sits beside me, his shirt fluttering in the wind. "What do you think of the view?"

I take a deep breath, drawing my legs closer to myself. It's a good thing the air is chilly. It jostles my senses, making me aware of every little thing around me. The fields of flowers below blend together like a confused rainbow. The sun kisses the lake with thousands of rays. The island on which Omniscius resides provides a boundary to the east. To the far west is the Dark Forest. The sun's rays somehow don't seem to touch it, the clouds above the forest the color of tar.

"Discounting the Dark Forest, the view is beautiful," I say.

Wren traces a cloud with his fingers. "Whenever I come to this plane, the first place I go is always here. I might not be royalty, but when I'm here, watching over everything, I feel like a king."

"You might not be a king in the other plane, but certainly your life there matters," I say.

"I never said it didn't," Wren says.

The words come out of my mouth before I can stop them. "Your actions say otherwise."

Wren's face twists with several emotions before he wears a sheepish expression. "Maybe you won't believe me, either, but I've already exhausted my options there. I can't win against the prince in the other plane. And I'm certain I will die by his hands soon. He's tired of me."

The idea of Wren dying incites a feeling of dread in me that almost parallels what I felt when my family was attacked a year ago. I take deep breaths, my hands beginning to shake. I don't want Wren to die. I don't want to die either. Given Sam said it was likely I was about to meet the prince, death might very well be waiting for me. Even then, I can't pretend nothing is wrong. I can't live in the moment. How can Wren?

I pray my voice doesn't smack of judgment. "If you believe the prince is going to kill you, why are you so calm?"

Wren fixes me with his gaze. "Every moment I spend resenting the atrocities of Lake Forest is a little victory for the prince and his followers. I refuse to let them take any more than they've already taken, Alyssa."

I wish I could join him in his way of life, forget all the negative things in the other realm. But I have the fate of the kingdom riding on my shoulders. Not to mention, as Wren said, it's only a matter of time before the prince kills him. I refuse to just sit and wait for that moment, in this plane or any other.

Wren sighs. "There you go again, Princess."

"What?"

"You're thinking too hard. Focusing on the negative things."

"I can't help it. There's a lot at stake," I say.

Wren passes a hand over his face. "I can't do that. However, I am here for you until I draw my last breath." Wren is rarely serious, but his promise is heavy. He means what he says, and I find myself leaning closer to him. We might have our differences, but since I have arrived at Lake Forest, he has done nothing but help me. And with him, I have never felt more alive...more like my old self.

Wren's face is only a few inches away, but it feels like time moves slower as our lips get closer. Desperate and burdened with so many emotions, we are just about to kiss when my bracelet breaks. The beads scatter all over the hill, as if there is some invisible string pulling it far away from me. Wren and I jump apart, breathing hard.

He picks up a bead that landed by his feet. He does not smile, pulling out a silver broach shaped like a horse from his pocket. "I'm sorry, Alyssa."

I swallow hard, not sure what to say as I get up and pick up the beads one by one. "I don't understand. How could it just break?"

"It didn't just break," Wren says, a glimmer of a possible tear in his eyes. "The prince has secured what you hold most dear."

CHAPTER
13

LAINE

When I dropped Alyssa off at Lake Forest earlier, Robert was nowhere to be seen. I could feel my heart sink as I hopped into the SUV, the jumbie on my shoulder cackling.

You took too long, girl. A man like him is not going to wait for the likes of you.

I mentally swat the jumbie on my shoulder, and she hushes for a few seconds. Hopefully, I'll see Robert when I pick up Alyssa this evening. And hopefully, Reena won't be around to glare at me.

I can feel the muscles in my face twitch as I smile. Things are finally starting to look up, aren't they? My chest feels warm as my mind plays with the thought of Alyssa...how yesterday when Marcella and I were discussing the date, Alyssa said *go*. Sure, it might be a one-off. However, the part of me that likes to think of my sister as more than a shell of a person thinks she's improving. She just might have understood Marcella's mention of our neighbors gossiping about me, my reservations about dating.

I pull into the driveway and hop out of the car, the breeze whisking through my short hair. I wasn't able to get a shift at the coffee shop today, and I don't have any lessons at the stables.

No choice but to enjoy the day off, I head upstairs to my room. My eyes trace the herd of sticker horses racing across my purple walls. I stuck them there ten years ago. I was so certain back then of my life's trajectory...that by this time I'd have made a name for myself in the equestrian world. In all three forms of eventing, of course, but mainly cross-country. With the variety of natural obstacles and exposure to the elements, it has always been my favorite.

If not for the accident, I'd have gotten my degree in animal nutrition at Virginia Tech and would be in vet school, working toward becoming an equine veterinarian.

I draw the curtains and climb into bed. I always spend minutes, hours even, imagining my life playing out the way I planned it. It never ends well. Daydreaming always turns into actual dreaming, with me back in college, telling my parents that I'm too sick to come home and visit. The next thing I know, they're always somehow outside my dorm room, asking me to open the door. I'm usually ecstatic. Until I see them.

Dad's face is barely a face, and Mom's skull is always spewing blood. Some of that blood gets into my mouth and eyes, yet I never back away. I just stare at Alyssa, most times standing between our parents, covered in blood, screaming, "You did this to us. You, Laine. You."

As expected, I'm plagued by this nightmare today. However, in an interesting turn of events, just before I can open the door and greet my parents and Alyssa, I'm able to rouse myself out of sleep.

"Jumbie zero, Laine one," I mutter.

Eyes still groggy with sleep, I head downstairs to the living room and turn on the television, knowing this is the best chance I'll have to do a little picking up.

The news has just begun to broadcast a segment on a high-profile murder from a few years back, one in which the accused was a rich man and the lawyer he hired to defend him was none other than my uncle.

The news anchor sings his praises on television, calling him a wolf in the courtroom yet a man with a tender heart due to a long list of philanthropic work. If only he knew Freidmore won't even acknowledge his orphaned nieces, much less offer to help them. As to why? If had to guess, it probably has something to do with my mother. Dad always said Freidmore didn't approve of her. The reason? Well, why does the British media harp on Meghan Markle so much?

Refusing to let my uncle get to me more than he already has, I turn off the television and head to the bathroom. I stand in front of the mirror for a few minutes, observing my face like it's a painting I'm seeing for the first time. My curls are growing at an alarming rate, already long enough that I can probably pull the front of my hair back with a headband. I have dark circles around my eyes. My skin, much like Alyssa's, doesn't glow soft honey anymore but is patchy. Really, what did Robert see in me?

If my mother were here, she'd probably say a goddess. My dad would probably say a queen. Both of them are compliments they'd occasionally give me, compliments that made me cringe because they sounded so cheesy.

If only I internalized their words back then, maybe I'd feel more like a goddess and less like a shriveled-up witch right now.

I step into the shower, letting the hot water beat down on me like a storm cleansing a forest of any impurities. I'll go treat myself to a nice meal. I haven't had a burrito bowl at Chipotle in so long. I'll also stop at some beauty supply stores...see what kind of makeup I can buy on a twenty-dollar budget. Might not be much, but some eyeliner and blush will do. And I'll choose a nice outfit, one I haven't worn since I left college.

Hopefully, it'll make Robert forget about the way I shut him down. Hopefully, it'll make me feel more like what my parents said I was.

You really think that's gonna be enough? asks the jumbie on my shoulder.

"Yes," I belt out while turning the water to blazing hot. "So shut the hell up!"

I don't expect her to, but today must be my lucky day. She says nothing, and I hop out of the shower, excited for the day ahead until I add the final touch to my outfit—my bracelet.

While the string is a clear elastic band, the beads are dark tree bark. Hoping to maintain their color and gloss, I've always avoided showering with the bracelet on my wrist. But as I put it on my hand, the elastic snaps like it was yanked by some invisible force, and the beads scatter all over the room.

I swallow hard, bending down to pick up the beads...beads from my mother's homeland.

I'm half expecting the jumbie to whisper in my ear how this is a bad omen, a clear sign that I should give up on the idea of going out with Robert...give up on the idea that I deserve forgiveness from my mother. But the jumbie is silent.

CHAPTER
14

ALYSSA

The first thing I sense when I return to Lake Forest from the other plane is the foul energy from last time, the one that makes my stomach churn, my ears ache.

I take a deep breath, praying my vision will come into focus. Much to my gratitude, everything in the chamber, including *him*, does.

The best way to describe him is like a serpent wearing the mask of an angel. His blond hair shimmers under the white of the orb above, his gaze as soft as a mother staring at her baby. His energy, however, perforates the air like the scent of a blood-lily. I almost gag on that smell, painfully aware that the scent is the same one I encountered when I first came to Lake Forest.

"I see you're finally back," he says. His voice is like the song of a siren, beautiful but deadly.

I try to ask him what's happening, who he is. However, my words remain lodged in my throat.

He wipes his upper lip before readjusting his blue and brown robe. "Alyssa Highland, second princess of Mirendal. Nice for you to finally join me."

My eyes must scream my inner thoughts because he proceeds to answer several questions I have not voiced.

"I'm the third prince of Remwater, Robert Remson. It's a pleasure to meet you." He holds up a hand, and my muscles stiffen as I glance downward. The beads of my bracelet are still strung together, but Robert holds the small charm fashioned in the shape of my mother's homeland.

"Your sister's little magic spell was successful in that it hid your bracelet from most mortals, but there's just one problem. I'm not most mortals. I have been trained in spell-casting and dissolution spells since I was a little boy. My father saw to that. So you can imagine my surprise when I come and see such a beautiful young lady here, with a charm only the Mirendalian royal family is known to have."

I can feel acid rise in my throat and tears well in my eyes. He knows who I am, which means he knows Laine's true identity as well. I need to warn her that Lake Forest isn't safe. I need to tell her that he's behind the attack a year ago.

Robert walks the periphery of the room like a tiger stalking its prey. "Remwater needs to expand. And as Mirendal is situated on prime land, it only makes sense to absorb your kingdom into mine. I'd be able to feed off more energies of those around me, especially the weak." The dark prince chuckles. "You look at me with such disgust. To be honest, I used to look at myself the same way, thinking Terra made a mistake. But, over time, it became clear." Robert smiles wide, his voice booming with excitement. "It was Terra's will."

He's crazy. He has to be. Terra would never will someone to be cruel. Would she?

Robert stops circling the room. "To think I doubted her. I mean, my plan, which I enacted a year ago, was pristine. Destabilize the kingdom and swoop in as a savior when the people are most against the royal family." He shakes his head. "But your sister managed to keep the kingdom's affairs in order. I was just about planning to take other measures, certain I failed, but Terra has blessed me thrice."

Robert sniffs the air like he's inhaling a hot meal. "You, Alyssa, have one of the sweetest energies I've ever tasted. It makes me wonder how your sister—"

Reena enters the chamber before Robert can finish his spiel, and I can't help but rejoice. If Robert continued talking, I just might lose my mind. My inability to do anything has never before been so upsetting.

Reena stares at me with a pale face before looking at Robert. "Did you..." She can't seem to finish her question and opts for a statement instead. "Tell me you didn't reveal yourself to her, Robert! We can't afford being compromised." Her usually stoic face contorts with emotions I know well—fear, anger, sadness.

Robert pins her against the wall, and I jump in my chair. "I think you forget your place. I must have forgotten it, too, constantly abiding by your rules. You're so worried about what I'm doing, who I'm with. You failed to realize that the girl who sits before us is the second princess of Mirendal."

Reena's eyes widen only slightly. She doesn't say anything, letting silence fill the room.

When Robert speaks again, he practically growls. "You

already knew, didn't you? Did you purposely try to deter me by giving her the sleeping potion?"

Reena stutters. "O-of course not. I just thought it would be easier for you to acquire what she holds most precious without a fight."

Robert arches a brow. "What is victory without a fight? Besides, how much of a fight can a changel really muster?" He unpins Reena slowly. "There was a time you rejoiced in the treacheries of magic and war. What happened?"

"Nothing, my prince. That woman is still here, still doing her best to protect you. But we must be careful until the battle is won. For now, can't I be your one and only source of energy?"

Robert's face morphs into a blank canvas. "Her sister, Laine. Do not get involved. Just like I didn't get involved with your little courtship with the clown."

"You know about Bennett?" Reena asks.

Robert nods. "I did, but why interfere? Someone needs to keep the imp occupied...make him feel loved. That way he'll stay right here, ready to serve a purpose."

Reena's eyes briefly glint with anger. As she bows her head, he catches her chin in his hand. "You will stay away from Laine Highland. Understood?"

Reena's voice cracks as she glances in my direction. "Yes, my prince. Shall I take her to the hall? Her sister should be here soon to retrieve her."

Robert holds up a finger. "There is something I must do first. Actually, two."

"What's that?"

Robert takes a step away from me. "First, I must commemorate this moment with a portrait."

It's no ordinary portrait. Without uttering words, there's a bright light. Seconds later, in his hands, is a drawing. Of me.

He holds it close to him before stooping low beside me. "Your sister denied my advances yesterday, but women always come around. I can't risk you getting involved. So, how about you keep yourself occupied with Wren in the other plane? You should view this as a favor."

I have to remind myself to breathe. My sister denied his advances yesterday? Beads of sweat flood my eyes as I piece together another nasty puzzle. He's the scholar Laine was talking about? The one who makes her feel happy? The one I told her to go and fraternize with? No! Terra, please no!

Robert rests his fingers on my temples while inhaling a big breath of air. And like he's whispering sweet promises, he says, "To the next plane you go. In the next plane you shall stay. Forever crowned. Forever bound. Silentium est aureum."

He grins. "The curse should let you revel in this plane for a few more minutes. I'm courteous. I'll let you say farewell to your other changel friends."

Each breath I take is hard, a conscious effort. Dread, unparalleled and stifling, sits on top of me as Reena guides my chair back into the hall. She takes a quick leave, her eyes teary. I imagine my eyes look the same, if not worse.

"*What happened? Are you okay?*" Veranda asks.

Sam's face is pale. "*You met the prince, didn't you?*"

"*I did. He knows who I am,*" I say. "*He's planning to take over Mirendal. I need to tell my sister before the curse takes hold!*"

"*Come on, Ferra. Answer us,*" Sam yells.

My brows shoot up. "*I just did.*"

"*Why aren't you responding, Ferra?*" Veranda asks.

My shocked expression must clue them in, because theirs twist into ones of horror.

I can no longer communicate with changels in this plane. I don't have time to process the fact for very long. Laine enters the hall to retrieve me, and Robert enters shortly after, almost as if timing her arrival. I try to tell Laine he's behind all our problems. However, before I can try to say anything, everything goes black.

PART 2

TWILIGHT REALMS

CHAPTER
15

LAINE

The evening sun beats down on me as I stare at my reflection in the bar's window. I'm in riding breeches and a green V-neck, definitely not dressed for a date. But I don't have time to go home from the stables and change before I'm due to meet Robert. I knew the schedule was going to be tight, but it's still been over a week since we agreed to get together and exchanged numbers.

I pray that I don't smell too horsey as I enter the quaint bar not too far from Glenn's coffee shop. Citrus and hops fill my lungs as my eyes scan the dim area.

I adjust my belt. They rode horses in the Middle Ages. Hopefully, Robert will think I ran with the theme after his suggestion that we come here—the Headless Horseman.

My eyes find him the same time he looks up from his drink menu.

"Can I get you a table?" the host asks.

"I actually see the person I'm meeting."

"And who is that?" she asks.

I point to Robert, and she glances at him, then me. Nose crinkling, she looks me up and down, her eyes settling on my jodhpurs.

She smiles wryly. "Right this way."

She gestures to the chair on the other side of the table. "Hello, sir, your friend is here."

I'm going to let it go. After several hours of dealing with kids cuckoo for horses, I'm mentally and physically drained. Plus, she's right. I look like a hot mess, definitely not someone Robert would be interested in.

Robert cocks his head. "Pardon?"

"Your friend is—"

"My *date* is here," Robert clarifies.

Satisfaction shoots through me like a live wire, renewing my energy. I don't hide my smile when the host looks at me, seeming to seek affirmation.

"Give us a few more minutes to decide on what we'd like, please," Robert says, and the host heads back to her post.

I huff at the exaggerated sway of her hips; she's so clearly putting on a show. It pisses me off, but I'll readily admit she has a wonderful figure.

Refusing to compare us, as I'm sure my jumbie would want to, I sink into my chair. Immediately, self-satisfaction is replaced with tiredness.

I muffle a yawn. "I'm sorry I'm late. One of my students at the stables had a little bit of a fall."

Robert raises a brow. "Is he okay?"

I nod. "Yeah, he's fine. All riders fall at some point."

"I remember you mentioned you worked at a stable, but it didn't quite register until now."

I look down at my drink menu. "Did it not register because I'm black?" I voice the question impulsively, regretting the words as soon as they're in the open. But I'd dealt with that reaction for years. Whenever I told people I rode, they'd always be surprised. They were never surprised when my white friends expressed their interest in horses.

Robert's eyes flicker for just a second. His grin widens, his face breathing an air of calm. "That's true. There aren't many black equestrians. But I was more referring to your outfit. You look like you're about to ride in a hunter-jumper competition."

I shift in my seat uncomfortably. *That's right. You're dressed like a horse girl, Laine.* "I'm sorry. I didn't have time to go home and change."

Robert reaches a hand out to mine. His warmth makes my entire body relax. "Don't apologize. I'm just happy to see you."

Our host approaches us before I can respond. "Have you guys decided?"

There's no point in looking at the menu. I already know what I want. "Can I have the Dogfish IPA?"

"I'll have the same," Robert says.

The host's eyes remain fixed on him, her grin eager.

Robert doesn't spare her another look. "Are you hungry, Laine?"

"Um...yeah. Can I also have an order of french fries?"

The host fumbles with her pen as she writes down the order, her gaze still glued on Robert.

"I'll have an order of fries as well." Finally he smiles at her. It's a radiant smile that just might make her fall to her knees. However, for the first time since I've met him, Robert's smile doesn't travel to his eyes.

"Annoyed?" I ask once the host is out of earshot.

Robert perks up in his chair. "You noticed?"

"Hard not to. Does it happen often? Women gawking at you?"

Robert isn't coy. "It does. But I must say that you have a sharp eye. Most people can't tell when I'm peeved. What gave me away?"

"I just noticed that your smile didn't travel to your eyes when you looked at her."

Robert leans forward. "Does my smile travel to my eyes when I look at you?"

I swallow hard, my mind fueling my anxiety.

Thankfully, the host spares me from answering Robert's question, setting our drinks in front of us. I take a hearty sip, praying the alcohol will ease some of my nerves.

"You love IPAs?" Robert asks.

"I love all beer except Miller Lite."

Robert takes a sip of his own drink. "That's quite specific. What don't you like about it?"

Well, Miller Lite was the beer at most of the college frat parties I went to. It was also the beer I was drinking when I found out about the accident. "Not sure really. Maybe it's the taste."

Robert doesn't hesitate to call me out on my bullshit. "I don't buy it. There's a story in your eyes that you're not telling."

I tap my fingers against the glass, a little unnerved even though I'm sure he's just being flirtatious. "You're right. There is. If it's okay, I'd like to save that story for another time."

Robert frowns. "I'm sorry. I didn't mean to upset you."

"You've done nothing wrong," I say quickly. "It's just something I don't want to talk about right now. Hopefully, one day, when we're closer, I'll tell you." It's a lie. I plan on keeping the truth about my part in the accident a secret forever.

Robert leans even closer. "You plan on going on more dates with me?"

My stomach does a cartwheel. "I wouldn't be giving you the time of day if I didn't think that was a possibility."

Robert chuckles, redness suffusing his cheeks. I feel a surge of confidence. He must really like me. No man can fake a blush like that.

He runs a hand through his hair. "You don't play games, do you?"

"I don't have time for games. I have my sister to care for. Bills to pay."

"Was your sister much like you before the accident?"

The question catches me a little off guard; I'm not quite sure why. "In what way?"

"Full of energy," Robert says, "Hardworking."

I smile, not because of his crafty way of giving me a compliment, but because my thoughts return to a time before the accident, when Alyssa was still in high school. "She was always upbeat, working hard to make good grades, be the best rider. We're mixed, but America identifies us by our blackness. Nothing is wrong with that, but growing up there was always this pressure.

"We needed to prove we deserved to be in the space we took up. It drove me up a wall, made me bitter. But Alyssa didn't let it get her down. She thrived on the pressure. That energy, that confidence, was so all-absorbing it made her a lot of friends." I close my eyes, remembering how my sister would dance in the living room while Dad played the piano and Mom clapped her hands in rhythm. "She was like a flame, attracting anyone who could sense just how truly magnificent she was."

"She still is, you know?"

I open my eyes. "Pardon?"

Robert smiles. "She's still magnificent."

I take a moment to wrap my head around the intonation in his voice. "I guess you're right. She's still Alyssa at the end of the day, the same beautiful soul I love."

Robert grabs both my hands in his own. "And I'm sure if she could express herself, she'd say something similar about you."

"How can you be so sure?"

Robert's grip tightens. "I'd like to think it's because of my experience around those at Lake Forest. Some of our guests were born with their disabilities, some acquired them later in life. Regardless, they're still human, still seeking the warmth of a family member...a lover."

I break Robert's hold to take a sip of my drink. Is that why Alyssa seems to focus so much more when she's at Lake Forest? Have I not been giving her warmth? I provide for her, dress her, feed her. Even in our conversations, I try to talk to her as I did before the accident. I ask—most times—for permission before doing anything. I tell her our plans for the day. I don't curse the fact that our parents are dead and she's now reliant on me, always tiptoeing around it as if it'll trigger her.

But have I been warm? I scratch the back of my head nervously. I haven't, have I? "That's really admirable of you. Your parents must be proud."

Robert frowns. "Not quite."

Shit! I've made an assumption that I shouldn't have. Suddenly I'm praying this is not gonna be another Caroline moment where he tells me his parents are dead.

The host brings our fries. Robert eats one before explaining.

"My father has always been about business. How to crush the competition. How to make sure our family is on top. That's good to an extent, but not when taken to an extreme. When I told him I didn't want to join the family business, he threw a hissy fit and kicked me out. He doesn't care about the work I do at Lake Forest."

Okay. That sucks but isn't nearly as bad as I thought. Crisis avoided. "I'm sorry to hear that."

Robert eats another fry. "I'm not. The last thing I want to do is head E. Remson Industries."

I almost choke on my drink, his words whirling around my head like bees in a capped bottle. E. Remson Industries is a big investor when it comes to motors and a bunch of other things that scream dollar signs. And it practically owns half the businesses in our town.

I look Robert up and down. He wears a blue T-shirt and black jeans with clean brown shoes. He could easily be mistaken for a model, but his outfit doesn't scream millionaire.

I stare at him like he's crazy. "I gotta say, I respect your strength."

Robert laughs. "Thanks, but I'm sure plenty of people would do the same in my situation."

I take up a handful of fries, deliberating how to reply as I chew. My response is honest. "I wouldn't."

Robert's brows shoot up. "Why?"

"Maybe before the accident I'd be more inclined to agree with you. I wasn't struggling back then. But now? Well, money can solve almost all my problems." I can almost hear my mother's voice echoing in the background. It can solve most problems but create some nasty ones, too.

Robert taps his fingers against his glass.

"What?"

"It's just the few times I do tell people about my family—and I rarely do on a first date—they're always quick to agree with me. You, Laine, are something else, aren't you? Alyssa is truly lucky to have you."

Is she lucky to have me? I'm the reason she's at Lake Forest.

Speaking of Alyssa and Lake Forest, when I picked her up last week, her bracelet was missing one of the very things that made it special. And while I told myself I wouldn't blow a fuse over it, I can't let it go. Not when those bracelets tie us to Mom. "By chance, any updates on the charm shaped like Trinidad? The one from Alyssa's bracelet?"

"Unfortunately not, but I'll continue to keep an eye out. Reena did say it might have broken off during one of the nearby outings to the park last week."

Reena. We've had minimal interactions in the past week, but I can't stand her. "I'm gonna come right out and ask. Reena likes you, doesn't she?"

Robert stares at several patrons in the bar before looking at me. "Do you mind if I show you something?"

Interesting way of dodging the question, but I've never been one to push. "Sure."

He fishes in his wallet for a few seconds before handing me a photo of a family dated twenty years ago. It has some sun damage and is worn at the edges, but I recognize him almost immediately as the boy in the center of the photo with the big smile. "It's you," I say.

He nods before pointing to a young girl at the very edge of the photo. The washed-out tint to her red hair and the vibrancy of her stare as she lifts a cat for the photo throw me off, but eventually it registers. "Wait, you and Reena are related?"

"Oh God, no. Her mother used to be a maid for my family and, along with Reena, lived in one of our guesthouses." He puts the photo back into his wallet. "She was always there to piece me back together when my father would crack down on me. She was also there afterward, when we'd pretend nothing happened. When I left the house, so did she. And when I said I wanted to help people, she decided to do the same. But it's gone beyond that, developing into some kind of dependency on her part. I mean, we work at the same place. Even have apartments in the same complex." He exhales loudly. "To be honest, sometimes I wish I could just wake up and be passionately in love with her. But while I love her dearly, I've never been able to reciprocate *those* kinds of feelings."

I finish my beer. She put all her energy into Robert, all her time. However, he can't give her the one thing she wants. No wonder she eyed me like I was taking what was hers. "I don't think she likes me very much."

"She has never liked any of the women I've been interested in, especially you," Robert says.

"Why especially me? Am I not what you usually go for?"

"You're not," Robert answers.

My tone is apprehensive. "And what am I not?"

Robert smiles. It's the kind of smile that sets my entire body on fire. "Ordinary. You said your sister was like a flame, Laine. Well, so are you." Robert grabs my hand and brushes his lips against my wrist. "Would you humor me with another date?"

Every fiber in my body screams to me the obvious answer. "Of course."

CHAPTER
16

ALYSSA

I pace back and forth in front of Omniscius, sobs slurring my words. "Please, there must be something I can do to return to my plane."

The leaves don't fall; there is no whispered advice. They haven't spoken since they fell nine days ago when I first arrived, and they said quite bluntly, *Forever bound you will be.*

"I'm begging!" My voice cracks as I collapse to the ground, my hands digging into the earth.

Even though I'm a changel, I fooled myself into believing that Terra would be on my side...that I'd find a way to defeat the evil at Lake Forest and rescue my parents. But I'm nothing but a girl...one cursed and unable to save her family. Why does Terra forsake me so? The one who has prayed to her since she was a child, even after the attack one year ago?

Why does she...? I suck in a big breath, so deep my chest aches. Mortals aren't to question Terra, why she allows certain things to happen. To do so is not only blasphemy but certain to do one thing only—make me give up. And I won't give up. There must be another way, even if Omniscius tells me no.

"You've come to see Omniscius again?" Wren's words are spoken with the slightest tinge of sadness and, even though he might not realize it, judgment.

"I need to get out of here, Wren. My sister needs me! My kingdom needs me!"

"But Omniscius said—"

"I don't care what Omniscius said!" The words erupt from deep within me before I even speak them aloud. I'm tired of him and the Great Tree, telling me what I can and cannot do. I'm tired of letting curses bind me to certain doom. I'm just...tired of it all, and that causes my sobs to erupt more vigorously.

"Alyssa," Wren starts, but I shake my head.

"Don't bother."

The first few days after being trapped in this plane, I let myself slip...let Wren take me swimming in the lake, let him take me riding on Nerra. At first, I thought it was his way of cheering me up. But after he suggested I stop fighting to leave this plane, I put distance between us. I refused to go anywhere else with him because for a second, just a second, I thought about how nice it would be—living in this plane, where I have complete use of my body and magic.

"But, Alyssa, at least let me get you something to eat. We can get fish from the lake. Start a fire. You'll pass out if you don't—"

"Don't give me that. You know as well as I that we don't need to eat here unless we will it."

Wren's face reddens, the reaction enough to confirm what I had only suspected.

I wipe my eyes, clambering to my feet. Again, I face Omnis-cius. "Please. I'll do anything! Sell my soul if I must. Just let me get back to the other plane!"

Wren rests his hands on my shoulders, squeezing, but I refuse to be soothed. "That won't work," he says. "Omniscius has already spoken. I'm sorry."

Won't work—the words rattle my brain, bringing on a stab-bing headache. My knees begin to shake as the pain zips through my body, growing more intense until the entire earth feels as if it's shaking. Wren reaches out to steady me.

"Hold on," he says, and only then I realize that the ground has begun to crack, light spilling out of deep grooves.

Glior emerges from one groove, his beady eyes pinning Wren and me in place.

"I'm tired of hearing you whimper, girl. You mortals are unrelenting creatures, let me tell you. And I'm a goblin."

"I'm—I'm sorry," I mutter. "It's just that—"

Glior silences me with a wave of his staff. "I know. And as Omniscius said, you'd be forever bound to this plane."

"So what? You've come to rub it in? Tell me to leave?"

Glior walks around Wren and me like a predator circling prey. "I thought about it. But I can't bear to hear any more of this racket. So, I've come to tell you there might be a way to leave the plane . . . one that Omniscius might not know."

"But the Great Tree knows all," Wren says quickly.

"He does know all . . . in this realm. But there are other realms, boy. Ones that your mortal minds cannot dream to fathom. In one of them might await another tree—deity, even—who might be able to give you the answer you seek."

"And why are you helping us?" Wren asks.

"Because you annoy me, obviously. I'd like you gone." A snide grin snakes across Glior's face. "*And* there is also something I want, something you must get to access the next portal."

"What is it?" I ask, determined to get whatever he asks for, no matter how dangerous or impossible it sounds.

"A mermaid's scale," he answers gleefully.

"A mermaid won't just give her a scale," Wren protests. "It's a painful thing, damn near the equivalent of ripping off a nail. Even if we did find a mermaid willing to endure the extraction, scales are a mermaid's most prized possessions. The scales' color, number, and pattern determine the mermaids' place among one another."

I turn away and start trekking through the brambles.

"Where are you going?" Wren asks, hurrying to catch up.

"I'm going to ask one of the mermaids to give me a scale. I have to try. I have to...It makes no sense explaining things to you. You want me to stay here."

Wren whirls me around to face him. "That's not true, Alyssa."

I cross my arms. "Don't lie. If you had your way, we'd stay here together forever."

"Yes, we would. But if having you stay here forever with me means you'll end up hating me, I want no part of it. So, Princess, I'll help you on your quest. Reluctantly so, but I will."

His answer is not what I would have expected, and retorts lingering on the tip of my tongue retreat into the depths of my throat. I stare at him warily. "Okay, so where do we start?"

Wren bursts into laughter, the sound of which makes my heart, begrudgingly, skip a beat. "You didn't have a plan, did you?"

"Aside from going to the water and calling to the mermaids? No, I didn't."

"Well, it's not going to be that easy," Wren says. "We're going to have to take a swim. And it's gonna take us deep below the surface. Hopefully, Freah will provide us with a scale."

"Then let's get to it!" I march forward toward the sandy banks, the coolness of the water washing over my feet.

Wren grabs my right hand, interlacing our fingers. "Don't let go of me, understood?"

I nod, and Wren sucks in a big breath. "Spiritus aqua, grant me this power." He chants the words three times in quick succession before guiding us deeper into the water until our feet can't touch the ground. "Remember, don't let go, okay?"

"Don't worry," I say. "You'll be begging me to let go because I'll be squeezing so hard."

Both smiling, we start to dive, Wren using his weight and speed to guide our descent. The sun's rays dance through the crystal clear water until we've reached a point where they have been blocked, darkness wafting over Wren and me like a cloak that steals our senses but not our breath.

Breathing and speaking underwater—they're the main goals of the spell he cast earlier, in addition to the ability to withstand the pressures of the deep sea.

"We're almost there," Wren says, and sure enough, the darkness starts to lift. Blue light, like that of a drunk moon worshipped by the stars, coats the bottom of the sea, giving it a warm glow. That glow illuminates castles made of coral, home to fish and, much to my delight, merpeople.

A merman with a green tail the color of Wren's eyes swims up to us. "Mortals venturing this deep below the surface? How can I help you two?"

"I'm looking for the princess," Wren says, and the words garner a dubious look from not only me but also the merman.

Freah, the mermaid who danced through the air and into the sea on our first journey to visit Omniscius, is a princess? I had no idea.

"The princess is with her father. You have wasted your time, creature of the land."

"But we must see her. It's urgent," I say. The merman's dark eyes bore into me like I'm an ant on the surface, one he deems very vulnerable to his mercy.

Here, under the sea, I guess I am.

"As I said before, girl of the land, she is unavailable. Now you best be on your way. The spell you use can be canceled with a quick counter, and I don't think you two have enough energy to swim back to the surface, do you?"

Wren swims forward, stopping just an inch in front of the merman. "Is that a threat?"

"It is whatever you deem it," the merman replies, and I insert myself between the two, hand throbbing as I twist my arm to ensure I'm still holding on to Wren. "We don't want any trouble. But I need a mermaid's scale if I'm to save my kingdom of Mirendal. If you can just give me one, we'll leave. Won't even have to talk to Freah."

The merman's eyes no longer haze dark brown but a deep red, one that instills fear so palpable it makes the water whirling around us run cold.

My breaths begin to hitch, becoming more and more rapid until they don't come at all. I look at Wren, my limbs beginning to feel numb. Our fingers are still interlaced.

"Creatures of the land coming to ask merpeople for their scales? The entitlement! From people from Mirendal no less! I thought the king and queen had struck up a treaty with us . . . ensured we won't be hunted for our scales. And now . . ."

"The king and queen were kidnapped a year ago." The voice comes from behind us, followed by a warm current of water that whirls around my head first, then my lower body. Wren's tight grip on me slackens, and his face, puffy under the glow of the light of the merpeople, relaxes.

"Princess," the merman mutters, and he bows his head. "I thought you were convening with the king."

"Clearly, I wasn't." Freah takes one look at Wren before staring at the merman with eyes that might very well turn him to stone. "Leave my sight before I deal you a punishment worse than what you were about to do to these people."

The merman's tail beats the water into a stream of bubbles as he swims away.

Wren and I look at Freah, her tail shimmering as if each scale has been kissed by the sun. Her dark skin smooth, she gently plucks a little fish that has latched on to her arm before setting it to swim in the other direction.

"Come with me to my chambers. Your legs will catch too much attention in the open," she says as she leads us through the winding corals that tower like mountains. We follow her for quite some time, watching the way the rocks gleam as if they are the source of light that illuminates the kingdom below the water. It's so beautiful that for a few seconds I forget about all the negatives that await me on the surface.

How nice it would be to stay down here and swim among

them...live under the water in a kingdom as glorious if not even more glorious than my own. How...

The thought is stolen by Freah, who closes the doors to her chambers. Like the rest of the castle, the structures inside are made of coral, and there is a glow that casts shadows on the sandy ground.

Freah perches at the edge of her bed. "So I overheard part of your conversation. You want a mermaid's scale. Why?"

"I need it to get passage to the other realms," I say.

"And why do you need to go to the other realms?"

"Because I've been forever bound to this plane by the prince of Remwater, and he has his eyes set on my sister, the first princess of Mirendal."

Freah's brows shoot up. "Aah, a princess like me. Tell me, are you forced to bear the weight of your crown?"

Her question, or rather the answer to it, bounces around the caverns of my mind. I'm not. Even before the attack, it was clear that the kingdom's rule would be passed to Laine, the firstborn.

I hadn't really cared, and I still don't. Even though I quite enjoyed court life, the adventures of the unknown world intrigued me far more.

"Well, are you?"

My voice comes out hoarse. "I'm not."

"How unfortunate. Maybe, if I felt like I could relate to you, I'd want to assist you. But..."

"But what?"

Freah chuckles. "But you're just a creature of the land...one whom I don't feel too keen on helping."

My heart stutters in my rib cage. She can't be serious, can she?

She is because she yawns, the sleep in her eyes so evident her boredom cannot be faked.

"Please, I'm begging you. I need to rescue my parents," I say.

"The king and queen of Mirendal? They were lovely rulers, but what about your father's ancestors? The ones who hunted merpeople for their scales?"

My mind dredges up old lessons from spell-caster and history classes. Most of those books didn't speak of the atrocities of the kings before my father. What I learned about the sins of my kingdom came from the king and queen themselves.

"My mother and father are different. They stopped the persecution of magical creatures in our kingdom. They—"

"I'm not saying they didn't. Your mother is loved by the merpeople. And your father, King Gerald, was trying to make up for the mistakes of his forefathers. But what have you done to prove yourself as an ally to the merpeople?"

"I've . . ." I've done nothing. But how could I? I was cursed. I still am.

I try to steel my voice, sound more confident than I am. "I've done nothing yet, but I promise if you help me, I'll ensure that the merpeople will forever be under Mirendal's protection. So please, if you could give me a scale or direct me to a merperson who will, I'd be forever in your debt."

"I know Alyssa Highland might seem weak and a bit of a know-it-all"—Wren winks at me—"but she's a good person. If she promises to ensure the merpeople are forever protected, she will."

Freah's eyes latch on to Wren. She gets up from the bed and swims a circle around us. "Men. Handsome creatures you are, especially you, Wren. I've always taken a liking to you. But two princesses are talking here. What makes you feel your word holds more weight than Alyssa Highland's? If she hasn't managed to convince me herself, what makes you think that your word can weasel its way into my heart?"

Freah's words are little less than a slap to Wren's face. His eyes brew like the underbelly of a storm, but he says nothing.

Hoping to cushion the blow, I give his hand a little squeeze, then turn to Freah. "I understand it…your annoyance. My mother often spoke of how her voice went unheard when she was young. When she met my father and became queen, people started to listen. But, as she phrased it, it was then that she felt her voice mattered the least. Because it was then that she had confirmation. Her words mattered not for what she said but for who backed them."

Freah's gaze electrifies the water. "Men and mermen. They're the same aside from one having a tail and the other two legs."

"Look, I know you don't know me well. But I'll do anything in exchange for a scale," I say.

Freah's brows snap together, her dark hair rolling off her frame in rivulets. Her lips turn upward into a half-smile. "Anything I want? Are you sure about that?"

"Yes."

The silence that proceeds is palpable.

Finally, Freah exhales loudly. "So be it," she says, brushing her fingers against her tail. She then closes her eyes and pulls at a scale, letting out a scream that resounds throughout her chamber. The scale, shimmering gold, loses most of its glow.

I reach for it, but Freah looks at Wren. From in her chambers, we can hear the voices of worried mermen, guards ready to defend their princess. But Freah continues to stare at Wren, her face ripe with unutterable grievances. Did his speaking out earlier upset her that badly?

It must have.

I clear my throat, hoping my voice conveys the urgency she seems to be lacking. "What do you want in return?"

Freah breaks Wren's gaze and hands me the scale. "Oh, didn't you realize? I've already gotten it, girl. Something exceptionally rare."

"What's that?" I ask, confused.

Freah smiles slyly. "You will find out soon enough. Now go before the guards come, or you'll never see the surface again, much less the other realms."

I heed her warning, wasting no time swimming back to the surface with Wren. However, as we breach the surface, I can't help but feel uneasy. What exactly did she get?

LAINE

Caroline winks at me while blowing on her latte. "Someone's flirting via text."

I shove my phone in my pocket, smiling. "It's been a long time since I've dated someone who gets me this worked up."

"Sure it's not just a long time since you've gotten laid?"

I roll my eyes but don't pretend. "That, too."

Chuckling, Caroline nudges me in my side. "So, have you two finally set up a day for the next date?"

I begin working on a caramel frappé for a customer. "We originally decided the end of the week, but I don't know."

Caroline rests a hand on her hip. "What do you mean you don't know? I've stalked this guy's Instagram and Facebook. Not only is he hot, but he's also hella rich."

I'm about to tell her that his family cut him out of the will, but it's not my business to share. Still, the idea that he'd give up all that to do what he really loves is a testament to his character. "Believe me, I want to go on the date. He's amazing. It's just that Alyssa's been . . . off."

Three days ago, after I came back from my date, I decided to detangle Alyssa's hair before bed. I was expecting a battle of tears and flaying arms. But Alyssa didn't put up a fight. She didn't even cry.

"Sure you're not worried for nothing?" Caroline asks.

"Maybe. I've been giving her the medications, as prescribed, and for the most part, she's fine. No fever or anything. But I don't know. She just seems a little different? Besides, it's not like that date is going to be this weekend. Robert is gonna be in Philly for the next two days for a conference."

"So what? You're not gonna go out with him as long as Alyssa is giving you weird vibes?" Caroline logs another order, and I hand the customer his frappé. When we resume our convo, her eyes still hold the same intensity as before. "Come on, Laine. You work so hard! You deserve a break! And a date!" She waves a finger teasingly. "Though, I must say the vibes you're getting could just be universe's way of steering you in another direction."

"And what direction is that?" I ask while working on the next order.

She gestures playfully toward Dr. Jeon, who readjusts his scrubs as he enters the coffee shop. He doesn't make eye contact, just finds a chair in the corner.

She frowns. "Maybe he's getting yelled at by his boss like last time. Poor thing looks like he's about to have a breakdown."

I ignore her, wiping down the counters after giving the only other customer in the shop her drink. "Not my business."

"Oh, come on, he looks like he needs someone to talk to."

I look up just enough to get a glimpse of Dr. Jeon, head in his hands. Caroline slings an arm around my shoulder. "How about this. If you go talk to him, I'll give you all the tips for the shift. No split."

I damn near stand at attention. The tip jar is about forty-five dollars, excluding coins. Might seem like a chump change, but to someone who's struggling to put food on a table, it's plenty. "You're on."

Squealing, Caroline pours Dr. Jeon's usual large iced coffee with two shots of espresso. She hands it to me. "Tell him it's on the house. Also, be nice."

"And what if he snips at me?"

She pauses, seemingly envisioning it. "Then I guess I'll have no choice but to let the idea of you two die." She tucks an over-grown curl behind my ear. "I have a feeling my ship won't sink, though. Well, that's if the snippy back-and-forth is anything like last time."

Desperate to show her she's delusional, and happy to make some money while doing it, I slip out from behind the counter. And, almost as if perfectly timed, the jumbie on my shoulder rears her head. *He's gonna think you spit in his coffee. Why would you be nice to him? You're not nice, Laine. You're evil.*

My feet stall. Actually, I'm not sure I can do this.

You're a bad seed, Laine. A killer. Your parents...

I shake my head and trudge forward. I won't let my jumbie win today.

I stop at Dr. Jeon's table in the corner of the shop. He doesn't look up immediately, not until I set down the coffee. "Um, on the house. Think of it as a peace offering."

He glances at the coffee cup, then me. "You actually think coffee's enough for a truce?"

I wince a smile. "Well, this is the best I could offer someone who's prone to snapping at his barista. Also, probably those in retail and the like."

Dr. Jeon's lips mash into a straight line. "I get it. You think I'm a total asshole, but I'll have you know I worked as a gym attendant while in medical school. Also moonlighted as a store clerk at Target in undergrad. But..."

"But?"

He fiddles with the lid of the coffee cup, his voice dropping several octaves. And suddenly he seems less of an ass and more like a child—vulnerable. "But I don't know. Being a doctor...residency...it's not all it's cracked up to be. I get bitched out at least six times a day from my attending, see more paperwork than patients, and the coffee in the hospital cafeteria is garbage. Honestly, it's all making me a bit of a bitter person. Although I gotta say I'm usually much better at keeping my emotions in check. The two times I dropped the ball..."

"I served you your coffee, huh?"

He throws up his arms in defense. "You did. But hey, there's no need to worry about you shouldering any more of my *redirected aggression*. I plan to quit."

Dr. Jeon quitting is none of my business, and it probably won't have any direct impact on my life aside from fewer of these snippy interactions. However, it leaves a bad taste in my mouth...the fact that he seems to be giving in to a pressure that wants to break him.

I don't want him, or anyone, to break. Not when I know just how painful that can be. So I ask him if he'd still quit if all the issues he mentioned earlier disappeared.

"Of course not," he says without hesitation, and I cross my arms.

"Then you shouldn't quit. Shit's tough, I get it, but wouldn't it be better to finish? Become an attending who doesn't chew out their residents six times a day? Oh, and also one who puts patient care above money? Honestly, we need more of those kinds of doctors. Won't happen if you quit, though."

Dr. Jeon's eyes widen. "You sound like you're talking from experience. Are you a student in med school or something?"

I shake my head, a little flattered that he's entertained the possibility. "No. I've just spent a lot of time in hospitals and happened to see a lot of what you're referring to."

Dr. Jeon's eyes flicker, just for a second. "Guess it's a good thing I came in here today, huh?"

"Guess so," I say, and before I can say anything else, my relief for the shift pats me on the shoulder.

I return to the staff area to grab my things, encountering a very excited Caroline.

"Spill! What did you say to him? He's smiling like a kid at Christmas."

I hang up my apron. "He was about to quit his job. I basically told him to hang in there."

Caroline does a little victory dance. "My canoe just upgraded to a full-blown yacht! We just need it to leave the dock now. Set sail."

She follows me to the back door of the coffee shop. "Be straight with me. If things don't work out with you and the hot associate director, think Dr. Jeon could have a chance?"

Marcella said a lover walked into my life; she also said something about wolves. I don't exactly believe her ramblings when it comes to her fortunes, but if I had to entertain it, Dr. Jeon just made his way out of *wolf* territory, no?

Doesn't matter. I already have someone I'm interested in. "I'm hoping things work out with Robert, Caroline. He's absolutely perfect."

Frowning, Caroline holds the door open for me. "But you know what they say about perfect people, right?"

I step outside with a sigh, certain I won't like her answer. "What?"

"They usually have the most to hide."

I roll my eyes. "This isn't a Lifetime movie. He's just a nice person."

"But what if he isn't?" Caroline asks ominously.

I bite back a chuckle. "Then you'd be first to know. Now I gotta go. See you tomorrow."

I know Robert is away and won't be waiting for me at Lake Forest, but I still have butterflies in my stomach as I pull into the parking lot.

Unfortunately, those butterflies die when I realize my *favorite* nurse has been waiting for me. Reena taps her foot against the ground, her hands balled at her sides.

I get out of the SUV. "Is everything okay?"

"No. It's not."

My heart begins to plummet into my stomach. "Did something happen to Alyssa?"

"Did you sleep with him?"

I almost choke on my own saliva. "Excuse me?"

"Did you sleep with him?" she asks again, incensed.

I take a step back. "That's none of your business. I know you two grew up together, but you need to ease up. Robert should be allowed to date whoever he chooses. He's a grown man. He doesn't need you policing his every move."

Reena's face goes berry red, the veins in her neck bulging. If I didn't know any better, I'd swear she wants to hit me. Part of me wants her to try. If she does, I'll make sure she doesn't approach me in such a way again.

She huffs. "If people find out, they'll move your sister to another day center. You think you can afford somewhere else?"

I do my best to remain calm, her threat settling on my chest like a weight. "Why don't you take up this issue with Robert, Reena? Right now you're just bothering me."

She looks as if she's almost had a stroke, her face going even redder than before. "I'm trying to help you!"

The words are so shocking, I rear back. "Helping? How exactly are you doing that?"

"You don't know him like I do," she says. "You haven't done what I've done for him. You and your sister?" Reena glances at the bracelet on my hand. Tears fall from her eyes, but I don't care. I can't care. Not when she's out here, using my sister to threaten me.

"Robert is going to hear about this," I say.

It all happens very quick. Reena's eyes going wide, her lunging at me, her grabbing my arms. "Please. Don't tell him!" she yells. "Don't tell him. I'm begging you."

I pry her hands off me, stifling the urge to pin her to the ground. "Get out of my face before I call him right now."

Reena instantly lets go of me. Eyes darting around the

parking lot, she holds her arms close to her chest and makes her way to a maroon car across the lot.

I don't stick around to see what she does. I run to the entrance of Lake Forest, slamming my hands down on the front desk. "Where's Alyssa?" I ask the receptionist.

"She's in the hall with some of the others. They're playing games," she says. Judging by the way she gives me a once-over, I must look as shaken as I feel.

After nodding my thanks, I head to the hall. Inside, Alyssa sits still. Her eyes focus on a red ball that some of the other people throw around the room. Two of the attendants stand in the middle of the room to make sure the ball isn't thrown with too much force and to assist residents in catching it, though they don't seem to do a very good job of it. If anything, the two men don't seem to care, chuckling when one boy—he has bandages wrapped over all his fingers—cries about not catching the ball.

"Good boy," the boy says, reaching for the ball. "Harold is good boy."

"Are you?" one attendant asks, his voice dripping with sarcasm.

Already fuming from my encounter with Reena, I walk into the room and look the man up and down. He smiles at me, revealing crooked front teeth.

"And you are?" he asks.

"I'm Laine Highland. I'm here for my sister."

He glances at the other attendant before directing me to go ahead and take Alyssa. However, I don't move, reading his name tag aloud. "Bennett."

"That's me," he says, way too chipper.

"I trust that you know Harold is a good boy?"

Although he doesn't say anything, he wipes that smug grin off his face, and I make a mental note to tell Robert about his behavior when I tell him about Reena's.

Nothing left to say, I wheel Alyssa out of the hall and into the parking lot. I look in each direction, afraid Reena might pop out and attack us.

As I buckle Alyssa into the back seat of the car and put the wheelchair in the trunk, I think of exactly what I want to tell Robert. Anger still coursing through my veins, my fingers are like wildfire as I type out a message.

I write: *You need to speak to Reena about us. I won't tolerate her grabbing me again. Matter of fact, get your entire staff in check. The techs/attendants have a haughty attitude. Reena is fucking crazy.*

There's no immediate reply, and I don't wait for one. I shove my phone into my pocket and drive home, seething.

ALYSSA

Emerald is waiting for us when we breach the surface. Her wings flap quicker than she speaks.

"What's she saying?" I ask.

Wren outstretches a hand to her, and she nuzzles against his finger after whispering something. "Apparently she got into a fight with one of the other fairies. They called her weak."

"Weak?"

Emerald remains nuzzled against Wren's finger but looks up at me with a prickly gaze.

"You know you're anything but. Without you, when I came to this plane, I would have been lost. But you helped guide me to Wren," I say. "You're strong, Emerald."

The fairy's eyes remain narrowed. Wren whispers something again to her in the tongue of the fairies. This time, Emerald perks up.

"What did you tell her?" I ask.

Wren chuckles. "I asked her if she wanted to come on the journey with us, get away for a bit."

"Is that even allowed?"

"Maybe it's not allowed, but if it is, I'm going. Emerald, too. We're going to help you find the answers you seek, Alyssa."

Wren's words cut through the tension racking my bones, the angst plaguing my mind. I smile.

"What?" he asks, and my smile grows wider.

"You do know how to make a girl's heart flutter, don't you, Wren?"

Heat creeps up his neck, his bottom lip trembling slightly. The sun beats down on us, almost matching the heat between us.

"And that only scratches the surface of what I do, Princess."

This time, I'm the one blushing. I avoid Wren's gaze and turn to trek into the woods, toward Omniscius. "Let's go. Glior is waiting."

When we get to the Great Tree, Glior is standing with his staff outstretched in our direction. "The scale," he says. "I can sense it. Give it to me."

My fingers work quickly, finding the scale in the pocket of my dress. Before Glior can take it out of my hand, I step back. "What do you plan to do with it? Will it cause Freah more pain than she has already suffered?"

Glior knocks his staff against the ground. He glances at Wren. "Do you also take me, the guardian of Omniscius, as someone capable of cruelty?"

"No, Glior," Wren says, and guilt wafts over me.

I drop to my knees, scared my words will make the goblin think twice about helping me. I shove the scale at him. "Please forgive me. I was out of line. I just thought..."

"I don't care what you thought. I'm not a mortal like you. Cruelty isn't second nature to me."

I want to protest, but I don't. I can't. Mortals have a long history of subjugating magical creatures, and I can't cure Glior's apprehensions in a day, especially not when I have a mission to fulfill.

Mumbling something under his breath, Glior takes the scale. He grinds it up with his hands, despite its incredible strength and durability, and puts the dust from the scale into a vial. He then shakes it, whispering something I can't quite make out.

"You must drink this to allow you passage to the other realms," he says, extending the vial.

Wren steps forward. "Is there enough for me as well? Also, Emerald?"

Glior rolls his beady black eyes. "Of course there is. I wasn't aware of the fairy, but I knew you'd want to join her, lovesick mortal. I can't say that I'm surprised you—"

"Thank you, Glior," Wren says.

The edge in his voice doesn't go unnoticed. Glior huffs. "Are you sure you'd like to join her on this journey, Mr. Sidorov?"

Wren steps forward. "I am."

"Then I must warn you, if you're separated from the princess whenever the sun sets in the other realms, you'd be forever trapped. Although I'm quite sure that's not your biggest worry, is it?"

I swallow hard. My time with Wren has been short but each moment grand, each moment tethering my heart to his like a lifeline. I can't risk anything happening to him. "You can't come. I won't allow it. You and Emerald will stay," I say while holding on to his arm.

Emerald rattles off something I don't understand, the intonation in her voice stinging.

"What's she saying?" I ask.

Wren glances at her before resting a hand on my shoulder. "That you should know better, and I agree."

His tone is sharp, but I won't buckle. Wren trapped in another realm won't be insufferable for just him. It'll also be insufferable for me, and I don't know if I can bear it...that pain.

He locks his eyes on mine. "You are, in fact, a princess, Alyssa. But need I remind you that you are not my princess. As a citizen of Remwater, I am not required to obey your commands." He gestures to Emerald, her arms crossed. "And neither is Emerald."

The embarrassment lasts only a second, but the dread that something might happen to him...the relief and gratitude that I won't have to face the unknown alone, remain as Glior presents me with the vial. Inside it is an ever-swirling purple liquid carrying not the faintest glow of Freah's scale.

"A sip for each of you except the fairy," Glior says.

I squeal as I take a sip, the concoction bitter like molasses yet sour like unripe grapes.

At first, nothing happens aside from the wrenching of my stomach. No humming of my body in tune to an unnatural force. No haze of my mind. But then I see it—a hole in the ground opening up. Glior points to it with his staff. "Down the hole you three must go."

I look at Wren, tempted to ask him one last time if he's sure about going. However, he gives a half-smile, that earlier adamancy flaring in his eyes.

"To the ends of the realm and back, I'll follow you, Princess. Whenever you're ready..."

I slip my hand into his and squeeze hard. "Stay close, you hear?" I glance at Emerald. "You, too."

And with no more time to spare, we jump into the hole.

The first thing I see when I wake up are the blue eyes reflecting back at me in the mirror. Then it's the golden-yellow ringlets of hair that fall over dainty, ivory-colored shoulders. Lips, my lips, tremble. *What is this? And where is Wren?*

"Alyssa, are you alright?" a woman perched over my shoulder asks. Blond hair curls at the edge of her jaw, and her eyes are the same blue as mine. However, her voice is Laine's.

She brushes my hair before pinning it into a low bun. "Ready for the afternoon meal? The servants should have set the table by now, and we have a special guest today."

"A special guest?"

Laine, this Laine, nods. "But of course. It's Father's birthday. And you know he loves having a small celebration."

She's right. Today is Father's birthday, isn't it? I want to see him, but I have to look for him ...

Mind foggy, I follow her through the winding hallways of the castle, eyeing the walls burnished with light. Laughter seems to echo from the mere walls itself, and quickly the haziness in my mind is replaced by a sense of excitement.

Laine wraps her hand in my own, and my lips automatically curl upward into a smile.

"Let's hurry," she yells. And we pick up our pace, running through the hallways until we get to the hall.

A dining table has been placed in the middle, and silver

platters of meats and greens decorate each plate. My mouth waters as the scent of smoked meat floods my nostrils.

I can't wait to eat! I can't—

"My daughters," Father says. "Please have a seat."

Father sits in a chair at the head of the table. His voice is like the skies opening, and before I know it, I'm running into his arms.

I hug him tightly, inhaling his scent. He smells like pine and something else. I'm not sure, but I don't care. I've missed him so much. And he's here. With me. That's all that matters.

He gestures for me to sit down. "What's gotten into you today?"

Laine chuckles. "She's been a bit strange. Must be excited to leave for Tergo in a few weeks."

My chin snaps upward. "I'm going to Tergo?"

Laine and my father look at each other before staring at me wide-eyed. "Of course, darling," Father says. "You graduated at the top of your spell-caster classes. Why wouldn't you be going?"

"We can finally share a drink in the taverns, served by giants." Laine winks at me. "Well, actually, you're not allowed. But I'm sure I can—"

Father snaps his fingers. "You know I will not allow such transgressions." He lowers his voice. "At least not if it's spoken about at the dinner table."

Laine and I share a small smile. We shall keep it to ourselves. For now.

I look around the table, getting a good look at all the faces. There's Marcella, dressed in a gown as bright as the sun. There's Ana, who tends to our kingdom's dragons and horses alike.

"You're due for a lesson," Ana says. "Tergo is home to some of the best riders. We need to make sure you're in tip-top shape before going."

"I'll be there as soon as the sun rises tomorrow," I say before letting my gaze continue to skim the table. They stop at an empty chair.

Someone is missing. Who?

"Father, who's this open chair for? Aren't we missing someone?"

Father's eyes widen, as do Laine's. They stare at me, and all the people at the table stop eating.

The silence only breaks when a man, tall and lanky but with a strange likeness to Father, enters the hall. He takes a seat at the table, and everyone seems to pick up conversations where they left off.

"What a pleasure for you to join us, Uncle. I take it your trip to the dragon pit was fruitful?" Laine asks.

"'Fruitful' won't do it justice. A fine dragon paraded the square, bred from prime lineages and no more than two years old. I believed you would take interest, so I bought him."

Laine rests a hand on her chest. "Uncle, you shouldn't have."

"I should, and I did." He rests a warm gaze on me. "And fear not, sweet Alyssa, for I brought you a gift as well."

I shift in my chair, skin prickling with nerves. He shouldn't bring anything for me. He hates me...hates us. Or at least, he did. Yes. He's made it clear before he...I can't finish the thought. I can't remember. Everything seems so jumbled...like I'm missing something, someone, but can't bring my thoughts together long enough to figure it out.

"Well, Alyssa, I brought you a gift crafted by the best

bookbinder in our kingdom." He hands me a brown book, the leather tooled with an intricate pattern. "It's beautiful."

Father sighs. "You shouldn't have, Freidmore. Margaret always said you spoiled the girls too much."

"Margaret, may Terra rest her soul," Uncle says.

"May Terra rest her," Laine adds, and in perfect unison, the table echoes her blessing.

My brain tries to process it, understand why an air of sadness has wafted over us, but I remain confused, finally working up the courage to ask, "Who's Margaret?"

Much like earlier, when I asked about the empty seat at the far end of the table, there's silence. Everyone stops eating, staring at me like I'm a horse amongst dragons.

They only stop staring when a guard, dressed in armor and a green mantle, enters the hall. His breaths come quick, and he stumbles over his feet, his hands swatting the air.

"What are you doing?" Father asks, his tone making me jump. And the guard points at something whisking through the air. It flies directly toward me, getting closer and closer until I can see it. No, her. A fairy, saying something I don't understand.

Wait. Why can't I understand? I'm going to Tergo. I should be well-versed in the tongue of the fairies. Does this fairy have a problem with her speech?

She screams as the guard takes a glass bowl from the table and covers her with it.

I reach to move the lid. "Fairies are creatures to be cherished and respected."

"They're more like pests, if you ask me," says Uncle, and Father laughs.

My eyes snap in their direction. "They're meant to be cherished. Mother said so herself!"

Mother. That's right, isn't it? Mother is missing. Where is she?

"Where is Mother?" I ask, and just like before, everyone freezes. The only thing moving or speaking is the fairy under the glass bowl.

I extend an arm to free her, but the play I'm seemingly in resumes. "Your mother, Margaret...she..."

"She died," Laine snaps. "How dare you pretend you don't know?"

Margaret? Was that my mother's name? It feels off.

"Get him!" a voice bellows, and we're joined by more guards and a young man, his eyes boring into me as he runs to the table. "This isn't real."

My face feels taut as my brows snap upward. "What do you mean?"

Father commands the guards to catch the boy, but he evades their hands with a simple turn of his frame. He grabs one of the silver platters and holds it up to me. "This isn't you, Alyssa!"

I run my fingers over my face. "This isn't me?"

"It isn't," says the boy. And he smiles at me so reassuringly that I can't help but smile back until a guard grabs him from behind. Four more guards enter the hall to help pin him down, but he doesn't lose any of that fire in his eyes. "Remember your mother," are his last words as he and the fairy are taken out of the hall.

I rise from my seat in protest, or at least I think in protest. Why does my mind feel like it's in such disarray?

"Margaret, our mother, the queen, died in a riding accident years ago," Laine says. "We have her to thank for our beautiful looks and Father to thank for our wittiness. Isn't that right?"

All I can manage is a nod before stumbling over. Laine manages to rise from her seat and catch me before I can hit the ground. "Oh my, my little sister. You don't look too well. How about you go and rest?"

"I think that'll be for the best." Father gestures for a guard to take me back to my room.

I don't say anything. Mind hazier than before, I exit the hall and return to my room, the world spinning.

CHAPTER
19

LAINE

I stare at the text from Robert agreeing to meet with him at two thirty, and deliberate whether to cancel our date.

I mean, can I even call it a date? It's more of a meeting to discuss what I witnessed at the day center three days ago. And if he wasn't at a conference for the past few days, we would have met sooner. Shit, within the same hour of the same day.

My blood curdles at the thought of Reena. It curdles more when I think of the man with chipped teeth who taunted Harold. As one of the volunteers explained to me yesterday, the twenty-seven-year-old has Lesch-Nyhan syndrome—a genetic disorder that usually affects male children. The volunteer tried to explain the disorder in so many words…how it leads to self-mutilation and intellectual disability, but I couldn't really focus past that. All I kept thinking about was Alyssa. Has this man taunted her in a similar manner?

I push open the doors to the pharmacy. *Lights on but no one home* is how one doctor described her state after the accident. *Vegetative* was the term another doctor used. Neither of them expected her to be able to speak again, but she did. Even if her muttered words mean nothing to us, they mean something to her. Certainly some part of her understands what's going on.

The worker taunting her? Taunting anybody at Lake Forest? Robert needs to know and make sure it never happens again.

But did he actually taunt him? the jumbie on my shoulder asks today. *Technically, he just made a comment. Did he actually do anything wrong? What if you make this man lose his job for nothing?*

My fingers twitch, and I clasp my hands together. I'm not going to second-guess myself. That man's treatment of Harold made me uncomfortable. Robert should be made aware.

But what if he dumps you because of it? And, I mean, you're no saint, Laine. Can you even take care of Alyssa?

"I can take care of Alyssa," I snap, and look around the pharmacy's medication aisle. Thankfully, no one is around to see my outburst, and a relieved sigh escapes my lips as I reaffirm to myself that I will take care of Alyssa.

One of the more recent ways I did so was by calling her doctor yesterday to see if he had any thoughts about why she could be acting so differently lately.

"Different how?" he asked, and I fidgeted with the buttons on my shirt as if we were face-to-face, his gaze drilling into me.

Alyssa had no fever, just a runny nose. Her J-tube was clean, the skin around it showing no signs of infection.

Finally, after a long period of silence, her doctor suggested she was likely suffering from the common cold. Acetaminophen could be given in the case of any aches or fevers. But keeping her hydrated and comfortable was—is—key. I throw a bottle of Tylenol into my basket.

My feet pick up the pace, planting me dead center in the

aisle of candy bars and chips. I grab two Hershey bars, making a mental note to get a Coke from one of the little fridges near the register.

Sweet to cancel out the bitterness of the past three days. Sweet to cancel the worry that Alyssa might come down with something worse than a cold, something her body can't handle.

Yes, sweets surely are the remedy I need. I put the chocolate bars, Coke, and meds on the counter, then hand the clerk a script for the anticonvulsants Alyssa's been on since the accident. She nods at me, and I nod, too, finding it funny that even though we both know each other—or rather of each other—a nod is the most we can manage.

Actually, a nod is plenty. Her daughter was in Alyssa's grade school and used to pull her hair, tell her it looked like tumbleweed. Mom wasted no time filing a complaint. But the girl's mother didn't come into the school, and the school didn't make much attempt to hold the girl accountable aside from a slap on the wrist. Well, that was until Dad had a chat with the principal. Apparently, he had no clue Alyssa's father was the great Gerald Highland.

She holds out her hand. "That will be $86.95."

Her words are like a zap of electricity. "Why is it so expensive? Her prescription meds are never more than twenty-two dollars with insurance."

"Yes, but your insurance has expired," the woman says.

"You're wrong. My insurance—well, Alyssa's insurance—has not expired." It was about to, but when I got the notification email Friday, I paid it the next day.

"Well, darling, I'm looking at the screen right here, and

it's not showing any deductibles. Either you didn't pay as you thought or—"

"As I thought? Are you fucking serious?"

Obscenities fly out of my mouth while anxiety rips through every other part of me.

It's possible, isn't it? That the payment hasn't been processed yet? It happened before. A short period where Alyssa lacked coverage while the insurance was being renewed. But certainly, there's a way to avoid situations like this.

The woman clears her throat. "There's a line forming. If you can't pay—"

My neck doesn't crane to see the line trailing behind me, the faces staring at me with annoyed expressions. It'll just cause my heart to beat faster than it is already, my skin to burn with more embarrassment. So I shove the candy bars and Coke to the far side of the counter.

Last I checked, my account was bordering a measly seventy-six dollars, my direct deposit not scheduled to hit until tomorrow at midnight. I doubt I have enough in my account to afford it.

Fingers shaking as I hand my card to the clerk, I wonder if her daughter is in college. Living her best life while Alyssa is stuck at home. If she ever felt sorry for what her daughter told my sister.

The jumbie on my shoulder cackles, while I pray to the God I've lost all hope in that my card isn't declined.

He must be looking down on me today. It isn't.

I shove my card in my pocket, grab the meds from the clerk, and dart out of the pharmacy, refusing to be embarrassed any further.

Once outside, I breathe in as much air as possible, willing it to cool my flushed cheeks. Just my luck that it's raining, too, and of course I have no umbrella.

I should hurry to the car, but I'm paralyzed. Not by panic but by something else. Whatever it is, it makes me stand there, in the middle of the sidewalk, letting the rain beat down on me as if it's water from heaven, sent from God, to wash away unforgivable sins.

My eyes close, and for just a moment, I think maybe the rain does have the ability to forgive me. Silently, I wish more of it to cleanse me. But a black umbrella appears over my head.

I look up, locking eyes with Dr. Jeon. He stares at me with a curious expression, maybe like I'm one of his patients in the hospital, one he can't quite seem to understand. He holds out a bag to me.

"What is it?" I ask.

He gestures for me to take it, but I don't grip the actual handle of the bag, just some other part. When he lets go, it falls and two candy bars and a bottle of Coke tumble out.

By all means, I should be thankful. He's being kind to me, maybe because of our exchange a few days ago. However, the sweets falling, for whatever reason, cues my unraveling.

I pointlessly reach for my bag usually slung around my shoulders, even though I damn well know I left it, and the medication in it, in the SUV. The pharmacy was only supposed to be a quick run. But now…now I can't even remember where I parked the goddamn SUV.

I try those breathing exercises my psychiatrist taught me, the ones that are supposed to help more than the anxiety meds if you do them right. But my heart is throbbing against my rib cage.

Dr. Jeon attempts to steady me as I slump to the ground. "Laine! What's wrong?"

I clutch my chest, stammering between sobs and exacerbated breaths, "Chest...hurts. Dy...ing."

Dr. Jeon slides his hands down my arms to my wrists, checking my pulse all the while looking me dead in the eyes. "Listen, Laine. And listen carefully. Your chest hurts because you're not breathing. You need to breathe!"

My peripheral vision begins to get fuzzy. I choke out the word *can't*.

Dr. Jeon lets go of my wrists and cups my face. "You can breathe. I'm sure of it. You just need a little help is all. So let me help you." Ignoring the rain beating down on us, he points to one of the passersby who's stopped to observe the commotion. "What's that right beside them?"

My chest is on fucking fire, but I look at the golden retriever on one of those retractable leashes. "Do...dog."

Dr. Jeon points to a little section of the curb where there are no cars. "Good, and what's that there?"

"Fire...hydrant."

He points to the sky. "And those dark gray things above our heads?"

"Clouds."

He slips his hand under my own and holds out my right palm, letting the rain pool in the lifeline. "Okay, and what's falling from those clouds?"

"Rain. Cold rain," I stammer.

Dr. Jeon sighs. "Well, that's why you should have walked with an umbrella. Next time, I hope you make better decisions."

"Don't patronize me, Dr. Jeon!"

"I prefer Eric, actually."

"My bad, Eric. But as I said, don't—"

My words lodge in my throat. He's smiling at me. Takes me a few more seconds to figure out why, but when I do, I'm smiling, too. "I...feel better."

He helps me up to my feet, his clothes completely drenched like my own. "Great. So what do you say we get out of the rain, huh?"

I'm about to say yes. I should say yes. I feel better, but I'm in no way completely healed. However, it'd probably be best for me to get to the SUV, something more familiar to me. Besides, people are staring, a few even asking me if I'm alright. And most importantly, I can't look at Eric without feeling embarrassed.

"It's fine. Um, thank you. For just now." I shove the candy bar and Coke back into the plastic bag. "And this."

Eric holds out a hand as I put distance between us. "I really don't mind—"

"It's fine," I say, and I don't let him make me have to repeat myself. I dart down the street to my SUV.

CHAPTER
20

ALYSSA

Alyssa, you're running out of time. Wake up. You need to wake up. The words come from somewhere near me but nowhere at all, rousing me from the light sleep I fell into once I returned to my chambers. A chill shoots up my spine as I let my feet touch the floor, testing the ground to see if it'll give way as I feel it might.

My head begins to spin, and I rub circles against my temples. Why do I feel like I'm missing something?

My eyes flicker to the portrait of my parents on the wall. Father and Mother stare at me with warm gazes, Father dressed in his usual sandy-colored pants and white shirt. Mother is dressed in a gown made by our kingdom's best seamstress, a daisy come to life...

I approach the portrait slowly, each step deliberate. Something about Mother feels off. She stares at me with eyes as blue as the morning star, her hair blond like my own. Her button nose is the perfect shape, her lips as pink as her cheeks. She's beautiful. But...

Something is wrong. Find me before it's too late.

I spin around in a circle, searching for the voice, but again I'm not sure where it comes from. "Anyone there?" I ask, but there's no response. Just the sound of footsteps approaching.

I dart back into bed and cover myself with fur blankets, praying that the footsteps pass my room.

They don't, the wood moaning as the doors are pushed ajar. "Alyssa, are you awake?" Laine asks, but I remain cemented in place, not quite sure why but certain pretending is what is required of me.

Laine asks the question again, this time with a tad more vigor. However, my lips remain pressed together, my eyes shut. If she pulls the sheet back, she'll certainly see through my act, but her footsteps never draw near.

After another minute, the door closes. I get ready to pull the sheets back, but again there's that voice. And this time I realize it comes from somewhere deep inside my head...a part of me I can't quite understand.

Don't move. She's still in the room, it says.

I do as told, and this time, when the door opens and closes again, there's a loud click.

Heart pounding in my chest, I pull the sheets back and run to the door. The knob catches on something as I turn it, and my breath hitches. As I feared, it's locked.

But why would Laine lock it? *Is* she Laine? Why do I feel like she's a stranger? Like my mother is a stranger?

I make my way to the window. Evening sun gleams through the window, casting shadows on my walls that remind me of fairies dancing under firelight. I appreciate the beauty for only a second, staring at the ground. To jump would be certain death.

To stay in my chambers, for some reason, feels like it will have the same outcome.

So, what do I do?

I pace my chambers, the question whirling around in my head until I settle on an answer. A simple spell I learned years ago.

Before I cast it, I change out of my dress and into pants and riding boots, for I must run.

But why must I run?

Because you must find me.

Who is "me"?

The questions and evasive answers prickle my scalp as I climb onto the windowsill.

I suck in a big breath, so big the rise in my chest is visible, and mutter, "Volant."

There's no hesitation as I jump off the ledge, several stories above the ground. The first thing they teach you in spell-caster class is *never doubt your magic. To doubt one's magic is to doom one to certain failure, nullify one's success before it has a chance to bloom.*

The lesson serves me well because even though I don't soar through the sky, my descent is slowed, gravity my willing assistant.

When my feet kiss the ground, I hunker behind some rose-bushes, the scent failing to tickle my senses as it has done in the past. I remain hidden behind the bushes until two guards make their rounds. Once their footsteps have well faded into the distance, I dash through the garden, weaving between paths of lilies, daisies, and more roses until I hear it—my sister's voice. It's joined by Father's, then Uncle's.

Heartbeat thundering in my ears, I hide behind the tallest

oak in the garden and watch Laine, Uncle, and Father walk along a stream that spills into a dark pool. A sharp pain zips across my scalp. Was there ever a lake in our garden?

"Bring the girls!" Uncle hollers, pulling me from my thoughts.

Wide-eyed, I watch as six guards come into view.

In the middle of them is a girl dressed in tattered garb the color of dirt, her skin the color of earth. Her hair is wiry, like bramble, and her lips plump, as if stung by a bee and forever swollen.

"Please," she begs. "Spare me."

But Uncle gestures the guards forward. Tight-lipped, Father and Laine watch as the guards march the girl into the water until her lower body is submerged.

"Please!" the girl screams, but the word is forced back down into her throat as the guards dunk her entire body.

My head throbs. Should I try to help her? What if they do the same to me? I take a few steps forward at the same time the girl breaches the surface.

I retreat back into hiding, the fear very much still there, if not worse than before.

The guards don't hold on to the girl's arms as they march her out of the water. And the girl does not scream like before, smiling at my Uncle. She does a curtsy. "Thank you. I shall be on my way now."

Without another word, she takes her leave. But she's not the same girl. No, her hair shines yellow like hay, and her brown eyes glimmer a deep blue. Her wide nose has been pulled straight and upward, and her lips have shrunk.

Murder, the voice in my mind says, and I swallow hard, sweat dripping down my back as I watch another girl come. Then another.

I want to help. But then again, the girls don't seem hurt? Isn't my uncle making them better? But how are they better? What was wrong with them before?

Nothing, the voice responds, and this time I make up my mind to help, my eyes finding the next girl. Unlike the others, she looks familiar, though I can't put my finger on why.

Her skin is a tawny color, her hair curling like strands of yarn. And her eyes, brown with a smidgen of green, beg for help.

Once again, on Uncle's command, the guards lead her into the pool of water. And even though the voice in my head demands I rescue this girl, I hesitate.

Won't she be better once the process is over? Won't life be easier for her in this kingdom? Won't—

I think she's pretty the way she is.

The words are whispered in my head, but somehow they command me with an authority the other demands were lacking.

I dart out from behind the tree and outstretch my hand to the guards. "Nec motus," I mutter, and they freeze in place, their eyes the only things moving.

"What are you doing?" Uncle bellows, and Laine stretches her hand out to me. "Nec—" she starts, but I hold out my hand to her in the nick of time.

"Novis," I yell, and her magic is canceled by my own.

"You're not my sister," I scream.

The girl runs out of the pool and slips her hand into mine. "We must go," she says, and it's the only thing so far that has made sense.

Not stopping to catch our breaths, we run as Laine and the guards give chase.

Confusion begins to overpower fear as the girl skillfully guides us down secret paths and narrow passageways that take us from the garden to the bowels of the castle. "How do you know your way around the castle?" I ask her. "Have you been here before?"

"I've been here all my life." She leads me down winding stairs that lead to the castle's most dangerous place—the prison.

"Princess, what are you doing here?" a guard asks, but I can see him reaching for his sword, his gaze set on the girl beside me.

"Nec motus," I say, and he remains frozen as we walk down the aisle of cells. From each cell, girls with wide eyes stare back at me, begging for help. Their skin, various shades of black and brown, shimmer under the light of torches, and their black hair refuses to lie straight.

"We must help them," I say.

The girl beside me nods. "And we shall."

"How?" We stop at the farthest cell. In it, chained to the wall, is the same boy from earlier, the one who interrupted our meal.

"Alyssa," he calls.

"Who are you?" I ask. "How do you know my name?"

His eyes dart between me and the once prisoner.

"We'll get you out of here soon," she says.

"Hurry, Princess. The sun is about to set, and we need to be touching. No offense to you, but I'd rather not be trapped here for all of eternity."

My brows snap upward, their exchange making me even more confused. "Princess?"

"Yes," the girl says matter-of-factly. "I'm the second princess of Mirendal, Alyssa Highland."

"No. I am," I say quickly.

"In some ways, yes. But in many ways, no, you're not."

"You're a fake," I snap, and the girl flinches at my words.

"Whose voice do you think has guided you since your arrival to this realm?"

She reaches to open the boy's cell, and I grab her arm. "I'm not sure this is a good idea."

She snatches her arm from me, but I grab it again, this time refusing to let go. "I said wait!"

She jabs me in the side with her free hand before attempting to pin me against the wall. "I don't follow orders from you."

I tear myself from her grip, using her own weight against her to push her against the wall. "But you do! I'm Princess Alyssa Highland and you are..."

She stops resisting but leans her face closer to mine. "Go on. Tell me who I am."

I don't know who she is, I think, but as I search my mind for the answer, something strange happens. Emotions pour into me like a flood, ushering in memories that threaten to rip me apart with no promise to piece me back together.

I take deep breaths, everything spinning until there's a perfect stillness. In her. In me. "I know you."

"I know," she says with a faint smile, and I'm not quite sure at all how it happens. Just that my entire body, lit ablaze by the realization, morphs into air as I melt into her, assimilating until I am a part of a whole—a part of me—Alyssa Highland, second princess of Mirendal. A girl of mixed lineage with hair once described as fairy weed and skin the color of honey.

Well aware now that time is running out, I grab the ring of keys attached to the frozen guard's waistband.

Wren laughs as I unlock his shackles. "Took you long enough, Princess."

"Did you really think I could forget about you?"

Wren's eyes glint with emotions I've seen before—attraction, excitement, yearning. But there's something else, too. A sadness that makes me want to pull him into an embrace.

We maneuver our way out of the bottom of the castle, but before we leave, Wren stops by the guard. He hits him over the head as his limbs start to twitch, my spell wearing off.

From the guard's pocket, Wren pulls out a large vial. In it, squished into an uncomfortable position, is Emerald. "He planned to sell her on the market," Wren says, and he holds the vial tight, whispering something.

The glass melts with Wren's spell, and Emerald flits through the air just as dozens of footsteps approach.

"I'm not sure there's a way out," I say, my voice cracking. "The most we can do is pray they don't separate us before the sun sets."

Emerald says something, and Wren works quickly to translate. "Fairies can cast portals to travel short distances when in large numbers. If we lend Emerald our strength, she might be able to get us out of the castle."

I wrap my fingers in Wren's. Emerald perches on our intertwined hands and begins to chant, her voice starting off as a whisper, only to grow louder and louder as Wren and I let magic pour out of us.

"She says to close your eyes," Wren says, and I do.

I don't feel the jump. All I feel is weakness, the kind that makes me want to roll up in a ball and take a long nap.

Wren and I walk forward. Even in our tiredness, we marvel at the trees outside of the castle. They kiss the sky, now an array of dark blues and pinks.

"What now?" I ask.

Either Glior is watching, or my words are a trigger of some sort. The ground begins to shake.

I tighten my grip on Wren and Emerald, watching as a circle of earth gives way to a gaping hole.

"There they are!" Laine bellows, and I look over my shoulder, eyeing her and the army of guards running toward us.

There's no time to second-guess myself. I jump into the hole.

CHAPTER
21

LAINE

I never made it to the date I was supposed to have with Robert. Even though Dr. Jeon managed to calm me down, my nerves were still firing with panic when I got home. So I just called him to discuss things instead. In a way it worked out. Not being in the same space allowed me to get directly to the point without second-guessing things like how I look or what he thought about how I look. And once I said what I needed to and Robert promised to check into the bad behavior, the call ended. Understandably so. My concerns weren't something to just brush over with talk of favorite foods and future dates.

I enter Glenn's coffee shop, glancing at Caroline, who's running the register. She lifts her chin toward Robert, sitting at a table in middle of the shop. I sigh. We were supposed to meet at Lake Forest for him to give me an update on the situation with Bennett. But Glenn asked me to cover the evening shift.

"Hey. Thanks for meeting me here on such short notice," I say while walking up to the table.

Robert gets up and holds out a coffee. "No problem. And I hope you don't mind. I asked your coworker what kind of coffee you'd like, and she made this."

I look at Caroline, and she gives a quick wink before continuing to tend to a customer. I take a seat. I'm sure the hazelnut macchiato she made is delicious, but I can't drink it. Not if my conversation with Robert is going to end in him telling me my concerns are invalid.

Robert frowns, sliding his own coffee cup forward. "You must think I'm about to trivialize everything, given the way I'm acting. I'm sorry."

Shit. That's a damn good read. So good it's a little scary.

"Well, maybe just a little," I say, not wanting him to know just how right he is.

It's brief, barely noticeable, but I'm almost certain I see it. A hint of relief that he's reading me as well as he thinks. I'm not sure how to feel about it. "I want to assure you that's not what's about to happen here."

"Shouldn't I be the judge of that?" I ask, and while it isn't my intention for those words to sting, it appears they do. Robert purses his lips. "About my employee and his treatment of the guests at Lake Forest…it's not the first time I'm hearing of it."

"It's not?" I ask, voice going up at least two decibels.

Caroline shoots me a questioning glance, and I gesture to her as discreetly as possible that I'm fine before returning my attention to Robert. If he's gotten a complaint about Bennett before, why the hell has he kept him around?

"One other staff member said he seemed a little rough with one of the guests. When I checked the camera footage, there was no evidence of physical abuse. And to be honest, Bennett hasn't really had the greatest luck. When I met him, he was struggling. He begged me for a job, and even though he didn't have the best education, his experience taking care of his mother with multiple sclerosis was invaluable."

I'm patiently waiting for a *but*, and sure enough, it comes.

"But while many of my staff members love him, there are several who've learned of Bennett's history with drugs and petty robbery." Robert pauses, seemingly searching for words. "I firmly believe he shouldn't be judged for what he did in the past. But your complaint... it was the last straw. I've let him go."

I'm not sure if it's Robert's intention, but suddenly I feel horrible. Like I've kicked a man while he's down.

"I didn't see him hitting Harold, just his tone rubbed me the wrong way. Did it really warrant dismissal?"

My jumbie rears her head. *Of course it didn't. You overreacted and cost this man his job. What if he has a family to feed? What if he's struggling like you? What did he really do, Laine?*

"I love my staff. And I believe in giving people chances. But your complaint should be acknowledged. So don't make that face."

What do I look like in Robert's eyes? "What face am I making?"

"The face of someone who thinks they've made a mistake, and you, Laine, did not make a mistake."

It's funny. He's telling me what I want to hear, but my defenses are still up. After all, Bennett has been the focus of our conversation, but there's someone just as worrisome we should discuss while we're here. "Did you speak to Reena?"

"Spoke to her as soon as I got back from Philly. I'm sure you can imagine how that went."

"Maybe she's right. Maybe us dating is inappropriate."

Robert lets the silence between us linger for a few seconds. "I won't lie to you. While there's no law against it, some might consider it unethical. But my feelings are real, Laine. And, if it makes you feel better, Reena quit."

"What?"

He stares at his coffee like it's a crystal ball or something. "This would have happened sooner or later. I'm just sorry she attacked you in the parking lot."

I run my fingers along my collar, recalling the way Reena grabbed me. None of it gave "I'm going to quit" vibes. "I don't believe she's totally out of the picture just because she resigned. And honestly, do I want her to be? You two have known each other since you were kids. Making you choose between us when we've only known each other for a short time . . . it feels wrong."

Robert's head cocks to the side, much like a dog's when it's confused. "Strange."

"What?"

"With my father being the owner of E. Remson Industries, I'd think you'd say good riddance to Reena. She might hinder a relationship . . . hinder a possible fortune."

I take a big gulp of my coffee, hoping to hide the way his words make a tinge of pain race across my chest. I'm not a gold digger. "You must have had a bad run dating girls only interested in your money, huh? And you got cut out of the will, remember?" Not to mention, I'd be stupid to be dreaming about anything past this casual dating thing we have going on. Something's going to give sooner or later.

Robert leans forward, and the gravity of the way he's look-ing at me, eyes unblinking, makes me still. "I like you, Laine. A lot. But I am worried Reena hasn't been home since she quit."

"I didn't know that she hasn't been home," I say, not bother-ing to pepper my voice with more concern than necessary. "Is she okay?"

Robert shrugs. "She's been reading my text messages, so I'm sure she is, but I'm afraid she might do something stupid."

Reena doing something stupid to keep Robert on a leash—I can't say that I'm surprised.

But then again, couldn't the fact that she quit and is now avoiding the apartment she rents near Robert's actually be an attempt at moving on?

"If she reaches out to you and starts rambling about anything strange, although I doubt she will, please call me."

I arch a brow. "Strange?"

Blood visibly creeps up Robert's neck to his cheeks. "There've been plenty of times when I've refused to break things off that she's spread rumors about me being a horrible person… someone to avoid. None of it's true, of course, but still. I'd like to set the record straight just in case she pulls any similar stunts."

I take another big gulp of my drink. I like Robert. Our con-versations make me laugh, and he's a nice person. But he has baggage, and her name is Reena. I should steer clear of him. I should— My own train of thought pulls me up short. Did I just justify not dating Robert because he has baggage? Me of all people?

I run a hand through my hair, feeling ashamed. I'm sad-dled with debt, have a sister to take care of, and am prone to emotional outbursts. Yet Robert gave me a chance. Shouldn't I extend the same courtesy?

"I'm down, Robert. But if Reena threatens me again, that's it."

Robert clasps my hands. "You won't regret it."

"Better not," I say with a wink, and with everything now cleared up, somewhat, I head to the back to get ready to work the shift.

Caroline nudges me in the side. "Looks like he's staying here to ogle you some more."

I roll my eyes. "It's not like that. He has some important emails to send. And we do have good Wi-Fi."

"Oh, sure we do," Caroline deadpans, and almost as if to taunt me, she stays back even though her shift is over, observing "Dr. Jeon's competition."

Her teasing only stops when a child runs into the shop, mother following, face glued to her phone.

The child cuts in front of the one person in the line. I don't say anything, nor does the older gentleman who seems too tired to even care.

I paint my face with a little smile. "You have to wait your turn, sweetheart. Do you mind—"

She keeps her gaze fixed on the menu, pointing. "I want a frappé."

"Sure thing, but you have to wait," I say while glancing at her mother, still lost in whatever conversation she's having via text.

Annoyed, but not about to scold a child who's not mine, I ignore the girl and finish ringing up the gentleman's order.

But the little girl isn't too happy about this. When I ask what she wants, she changes her mind several times with a cheeky grin.

Caroline, just as fed up as I must be, leans over the counter, tone so peachy it's more intimidating than kind. "Darling, why don't you take a minute to decide, then place an order when you know what you want, huh?"

"Excuse me? She knows what she wants," Mom says, finally looking up from her phone.

"Actually, she didn't," I add, but the woman is tapping her toe against the ground, eyes glinting with an anger I can only imagine given the sunglasses indoors.

"You know what you want, don't you, sweetheart?"

"I do. French vanilla frappé with chocolate syrup drizzle, which I told them several times."

Mom juts her chin in the air. "See? So how about you stop patronizing my child and make the damn order?"

The little girl smiles slyly, clearly thinking she's won. In a way, she has. Now that she's finally given her real order, it's just easier for me to ring it up and make it. By the time I'm taking the next set of orders, she's out of sight, out of mind.

Until the sound of something hard smacking against wooden tiles and a loud cry ringing through the shop.

"Well, that's some karma. Although, I gotta say I feel kinda bad. Looks like it hurt," Caroline says as we watch the woman scramble to help her child off the floor.

Robert helps, handing the mother some napkins to wipe the frappé her daughter is now wearing. "Sorry. It looks like she tripped over the strap of my laptop bag."

Caroline scoffs. "Damn, she looks more concerned about him than her daughter. Just look at the way she's ogling him."

She's not wrong. Mom stands extra close, saying, "No. She

should have also been watching where she was going. The bag isn't damaged, right?"

Robert responding, "No problem" is all I manage to hear before I must turn my attention back to the line that's begun to form. However, I do manage to glimpse the woman and her daughter walking out of the store. And Robert, staring in their direction, hint of a smile on his lips, if only for a second.

I ring up another order. That smile, for some reason, makes me feel uneasy.

CHAPTER
22

ALYSSA

Darkness greets me when I open my eyes, the call of frogs cutting through the hot night.

Once I've clambered to my feet, I dust myself off and look around. The moon, full and round, illuminates trees with trunks thinner than oak.

I look to my right. More trees, but these are different, the trunks also thin but shooting out of the ground at different angles. Emerald's dress is caught on one of the trunks, and she's trying to free herself. I unpin her. "Are you okay?"

I'm not quite sure what she says, but her tone is laced with an undeniable snark. I can't help but think of our encounter when we breached the surface of the lake earlier. She seemed downright angry with me. Wren said she wasn't... that she had a fight with one of the fairies, but was that truly it?

Unable to get an answer without Wren here to translate, I force a small smile. "Illumine," I say, and the tip of my pointer finger shines like a small sun. "Let's find Wren."

With a humph, Emerald flits forward, letting my light guide

her path. I'm not sure how long I've been walking—the moon has just slid behind a swath of clouds—when Emerald flutters into my hair.

"What's wrong?" I ask, but the question is like a call for action. She bundles my locks of hair, hiding herself.

"Shh!" she says, and I don't need much translation to understand that.

The light emanating from my finger flickers out as I cancel my spell and press my back against one of the trees.

My eyes struggle to adjust to the darkness. My clothes cling to my skin with sweat, the hot air heavy with humidity.

Mirendal has never been so warm, has it?

Emerald tugs tighter on my hair as the sound of insects is silenced by laughter.

It gets louder and louder until it's near booming in my ears.

My nerves feel shot as my eyes find the source.

Several yards away are the creatures of my nightmares. At least a dozen douens prance around in a circle, laughing and singing. Even though their featureless faces are covered by palm leaves dipped in silver, they're recognizable by their backward feet and knees, and potbellied stomachs.

I'm not in Mirendal at all, am I? No, this is my mother's homeland across the sea.

I cover my mouth, hoping to hide my gasp of shock, but the douens' heads snap in my direction.

My body feels as if it's been dunked in cold water.

Mother always said douens—known for persuading children to join them out in the woods—are friendly. But to those who are older, the creatures can be nightmares.

I don't wait to see whether I'd be considered friend or foe.

I turn and run through the woods, grasses cutting against my skin to make it itch and bleed.

When I finally stop to catch my breath, I'm pleased to see that the creatures have not given chase, but another fear sets in. I still don't know where Wren is.

I pace in a circle, Emerald hovering in the air until I get an idea for a spell to find someone. What were the words again?

Emerald perches on a branch and crosses her legs. She rolls her eyes, and for a second, I forget about the spell. She's definitely annoyed with me. Why?

"Did I do something to you, Emerald?"

Her haughty attitude simmers to a sad look. She avoids my gaze.

"I'm sorry if I did. And whatever it is, I'll right it once we find Wren and make it to the other plane."

My words garner only a nod. Clearly, I did something, but what?

My mind spins as I try to recall the spell we need. Once Wren is back, I can make amends with Emerald.

Much like before, I hold out my hand to chant the word *illumine*. When my pointer finger is showering our surroundings with light, I chant another spell. "To Wren, clamarem tota die."

It doesn't quite work, but I play around with the words a few more times. On the sixth try, the light from my finger frees itself to form a circle on the ground. That circle darts back and forth in front of me before moving north.

I don't need to tell Emerald we must follow. She's already ahead of me, chasing the light. And luckily for her, she doesn't have to contend with vines and branches that threaten to bring me to my knees.

Once we reach the edge of a clearing, the light fades away.

On either side of the field, four tall torches arranged in a square are stuck into the ground, pelting fire into the air. In the center is a dry rotted log on which Wren sits.

A woman bustles around him, her face hidden by a large straw hat that matches her long red dress. The fabric picks up dirt as she stirs a pot of something that makes my mouth water. She dishes some of the food into a bowl...a bowl she hands to Wren.

I'm tempted to call out to him, but something stops me, a gnawing feeling that something is amiss. At first, I can't put my finger on it, and I just stand there, watching. Why didn't Wren come looking for us? Who is this woman?

Terra must hear my question, for a gentle breeze picks up the woman's dress, and I see it—a leg of black fur, a hoof for a right foot. Wren should notice it, too. But he keeps eating, his face hazing red as if he's drunk too much wine. But it's not spirits that have caused his face to flush, is it?

My legs threaten to buckle as I recall my mother's words about La Diablesse.

A woman who wears a brimmed hat to hide a hideous face, La Diablesse was once very beautiful. That beauty was lost after making evil deals. Bitter, she now uses spells to lure men, especially those unfaithful to their wives, deep into the forest. By the time they realize what's happening, she's gone and the man is forever bound to wander forest paths, in search of his way out.

But why is she feeding Wren?

Wary, I move only when La Diablesse pulls something from the pocket of her dress.

I stretch my hand toward her. "Nec motus," I say, but her movements do not slow nor do her limbs lock in place.

"It took you some time, didn't it?" The demon's singsong words are clipped. "And you've come thinking you can beat me with your magic from across the sea. What an entitled child you are."

Emerald flits to Wren, tugging on his hair, but he stares at her aimlessly, in some sort of trance.

"Nec motus," I say again, but La Diablesse is unfazed, flinging purple dust in my face. I cough, attempting to swat away the dust that's still lingering. But my limbs are frozen, each muscle paralyzed by some unseen force that crushes my body and my spirit.

Fear races up and down my back like a horse. "Let Wren go," I manage to get out.

La Diablesse sits down next to Wren and strokes his cheek with her palm. "And why would I do that?"

Channeling what must be all her strength, Emerald emits a high-pitched scream as she flies toward La Diablesse.

I hold my breath, watching, hoping for what, I'm not sure. But in one swift movement, La Diablesse swats the fairy with the back of her hand.

Emerald falls to the ground like a leaf from a tree, and I scream.

"Oh, hush! She's fine. I just gave her a little tap."

La Diablesse nestles her head against Wren, and her hat shifts, no longer hiding her face. I recoil, stunned by the crackled skin, eyes completely white, nose that's barely a nose.

I try to steel myself, remain brave. But I know from the

moment I speak, my shaky voice betrays me. "Let him go. He's not a bad man. He's . . ."

"He is good. A little cocky from what I've gathered while siphoning his memories, but admirable. That's why I've decided to keep him. Make him my companion."

"No! You can't!"

La Diablesse stands. "I can and I will. Besides, do you think you deserve him? After what he gave up for you?"

"What he gave up?" Is she referring to Wren coming to this realm with me? I asked him not to come, and he did. "He does not belong with you. In this realm."

La Diablesse makes no attempt to hide her face now. "I'm sure the boy would choose me, even if I were to release my hold."

Wren would never choose her. She's a monster, a woman who sold her soul to darkness.

Wait! That gives me an idea. A rather dangerous one, but right now there's no other choice. "Fine. How about we make a deal? Release your hold on Wren, and let him choose. If he decides to stay, I'll leave. If he chooses me, you'll let us both go."

La Diablesse walks a circle around me, her limp more exaggerated than before, her jaw at an uncomfortable angle, her white eyes boring into me.

She won't agree to my idea. Wren would never choose her. I need to find another way to take him from her clutches. I need to—

"Deal. But if the boy chooses me, he won't be the only one staying. So will you, forever bound to this realm to languish in his decision." She smiles slyly. "Makes it more fun, no?"

Far from it, but there's no time to hesitate. If this is the only way to save Wren, I must take it.

Awareness materializes in Wren's eyes, his face no longer that of a man drunk in love. He looks at me just as I start to rise off the ground, my limbs no longer frozen. "Wren, come with me. We have to go," I say.

"Alyssa?" Wren steps toward me, stopping when a voice—all too familiar—calls to him.

"Wren. Don't trust her. She's an imposter." The words come out of La Diablesse's mouth, but the creature no longer wears her red dress and hat. Instead, she is in a dress identical to mine, her curls matted with twigs and leaves, face smudged with dirt.

Wren's confusion twists his features. "Alyssa?" he calls to La Diablesse.

My voice is a shrill cry. "Wren, remember how we raced up the hills in the other plane? How we spoke to Freah and got a scale to give Glior to come here? I'm the real Alyssa."

Wren takes several steps toward me.

La Diablesse trails a finger along her bottom lip. "What about a kiss that would have come to pass if my bracelet didn't break?"

Wren takes a step back to the imposter, and my heart plummets. La Diablesse mentioned something about siphoning Wren's memories, didn't she?

Wren's head swivels between me and La Diablesse until calm sets over him like some kind of blanket. "I have an idea."

"You do?" La Diablesse asks, and Wren gestures to Emerald, now awake and cowering by the log.

She flitters upward, glancing back and forth at me and my look-alike.

"Can you sing for us?" Wren asks.

Emerald nods, and Wren smiles.

"I'll dance with each of you. That is how I'll determine which one of you is the imposter. So who'd like to go first?"

A dance? He can't be serious, but he is, taking the imposter's hand before gesturing for Emerald to sing.

The fairy must pull from Wren's magic, because her voice is amplified, her melody seemingly enchanting the blades of grass that begin to sway beneath us.

Tears spill from my eyes as I watch Wren, the way he and La Diablesse move as one. Since we've met, he's been a masquerade of playful banter and boyish charm. However, as La Diablesse rests her head against his chest, gazing up at him so he knows he's in complete control, Wren seems anything but boyish.

He dances with perfect form, with his head held high and lean frame towering well above La Diablesse. Yet looming in height as he is, his touch—his gaze—remains gentle, just as the moonlight glimmering off his obsidian head of hair.

I don't like it. The only people I've seen move so gracefully together are my parents.

Once they're done dancing, Wren gestures to me. He puts his hand around my waist, but I don't look up at him. He uses a finger to lift my chin. "And what's your name?"

"Alyssa Highland, second princess of Mirendal. The real one."

"Is that so?" Wren guides me left and right, every few seconds spinning me in a circle. I follow his lead at first, but my despair hinders my rhythm, and I step on his feet.

"Owww," he hisses. "Can you be a little more graceful?"

"You're leading," I snap. "If you can't compensate for a few missteps, maybe you're not that good a dancer."

Wren's hand presses a little harder into my back, and a shiver runs up my spine. The last time we were this close to each other was when we almost kissed. Yet right now it's all aggressive stares and snide remarks...none of that tenderness he had with La Diablesse.

I step on him again.

"A princess should be able to dance flawlessly under pressure. You're not really a princess, are you?"

We stop moving, and Emerald stops singing. From the corner of my eye, I can see me—La Diablesse—smirking.

Tears roll down my cheeks again. I've failed to protect him. Just like I've failed to protect my parents.

Wren lifts my chin once more, and Emerald continues to sing. However, this time, the fairy's melody is slower.

As we dance, Wren and I stare at each other in an odd way, our glances a dance unto themselves.

"You're stubborn and annoying. You're also unnecessarily heavy-handed. But you're so much more than a princess who's a pain in my arse. You're hope, Alyssa. My hope."

Time seems to slow as the music ceases, and despite her ramblings, La Diablesse feels like a distant afterthought.

It's just me and Wren, lost in each other as his hands rest below my ears, his thumb caresses my cheek.

My legs tremble, but Wren doesn't let me fall. He leans closer until there's no space left between us and our lips have touched, our hearts coming to beat together, as one.

Each fiber in my body hums in tune to the same rhythm as we pull apart. "How?"

"Your stubbornness is one of your charms, Princess," Wren says.

"I won't allow it!"

Our heads snap toward La Diablesse. No longer does she have my likeness, but wears her dress that sweeps up dirt, straw hat that hides her face. "I won't let you take him from me."

I crouch into a defensive position and extend my hands, ready to yell spells my mind refuses to acknowledge might not work. Wren mimics my stance, prepared to fight. But just as we start to chant a spell, a deep voice booms throughout the clearing like a clap of thunder.

Letting out a screech, La Diablesse runs out of the clearing and into the trees, her half-hopping gait not slowing her as much as I'd expect.

Wren and I hold on to each other, and Emerald hides in my hair again as the deep voice lets out a laugh.

Wren gestures to our right, and I squint, trying to see what he's looking at. It takes only a few seconds to make out a tree that I'm almost certain was not there before. Taller than the surrounding forest, its four branches are oriented in perfect positions to mimic limbs. And it walks toward us, shrinking in size as it does.

Wren and I back away, but the tree is quick, its movements becoming more fluid as it gets closer and closer until it no longer has the likeness of a tree but of a man.

He sways with a gentle breeze as he closes the remaining distance between us. I'm tempted to back away, but his face, framed by matted locks of hair, is lit by a warm smile. He walks past Wren and me, and plops down on the log.

"Who are you?" I ask.

He dishes out food from La Diablesse's pot. "Hmm. Don't you know?"

"I don't."

The man chuckles. "I am the one you came to see—the moko jumbie in charge of this realm."

There's no hesitation. I plant myself down on the ground in front of him and proceed to explain my situation, but the man—the being—holds up a hand. "I already know, Alyssa Highland, of your dilemma. I've heard it every day since you were trapped in the other realm fourteen days ago."

"Fourteen days? Alyssa was trapped nine days ago," Wren says.

"Time is skewed in the other realms. It's been five days since the earth spirit, Glior, sent you into the hole." The moko jumbie takes up Wren's bowl on the ground, somehow still piping hot, and takes a bite of the food. "That devil woman is mean, but she can cook, let me tell you."

"How—how do you know all this?" I ask, happy that my confusion masks my fear. Also, my annoyance that he eats as if he has not a care in the world.

The moko jumbie huffs. "You told me."

"I told you?" My only recollection of moko jumbies comes from my mother's stories of spirits with the likeness of tall, long-limbed men. They're supposed to protect villages from impending danger, their height allowing them to see threats in the distance.

Emerald flits to the moko jumbie, perching on his shoulder. She says something to him and he nods.

"What's she saying?" I ask Wren, and he stares at me with wide eyes. "She told him his form here is much more interesting."

"Interesting?"

The moko jumbie smiles. "Different forms and faces for

different realms, but my goal of serving the people will always be the same."

I study him like he's a painting come to life. "So you're telling me you're Omniscius?"

He huffs. "And Omniscius is Terra. And I am Omniscius."

It takes a few minutes to wrap my head around it, and I'm not quite sure I do. Regardless, within seconds, I find myself begging. "Please tell me how to get back to the other plane. I need to help my sister. I need to save my kingdom."

The god cocks his head to one side, taking me in like I'm something he can't quite seem to understand. "Are you sure you want to know how?"

"Yes! Tell me!"

"Hmm, once I speak it, it cannot be undone."

"I don't care. I need to know."

The moko jumbie sighs, and I sigh, too.

"The only way you shall break the witch man's spell is through a sacrifice already promised."

Sacrifice—the word rattles around in my head like wasps, stinging my senses to make me feel dizzy . . . lost.

"What sacrifice?" My mind dredges up memories from the last few weeks, but I don't remember making a promise to give up anything. If I had, wouldn't I have already left the plane? Certainly, this must be some kind of cruel joke. "Terra mocks me, doesn't she?"

The moko jumbie looks up at the sky, no longer home to just the moon but an abundance of stars. "Some things, child, you shall never know. But rest assured, I have not abandoned you."

"Then give me the power I need to go back to the other plane! Give me the power to defeat the dark prince."

The moko jumbie raises his bushy brows. "But you already have it."

"But you just said I can only return to the other plane through a sacrifice already promised. What sacrifice?"

"Hmm, I did say that, didn't I?"

Talking to the moko jumbie is like pulling teeth. I bury my face in my knees, rocking back and forth. Wren crouches beside me, doing his best to comfort me, but I feel like I'm breaking.

His kiss, his love, is not enough to stop the hurricane of despair threatening to drown me.

"To cheer you up, I offer other words of advice," says the moko jumbie.

"And what's that?"

"The same way some changels, some non-changels, and some victims of dark magic communicate with one another, you can communicate with your sister. But, my child, it will require a sacrifice of the mind. You will have to break through the wall in her head, and that requires dooming yourself to certain suffering."

I'm almost certain now that the moko jumbie is hell-bent on throwing salt on fresh wounds. "You just told me the only way I can lift the prince's spell is through a sacrifice already promised. But you won't tell me what that promise is. How am I to believe I'll ever get to the other plane to even try and share thoughts with Laine?"

The deity takes a bite of La Diablesse's food, bobbing his head up and down. "You've asked quite a few questions, but I have a question for you."

"What?" I hiss.

The moko jumbie shrugs at my tone. "Why don't you stay in

Omniscius's realm? I understand you must help your kin. But there you can use magic. In the next..."

My eyes latch on to Wren, who's already staring back with a somber expression. It's a question he has asked before.

The moko jumbie knocks his spoon against the wooden bowl. "Well?"

I clear my throat. It's true. In the next plane, my abilities are limited. But life, despite its many ups and downs, has had its own magic at times, hasn't it? The times Laine took me out to the garden to watch the sunset. The days when the sound of Father's favorite instrument, emanating from her crystal ball, filled our kingdom.

I might not be able to wield magic there like I can in these realms. But I want to be with my sister and my kingdom.

The moko jumbie looks up at the sky. "Follow the comet. It shall lead you to where you are needed. Hurry."

I'm not sure how I clamber to my feet, just that Wren slips his hand into my own. I don't even have time to thank the moko jumbie before Wren is dragging me through the clearing and into the trees. I stumble a few times, struggling to keep up with him and Emerald.

He keeps his eyes on the comet. "You'll save Laine. And your kingdom. You can do this!"

Wren speaks the words as if they're fact, not a hope. How can he be so certain? I pick up my pace, wanting to believe him.

The ball of flame fades out of view, and Wren stops.

A few feet ahead, the ground gives way. My feet take me forward, my mind preparing for the jump. But we never have to leap, because the ground caves in all around us.

I'm not sure how long I float through the darkness, but I hear something. A voice…my mother's. She calls to me and I call back.

I'm still calling when I realize I'm no longer in darkness but lying in a field of white jasmine, the very one I awoke in when I first came to the plane.

Wren extends a hand. "Well, that was an adventure."

I dust myself off. "It was, but nothing was gained by it."

"But everything was," Wren says.

"What do you mean?"

The look in Wren's eyes can only be described as an unparalleled sadness, one that must drain through him, all the way to the ground. Muttering garbled words that make fear shoot through me even though I can't comprehend them, he collapses.

CHAPTER
23

LAINE

I know when Ana's going to tell me a lesson is canceled before she actually does. She always comes up to me, wherever I am, with three extra lines in her brow. Today, though, she's also holding a bucket of feed. "Got some bad news. Two p.m. lesson—"

"Let me guess, canceled?"

She sets the bucket down and pats the black Andalusian I tacked up in advance. "Before you say it, I'm working on the cancellation policy. I just gotta review a few more things."

She's been saying that for the past year, but I hold my tongue. The lesson getting canceled costs me money and time, but today I don't mind. Since I got here, my mind has been elsewhere, and an unfocused mind is never good while giving a lesson to an anxious student on top of an animal that can be unpredictable.

"You look like you're miles away," Ana says as she waves a hand in my face. "Is everything alright at home?"

"Fine," I say. "No complaints."

From her sheepish smile, she doesn't seem to buy it, but she picks up her bucket and returns to feeding the horses.

I watch her as she works, feeling annoyed at having to untack Oslo after just having tacked him up. He knocks his front hoof against the cobblestones, and I start leading him back to the stall. "Sorry about that, boy. Know you love the exercise."

He knocks his hoof harder, and I run my hands through his mane, thinking.

Last night, I went home and watched a Netflix show about horses with Alyssa. Once I put her to bed, Robert called, and we stayed up late into the night, talking.

A lot of questions were asked and a lot were answered, but only one stuck with me. It was, "Have you ever thought about just doing something for yourself? No thought of anyone else, not even your sister?"

I fiddle with Oslo's bridle. The answer to that question was obvious, but I didn't answer it, pretending to get a late-night call from Marcella.

"I should have answered it, huh?" I ask Oslo.

He bumps me in the arm before bobbing his head aggressively, and I laugh.

Oslo's been with us for only a few months, but Ana says out of all the horses in her stables, he's the most perceptive, feeding off people's energy. Maybe that's why although Oslo's knocking his hoof, seemingly desperate for a ride, I can't help but feel this is more a push to accommodate me than himself.

I hold both sides of his bridle and look into his eyes. "Are you psychic?"

He doesn't whinny, following some crazy cliché in a Lifetime movie, but he does blow snot on my shirt.

I don't balk, don't complain. Instead, I do something I never do: I lead him out of the stables, to the riding ring. Not the indoor one that Ana can see from the stables, but the outdoor one that requires a bit of a walk.

Tucked beneath the woolly clouds, the sun still manages to cast what feels like a spotlight as we enter the ring, sawdust crunching beneath us.

I stop dead center of the ring and stare at him. Since the accident, I haven't been able to ride without thinking about Alyssa...how I'm getting to do something she can't. However, right now, there's only one thing rattling around in my head.

Do I remember how to ride?

Silly. Even if you take a break, you never truly ever forget when you've been in the saddle for years. Still, when I think about how much I might have forgotten, my chest gets tight.

That said, there's an extra strangeness to Oslo today, a daring sort of mood that pushes me to take that risk. And I wonder why he of all horses is having that effect on me until it hits me.

Ah, that's right. The black mane...the spunky personality? It all reminds me of Sprinkler.

Holding my breath, I slide my foot into the stirrup and hoist myself up into the saddle. I need to hold on to this moment. If I don't, I might never get the chance to ride again.

As I pick up the reins, Oslo's explosive energy resonates with a part of me I haven't indulged in so long...with my dreams.

Smiling, I give Oslo his head, his freedom. And, in turn, he gives me mine. If only for a moment.

CHAPTER
24

ALYSSA

Wren's breaths are labored and uneven. When he speaks, his words are clipped, his voice hoarse. "I'm being rejected by the plane. I can't stay much longer."

"Rejected? What do you mean?"

"Freah asked for a sacrifice in exchange for a scale. I've been running on borrowed time and potions to come to this plane anyway, so it just made sense I be the one to offer something."

I think back to the way Freah and Wren stared at each other several days ago, how Emerald reacted when we breached the surface. "Emerald was never distraught because she got into a fight with the other fairies, was she? She knew of the deal you made, sensed it."

Wren coughs. "Yes," he says finally, a wry smile on his face.

My heart flutters rapidly. "What exactly did you give in exchange, Wren?"

Wren's hands shake, and he digs his nails into the soil, as if doing so can keep them steady. "I had an idea Freah would want years of your life in exchange for a scale. So I offered mine instead. But she wanted something she's asked me for before by way of a single look, something she knew would be much harder for me to give."

"What could be worse than your life?"

"My time here, Alyssa." Wren winks at Emerald, letting out a cross between a chuckle and a cry. "I've always enjoyed my time here. But who knows? Maybe you're right about the other plane. Maybe I didn't give the magic there a fair shot."

A sob warbles in my throat. "You're leaving because of me."

Wren shakes his head. "Don't you blame yourself. I didn't just give up this realm for you."

"You're lying."

"I'm not. I . . . before we journeyed into the realms, I learned my family has been making plans to move to a different kingdom. I'm to go to a new home for changels, somewhere near the sea in the west."

I should be happy by the news that Wren will be leaving the evil of Lake Forest. But given he won't be able to return to this plane, it's likely we won't see each other again. The thought swirls around in my head, along with images of our kiss, his words to me. It feels like I'm losing him forever.

Wren's eyes scour my face, searching, yearning. "If I never get to see you again, it'll be torture. But I'm tired of the dark prince winning. I think you—you—can beat him. Even if I cannot accompany you on the rest of your journey."

I speak through gritted teeth. "No. We'll fight and finish it together."

Whistling loudly, I pray to Terra that Nerra will respond.

Wren's eyes widen as the horse's whinny resounds throughout the plane. She thunders toward us, a ribbon of black parting fields of white.

"What are you planning to do?" Wren asks.

I look at Emerald. "Take care of him. I'll be back as soon as possible."

Emerald nods as I grab Nerra's reins. It takes a few tries, but I manage to solidify my seat after my third attempt.

"Alyssa, please don't leave me. Let's—let's spend this last bit of time together." Wren's words tug on my soul, so much so that I'm ready to dismount. But I can't lose him.

"I'll be back. Just hang on, Wren." With those words, I kick Nerra into a gallop. I can't relish her speed, the way her hooves kiss the ground. I'm too worried.

I spell her hooves once we get to the lake. Nerra doesn't wait for me to give her the command to gallop ahead, and I take it as a sign that she, too, knows she might never see her friend again. She races ahead, her breaths coming as quick and heavy as my own.

Wren's smug, but he's also kind. He's a rock I didn't expect to find at Lake Forest, someone to keep me going.

I love him.

We stop in the middle of the lake. "Freah," I call out.

The mermaid must have been expecting us. She breaches the surface in an instant. "Alyssa Highland. How can I help you?"

"Undo the deal you made with Wren."

"Why would I do that?" She stares at me like I'm a foolish child, one yet to learn the workings of the world.

Maybe I am.

"If anyone should have given up something in exchange for your scale, it's me."

"Wren took up your mantle of his own accord," she says. "It's regrettable that he won't return here, but what's done cannot be undone."

Nerra stomps her hoof, kicking up spray. I tighten my grip on her reins. "You're too cruel! Torturing him so can't be worth the brief pain of losing one scale."

"You ignorant girl of the land!" Freah dives down and breaches the surface several times, tail first. It's a show of aggression I've only read about in books about merpeople. "Do you know why a merperson's scales glow?"

The question pulls me up short. "I——I don't know."

Freah points to the sun above. "The scales glimmer like the sun. The sun is life. A mermaid's life force is held within her scales. Wren no longer able to return to the plane? It's a small price to pay considering the years I've given up. So, girl, you best return to the land before I lose my temper."

There isn't much that I can say except that I'm sorry. I scream it again and again before once again begging for her to undo her deal. However, Freah's response is a song, one that causes the water to churn beneath me. Without being told, Nerra gallops toward the land, her fear of the brewing water beneath us evident in her haphazard steps.

I sink to the ground when I'm back at Wren's side. His face is paler, his body fevered. I hold on to his shoulders and press his head to mine.

My heart thumps painfully, and my limbs go cold all at once. "I can't bear to continue without you by my side."

Emerald nods, her face streaked with tears. Her fellow fairies swarm around us like a whirlpool, their voices tinged with
fading hope.

Wren forces a smile at Emerald. "Tell them I'm fine. I just
need to get back to the other plane." The words are followed by
a rumble in his chest. He coughs green sputum streaked bright
red into his hand.

I have to remind myself to breathe, to think.

"Don't cry, Princess," Wren says, and I hold him tighter,
almost as if I can keep him with me.

"Did I ever tell you you're an ugly crier?" he asks.

My sob morphs into a laugh, and Wren struggles to wipe a
tear from my eyes. "My only regret is that I didn't meet you
sooner, Alyssa. Trust me, not one day will go by that I won't
think of you. I'll try to be happy. So do the same for me, will
you?"

My heart screams with agony, but I force myself to nod.

Forcing a smile of his own, Wren looks upward. The bright
rays of the sun darken until it hangs in the sky no longer. The
gray sliver of a moon embraced by blue sky peaks overhead. It's
a stunning display of both nature and magic, the transition from
sunny sky to a starry night enough to steal my breath.

"Hold on to me tightly," Wren says, and I do.

Interlinking their arms, the fairies form a massive circle and
begin to sing. It's a tune that makes me want to laugh and cry,
dance yet fall. The melody lifts me high yet sends me crashing
to the ground. It is a song of Wren's time here in this plane, the
promise of adventures to come in the next.

When it ends, Wren's body dissipates into the air like a fog
That fog hits me with so many emotions that I find myself

ripped from the plane, each fiber in my body screaming out as my chambers in the castle come into view.

A shrill cry escapes my throat.

The moko jumbie said the only way I'd break the dark prince's spell is through a sacrifice already promised. But it wasn't my sacrifice. It was Wren's.

CHAPTER
25

LAINE

We blast music the entire ride to Robert's apartment, a few miles away from Lake Forest. I almost topple over getting out of the car, and he steadies me with one hand, pulling me close.

"Are you okay?"

I smooth my dress as he releases me. "Never been better." Well, technically, I've had better days. From the moment we hit Fontaine Avenue, where his apartment complex is nestled, I've had this strange sensation kneading in my stomach. But it's been so long since I've dated anyone that I'm sure it's just nerves.

Arms interlocked, we make our way to the lobby, where Robert is greeted by a building attendant.

The man spares only a second to look me over with a questioning glance. "Morning lobby attendant said Reena came back to her apartment and got some stuff while you were at work."

Robert keeps a hand at the small of my back, and I have the sudden urge to move away. He stares at me before looking at the lobby attendant, who retreats behind his desk. "That's good. At least I know she's not dead."

The idea of Robert and Reena living in the same apartment complex never sat right with me the moment he told me. However, him having the lobby attendant providing updates about her coming in and out of her apartment doesn't land well at all.

Robert must sense it. He directs me into the elevator and explains that he doesn't have to worry about making a report to the police if he knows she's technically not missing.

"I get it, but I don't. What if Reena does want to cut ties completely? You can't expect to monitor her whereabouts."

The elevator spits us out on the fourth floor, and Robert leads me to an apartment at the end of the hall. "Trust me, I won't be opposed to Reena cutting all ties. If that's what she wants, that's what she wants. But I told you before, didn't I?" There's a broodiness to his words, barely noticeable and short-lived, but I've dealt with so many people at the coffee shop and the stables, I don't miss it, especially when he says, "This is just what she does when she doesn't feel like I'm giving her enough attention. How about we just not talk about her for the rest of the night, huh?"

Cancel. That's what I should do. After all, it's hard not to talk about someone who has almost defined our relationship since we started dating. But then there's a thought that surfaces from the caverns of my mind before retreating back into its murky depths. One that convinces me the red flag is more a burgundy than a flat-out red.

He wouldn't mess with Alyssa's ability to stay at Lake Forest if things were to go sour between us, right?

A risk I'm not exactly willing to take, I respond with one word. "Sure."

The best way to describe the interior of Robert's apartment is functional. Everything is put into its proper place. For a second, I'm unsure if I should sit down on the couch, covered with a white spread, but Robert insists. "I promise you I'm not a neat freak. I'm just always at work or traveling, so the apartment never really gets out of order."

"Got it." I sink farther into the sofa as Robert walks back into the kitchen, separated from the living room by an island.

"No complaints about spaghetti and meatballs for dinner, cookies for dessert?"

I shake my head. "That sounds wonderful."

"Perfect," Robert says, and he gets to cooking.

Our conversation progresses smoothly while Robert cooks, while we eat, and well after. I lean against him on the couch, matching him in his wordplay, and countering his argument that *Star Trek* is better than *Star Wars*. But it's there, in the back of my mind, lurking. Something close yet dangerously out of reach.

"Are you okay?" Robert asks. "You seem a little distracted."

I hold up my glass of wine and force a smile. "Ah, just a little tipsy is all. But how about we call a truce, huh? Both *Star Wars* and *Star Trek* are decent."

"I'll call a truce on one condition."

"And what's what?" I ask.

"A kiss..."

The cheesy line makes him lose some of his charm, but before I can overthink it, I lean in for a kiss. Our lips graze against one another's, tempting. However, just as his hand cups my face, sharp pain zips across my scalp.

I sit up straight and question whether I'm alright. I think I am. The pain might just be all that pent-up tension; dry spells are the worst. But then comes another shot of pain, and I can't deny it.

Something's wrong.

ALYSSA

Marcella stood over my bed, a hand on my forehead, urging Laine to go with the dark prince.

Once Laine left the castle and Marcella took me to the dining hall for a meal, I prepared myself to break Laine's mental barrier. The moko jumbie said it will break me, but who would I be if I didn't risk it? More importantly, I made a promise to Wren. He gave up his time in the next plane, the chance for us to be together, so I could save my kingdom. I can't—I won't— let him down.

Tuning out Marcella's words, I rack up every ounce of energy in my being. And by the time I feel the power coursing through my veins, at least two hours have passed.

Watching shadows cast by the moonlight trickling into my chambers, I reach out to Laine.

> *Elder sister, if you don't be careful, it will be forever night.*
> *Because the one who courts you is forever blight.*
> *Beware him, elder sister, I warn you, he is cursed by Terra.*
> *Only you can stop it, the dark prince's terror.*

Nothing. No connection. But I don't give up, chanting the spell again.

That's right. I repeat those words without allowing myself a break, casting out my energy like a net until I feel it—myself slipping into a void I can't quite comprehend. My body feels like it's being pulled apart in several different directions, but I don't stop, envisioning Laine, how danger lurks in her midst. Our parents were kidnapped, but I won't let the dark prince harm her, too. I refuse.

And that's when I see it—a small light gleaming from the side to cast infinite shadows on unfamiliar walls. It lasts only a second before the walls in my room fade back into view, but I'm certain I heard it—my sister's voice.

LAINE

I close my eyes as I try to breathe through the pain. Yet somehow I see an image of my sister and I can't quite understand it.

"Are you okay?" Robert asks as he slides closer to me on the couch.

"My—my head hurts. Can you just take me home?" I get up, but my knees feel weak, and my stomach begins to churn. I cover my mouth.

Robert points to the bathroom.

I dart inside, bringing up all the spaghetti and wine.

"Do you want to go to the hospital?" Robert asks while rubbing my back.

Hospital—the only times I go there are for Alyssa's checkups. To go there any other time? Unthinkable. My health insurance is stingy as shit. I'd get slammed with a copay I might not be able to afford.

"I'm fine," I murmur. "I think it's the wine."

"Are you sure?" Robert doesn't seem convinced. It doesn't matter. I'm not going to the ER.

"Let me run to the drugstore and at least get you some extra-strength Tylenol and something for nausea." He leads me into his bedroom, to the bed. "Rest till then."

I'm slow to move. The idea of going to his bedroom makes my head throb even worse. However, I'm too wobbly to make it back to the living room without assistance. He helps me lie in the bed, and I pray he hurries up and leaves. That there's as much distance between us as possible.

Wait, why?

I bundle up under the covers, pain and nausea welcoming another feeling into the fray—disgust. Why am I disgusted? Robert has done nothing to me. If anything, he's been excessively kind.

I glance at my phone once he leaves for the twenty-four-hour pharmacy. One missed call from Marcella. My first thought is for Alyssa: Is she okay? But as I'm unlocking the home screen to return Marcella's call, the phone slips from my hands.

Groaning, I roll out of bed and sink to the floor. I don't immediately see my phone, so I blindly reach under the bed and cast around for it.

My fingers fish out a small box, carved in the fashion of a mini–treasure chest. Definitely not my phone. My hand snakes its way back under the bed, this time emerging with what's actually mine.

Thank God!

I try to call Marcella, but my signal is weak. I'm hoping to get up and head to the living room, get service. But a bit of wine bubbles out of me, and I flop forward. As I slump there, my eyes land and stay on the little chest. Convincing myself a little peek won't hurt, anything to justify my actions, I open the box.

And I vomit all over Robert's carpet. How does he have this? My fingers shake as they reach inside the box.

I hold up Alyssa's missing charm, feeling like I might throw up again. I asked Robert several times to help me find it, and he had it all along? Why?

There are other trinkets in the chest, too. A metal pin shaped like a horse. A pair of gold studs. There's more, but I can't bear to look. I rest the Trinidad-shaped charm back into the box and take a few pictures, then shove the whole box back under the bed.

Panicked and covered in vomit, I grab my jacket and slide on my boots, not bothering to zip them up all the way.

My legs wobble as they carry me out of the apartment to the elevator. They wobble even more when I see the countdown at the top.

Two...three...

Someone's ascending.

I don't wait to find out if it's Robert, and dart into the stairwell. My stomach is on fire, but that doesn't stop me from ordering an Uber while bolting down the staircase.

"Is everything okay?" the concierge asks when I enter the lobby. I say nothing, adjusting my location to the McDonald's down the street as I track the Uber driver's distance.

Three minutes away. Two. The time it takes from two to go to one might as well be an eternity. I pace back and forth. Freeze when I hear Robert's voice.

"Laine!" He calls out to me from down the street, but it's too late. The Uber pulls up to the curb, and I get in the car.

"Let's go. Please hurry!"

The drive home passes in a blur: no traffic lights, no turning from one street to another. It isn't until we're on my street, red and blue lights prancing around the asphalt, illuminating faces of neighbors who rarely leave their homes, that I snap back to the present.

My eyes follow the lights, the gazes, my breath hitching when I see the object of everyone's focus: my house.

"That's my house! My sister! I need to get to my sister!"

The driver speeds up a little, hitting hard on the brakes at the edge of the crowd. I jump out of the car and run to the door of the house just as two burly men in EMT uniforms bring down a stretcher.

Marcella follows them, her green eyes red and face puffy.

"What happened?" I bark.

"I—I don't know. About thirty minutes ago, Alyssa seemed a little out of it. I thought she was just tired, but when I went to check on her, she wouldn't wake up."

"You should have called me!"

"I did, but you didn't answer. I..."

"Ma'am. We get that you're scared," says one of the EMTs. He gestures for me to move to the side so they can put Alyssa into the ambulance. "We're going to take her to Serca Grace Hospital. You're allowed to come with us or follow," he says, but I'm already in the ambulance, reaching for Alyssa as they close the door to the vehicle.

I hold her hand, squeezing tight as the ambulance makes its way to Serca.

Once the EMTs have hooked Alyssa up to an IV and run an EKG revealing her heart is beating fast, they look at me, asking a bunch of questions on Alyssa's medical history. However, one EMT pauses, glancing at my dress. "Are you okay?"

I look down at the vomit stains. I must smell rancid, but I have no fucks to give. "How much longer until we're there?"

"We're about five minutes out," the other EMT says, but each second feels like a sand particle refusing to trickle downward in an hourglass.

I stumble behind frantically as they rush Alyssa into a bay in the ER and a nurse helps me up. "We're gonna help your sister, but I need you to remain calm."

Calm? "I'm calm," I snap, but as the woman continues speaking, her words begin to mush together. "I don't understand what you're saying," I say, but she stares at me with a confused expression, breathing in and out slowly, gesturing for me to do the same.

Her words, *you're okay*, manage to get through after a few seconds, and then I realize it—I'm having a panic attack.

Suddenly I can feel the tension growing in my face and limbs, the way my breathing has become rapid.

I reach for my Xanax in the bag I don't have, heart palpitating even more.

Fuck! Fuck! Fuck!

Tears flood my eyes, and fear floods my heart. I'm not quite sure when I pass out. But when I open my eyes, I'm in a hospital bed, Marcella sitting next to me. I grab on to the bedsheets, the smell of chemicals burning my nose, the fluorescent lights stinging my eyes.

"Alyssa?" My voice comes out hoarse.

"In the room across the hall. In stable condition and awake."

"How long have I been out?"

"Sixteen hours," Marcella says.

I tug at the tube strapped to my arm, recalling how I was at Robert's. What I found. How I came home in an Uber. "I'm sorry. I didn't mean to yell...to run off on you. I..."

She squeezes my hand. "It's okay. I'm just glad you two are okay."

There's a knock on the glass door, and it slides open. Either I have no energy to care or the medication in my IV has apathy as a side effect, because I don't react to seeing Eric's familiar face.

"You're finally awake," he says with an exhale. "How are you feeling?"

"How's my sister?"

Eric pulls the curtains, that expression hinting at relief replaced with a look that says he's about to drop a goddamn bombshell.

"I need you to tell me how you're feeling. Once I know you're okay, we'll discuss your sister."

"I'm fine. No headache, no sore throat, no more nausea. No dizziness. So please, just tell me what's wrong with my sister?"

There is a beat of silence, a beat too long.

Eric takes a deep breath, his stoic expression for a second not so stoic. I can feel it—my heart plummeting to the lowest of lows, and I brace myself.

But nothing can prepare me.

"We ran some tests," he says. "Your sister had a stroke. We're still assessing the damage."

Eric's face is like that of a soldier, one still fighting a battle. But he's already told me the hard news. His battle should be over unless there's more to tell me. More bad news.

"There's something else, isn't there?"

Eric's eyes widen; he didn't expect me to read his facial expression. "There is something else that concerns us, something that warrants a discussion." His voice comes out slow, like he's treading water with his words.

I take a deep breath.

"One of the nurses noted your sister had some mild pelvic tenderness to palpation upon arrival and a bit of discharge when changing her diaper. It came up positive for chlamydia."

I clamber to the edge of the bed, ready to grab the chart from him to make sure he's read it right, but Marcella holds on to me as I scream that what he's said is impossible.

"We still have to do cell cultures, which are more specific, but the chances of it being a false positive are low, Laine. So, I have to ask, do you have any idea how she'd have contracted the STD?"

"I—I don't," I mutter, but the rest of my words stall in my throat, every encounter I had in the past few days hitting me like a train, scattering my body parts across the tracks.

As I lay there, reeling from the weight of Eric's revelation, I see a face...Robert's face. And somehow I feel it, deep in my bones: Robert is behind this. But there's no time to say that or even process how to go about convincing everyone. Because the next words out of Dr. Jeon's mouth might as well be the final nail in my coffin. "If it was just the stroke, it might be one thing. But the pelvic exam and STD have raised some red flags."

"Don't say any more," I whisper.

"Laine..."

"Don't," I plead. After all, it's obvious. I already had a hiccup with social services, and they made it clear then. Another hiccup, and I might not be so lucky to keep my sister.

PART 3

THE FIGHT FOR MIRENDAL

CHAPTER
26

ALYSSA

The light stings as I open my eyes, my ears ringing as Laine's voice calls out to me. She's hovering above me, pressing against my legs with shaky hands. Marcella has a hand on her shoulder, begging her to relax.

My head throbs, as if a thousand woodpeckers have been set upon it.

The last thing I remember is chanting the spell to communicate with Laine, and darkness washing over me. But I wasn't asleep. I was stuck in a form of stasis, alone in a dark chamber where somehow nothing else seemed to matter. Not my parents, not Laine, not Wren.

I'd nearly begged to stay there, embraced by that darkness. But just as complacency set in, colorful spots raced across my vision, the darkness becoming a vortex of color.

I wasn't quite sure what was happening. I'm still not. But here I am, awake, and all the emotions the darkness kept at bay hit me full force.

My chest aches as I suck in a big breath. Judging by the bright white orbs above and the crystal balls and potions on either side of me, I'm in a temple, but one much larger than Lake Forest.

The scent of leaves from an ash tree, from which many medicines derive, tickles my nose, but the stench of death characteristic of a healing temple makes me cough.

"Are you okay?" Laine asks. She's asked that question before, countless times while brushing my hair. But this is the first time she asks as if she expects an actual answer. I prepare myself to speak words that will make no sense to her, but I am too weak to open my mouth, and suddenly the temple's walls are closing in on me. Is this weakness an aftereffect of the dark prince's spell? Or is it an effect of the spell I cast to communicate with Laine?

Laine nearly collapses to the floor, but Marcella steadies her just in time.

The commotion must be heard from the halls. A tall man, dressed in blue garb with a white cloak, enters the chamber. Around his neck is a silver cord—the infamous instrument the white robes use to communicate with changels.

He looks at Laine, then me, then back at Laine.

She holds his gaze, her face conveying a pain she does not need to speak aloud. "Before my sister managed a few words, albeit broken. But now words seem to fail her altogether, and she seems in a stupor."

The white robe approaches me while keeping his eyes on Laine. "The spell cast on her was a powerful one. I'm sorry, but for now, we'll have to simply watch her and see how the counterspells work. If she'll regain any of her abilities."

Laine stifles a sob, and the white robe rests a comforting hand on her shoulder. I expect her to flinch. She's always shied away from touch, from comfort, ever since the attack on our parents. However, she stands there, feeding off the white robe's serene disposition.

Once he leaves, Laine collapses in a chair.

"Do you know him? There's a familiarity between you two," Marcella says.

Laine doesn't look at her. Only me. "He's the man I told you about. The one who I prayed I'd never see again. I thought he was the wolf but…" She bites her lip. "But I was wrong. The wolf is the man who heads Alyssa's temple for changels. He is a dark prince, and he managed to trick me."

I'm scared of what's happening to me. And I'm heartbroken to be without Wren. But Laine's words hint that she's learned that the man courting her is not to be trusted, and that is a shining light, a beacon in dark weather.

I hear the heavy footsteps before I see the faces. The white robe from earlier stands a step behind a white robe with skin the color of chestnut, eyes the color of dark gold. His wrinkles mesh into a frown as he sets his gaze upon my sister.

"First Princess, I am White Robe Thomas. It seems my underling, White Robe Jeon, failed to thoroughly discuss an important matter."

"I planned to. I was just waiting until—"

White Robe Thomas holds up a hand, silencing him. "You will not interrupt me, White Robe Jeon."

Laine glances at White Robe Jeon before resting a wary gaze on the head white robe. "Please do not upbraid White Robe Jeon. He was just waiting for me to get my bearings."

The white robe eyes me like I'm something pitiful. But when he looks at Laine, his gaze is hard. "Well, First Princess, I can't afford you that courtesy. As my robe in training mentioned earlier, we're doing our best to save the second princess. But it is concerning...the type of dark magic that has weaved its way into the second princess's bloodstream. Based on her state, she should not have had that exposure. Not unless she were in a precarious setting. Do you have any idea how this might have happened?"

Laine tugs at her curls that have grown at least two inches since I last truly saw her, as myself and not a spelled shell. "A prince from a neighboring kingdom, someone I let myself trust." She gasps, tremors running up and down her arms. Her breaths come quick, her eyes darting back and forth, seemingly unable to focus.

"Take a deep breath, Princess," White Robe Jeon says, but the head white robe's gaze remain steely. "This is a serious allegation, one that can put the kingdom at war. Are you certain?"

"You can't be serious? Are you questioning her? The first princess?" Marcella shakes her head, each word channeling a disgust she does not try to hide. "She told you what led to the dark magic in the second princess's veins. Would you like her to repeat it to you?"

What proceeds is a battle of looks between the head white robe and Marcella. However, during that battle, both fail to realize that my sister's panic has begun to worsen.

I want to speak out, even if it's a few broken words that no one can understand. But nothing but a muffled groan comes.

Terra must relay my thoughts to White Robe Jeon, because he grabs on to Laine. "Take deep breaths."

"I have a potion to help me with this," she says. "I left it at the castle. I..."

"I shall get you one of our own." The white robe quickly

exits the chambers, returning within the same minute to hand a vial to Laine. She swallows whatever magic pill he's given her, ensuring it's settled in her stomach with a sip of water.

For several minutes, the chamber is absolutely quiet, the only sound reverberating off the four walls that of Laine's breathing as it gets quieter.

When she's caught herself, she stands and dusts herself off. There is a glimmer of remorse in her eyes as she looks at the younger white robe. And there is a glimmer of something in his eyes, too, although I'm not sure what.

Clearing her throat, Laine faces the head white robe. "Is there a spell to learn when the dark magic was cast on my sister?"

The head white robe looks at me. "The spell that was used is one that sometimes has no effect at all, at least not immediately. One can go years with the magic lingering until they're finally made aware of its presence."

"So we can't learn the exact time such treachery took place," Marcella says, her tone half question, half answer.

The head white robe adjusts his cloak before reaching for a crystal ball on one side of the chamber. He looks deep into it, seeing things only those in his line of work must be privy to seeing, before turning back to us.

"We can perform a spell to check for the magic user's signature. But keep in mind, it's an invasive process. And the signature can be hidden. Also, if the spell was cast more than six days ago, it's likely the signature has faded, which means…"

Laine screams into her hand for a few seconds before looking upward, once again composed. Or at least as composed as she can be.

The head white robe frowns as he closes the distance between him and Laine. "Princess, I'm afraid I must call upon the blue robes, as obligated by the white robes' code."

Blue robes. Like the white robes, they hold high positions in our kingdom. However, unlike the white robes who heal afflictions, they specialize in upholding the law of Terra. While the royal family has a mandate over them to some degree, we are not totally above them. And it's not unheard of for blue robes to strip royals of their status, especially those accused of not upholding Terra's will and law.

One of the crystal balls in the room begins to cloud, the colors swirling around hazing blue, then black, until a voice echoes into the chamber. "White Robe Thomas, Regent Avyl speaking. We've received word of a man coming within a few minutes. He's suffering from an affliction of the chest."

White Robe Thomas looks at White Robe Jeon. "Please see to the princesses. And if anything arises, call for me. Understood?"

White Robe Jeon nods, staring at the back of White Robe Thomas until he's out of sight. Once it's just the four of us in the chambers, Laine pulls out her own orb. First, she calls the blue robes, telling them of our location and rather concisely the matter that requires their presence. Once they've confirmed they'll come to the temple, she shakes the ball.

Marcella runs her hand up and down Laine's back. "It's going to be okay. We're going to get to the bottom of this."

Laine shakes her head. "No. It's not going to be, Marcella. He didn't say it earlier, but I received a message from the auxiliator. I failed my sister. I failed her again. They . . . they won't leave her in my care. Not until the blue robes get to the bottom of this."

I can feel the tears swirling behind my eyes, desperate to rush out of me and flood the chamber. With responsibilities bridging between the white robes and blue robes, the auxiliators have served to help Laine and me adjust to life after the attack. However, it's always been posited that maybe being together has thwarted our progress.

No. No. No! They'll . . . they'll want to separate us.

CHAPTER 27

LAINE

My ass hurts, but I remain absolutely still, refusing to fidget in the cold steel chair across from the officer. He stirs a cup of coffee while looking at several sheets of paper laid out on the table. Only once he's taken a sip of the coffee does he look up to meet my gaze.

He's never gonna listen to you, the jumbie on my shoulder whispers. *Just look at the bags under his eyes. He's had a long day, so long you're the least of his concerns.*

Sighing, I look up at the ceiling. It's been a week since Alyssa had her stroke, a week since I found her charm at Robert's apartment. A week since I found out she had chlamydia.

Since then I've done a shit ton of research. Chlamydia can be asymptomatic in many women for years, only really proving a problem long term. At first, I wanted to hope this was the case, as sick as it sounds. Maybe Alyssa had sex in high school, before the accident, and we just never found out about it. But Alyssa and I told each other everything under the sun. Sex was the furthest thing from her mind, riding and getting into college paramount.

Mom always joked we were polar opposites when it came to boys. I had my first boyfriend at fifteen, although we broke up within a week.

I swallow down that invisible ball that's forming in my throat. Whether or not she acquired the infection before or after, though, it raised a red flag like Eric said it would. As of yesterday, I have been deemed unfit to be Alyssa's guardian. Per the judge, the only way to keep Alyssa out of the system is to have a willing relative or friend agree to take up the role. And unfortunately for us, we're a little lacking in friendly family members.

"So, Ms. Highland, we've been reviewing the case. Thank you for coming back to speak with us after getting our call."

"No. Thank you. Have you apprehended Robert yet?"

Robert—just saying his name makes my skin crawl, blood curdle, heart race. My mind tries to bury thoughts of him doing vile things to Alyssa, but it's unrelenting.

Alyssa had several stints in hospitals for UTIs since the accident. One of them would have picked up chlamydia, which means she got it after the accident...after she started at Lake Forest. Someone...

"Are you okay?" The officer hands me the napkin he had wrapped around his coffee cup.

My face is suddenly more chilled by the cold air blasting above me. I raise my fingertips to my face.

Shit. I'm crying.

As I dry my tears, the officer says nothing, cocking his head back and forth a few times. But as soon as I pocket the napkin, he clasps his hands. "Ms. Highland, the allegation you made against Dr. Remson was very serious. We have to run an investigation, ensure there's significant evidence that can prove a crime before taking anything to court."

My phone is on the table in seconds. "I showed you the picture of my sister's charm at Robert's house."

The officer runs a finger along the crease in his forehead, one of several that form as he narrows gray eyes. "That picture is not tangible proof. We'll require much more concrete evidence, especially when you yourself said you can't be one hundred percent certain he's the one behind this."

My jumbie cackles. *This is why you're shit, Laine. He's using your own words against you.*

I ask for a cup of water and try to gather my thoughts while the officer goes to get it for me.

When they took my report in the hospital, I did mention that several of the staff members seemed off. Reena was one of them. And so was Bennett. But Robert? I'm sure he's behind this. I'm sure he's the reason why my sister has an STD. Why else would he have kept her charm?

The officer returns and I take the water, gulping it down as if it can put out the fire brewing inside of me.

"Look, while we've yet to question Bennett Forbis, we've already interviewed Ms. Reena Harken and Dr. Remson."

"And?"

The officer sighs. "And right now, we do not have enough evidence to press charges."

I gulp down more water, and it trickles down my jaw. Is he even doing his job? Is he actually trying? "Did you look at the cameras? There must be something on there."

"Dr. Remson brought the footage to us himself. While there

were a few things that concerned us with other staff members, nothing implicated Dr. Remson in any crime."

I look at the clock on the wall, certain I can hear it ticking in my ears like a sledgehammer. "What kinds of things?"

"We saw the man named Bennett taunt several of the people at Lake Forest, also physically abuse a young male."

I have to search for my voice before speaking. "My sister... was she..."

The officer nods. "There was one instance in which he yelled at your sister. We also saw him removing her from the hall and leaving her in a room, alone. He is a person of interest."

As much as I thought Bennett was a real creep, I can't shake the idea that Robert is the one behind this.

I still can't.

"Robert could have tampered with the footage, had it on loop, taken my sister to a room where the cameras aren't working, go to a blind spot."

There's a loud knock on the door.

"Just a minute," he says before stepping outside.

I chew my thumbnail down to the flesh as I wait, the minutes droning on, until he returns with declaration of an update.

I sit up straight, my spine pulled taut like wire. "What is it?"

With no real intonation, the officer sits in the chair and says, "Colleague notified me that Bennett Forbis hung himself. Landlord found the body in his apartment."

My expression must not be what he expected, because he leans forward and begins to explain that the leading theory is that after they questioned Bennett about my sister, the guilt of what he did must have been too much to handle.

"I won't exactly call this justice...but keep in mind, Ms. Highland, some victims don't even get this much," he finishes with a sigh.

I crumple the paper cup, trying to remain calm despite my spinning thoughts. "Do you know for sure it was a suicide? I'm telling you, something is off with Dr. Remson. You need to look into him before he hurts anyone else!"

The officer shoves the papers into the manila folder in front of him. "I have to go by tangible evidence. *Something off* doesn't count. And the evidence says Forbis hanged himself. The evidence also says you'd been romantically involved with Dr. Remson. Some might wonder if things went bad and this is your way to get back at him."

My brows snap upward so quickly I swear I hear it. "Excuse me?"

He leans back in his chair and folds his arms. "You heard me. Wouldn't be the first time I've seen a bitter ex in here, making wild accusations to get back at a man."

Fluorescent lights might as well be fire, the chair a stake, the officer my executioner. Because suddenly Robert is a victim and I'm some witch trying to ruin a man's life.

"This is unbelievable," I say.

The officer shrugs. "Much like yourself."

Hauling ass out of the precinct, I listen to my jumbie laugh. But my torture isn't done yet. My phone rings. The number...his.

I don't pick it up immediately. My hands are shaking too much. But when I do, I don't say anything, just listen.

"Laine?" Robert's voice carries not the faintest sliver of anger or condescension, and somehow that makes his words seem all the more poisonous. "My buddy at the precinct said you'd just left. You must be experiencing so many emotions. Alyssa, too."

I bite back a scream. "You're a sick bastard. I should have known something was up from the moment you asked me out. Was it some kind of sick joke? Screw my sister, then screw me?"

Robert's tone remains light despite the topic. "I mean, is there anything wrong with asking someone out? Everyone deserves the warmth of a lover, Laine."

The words *warmth of a lover* shouldn't stand out to me, but they remind me of our first date at the Headless Horseman. How Robert held my hand and whispered those words to me after we talked about Alyssa, how he told me she was such a bright light, how she deserved warmth. Is this the fucking warmth he was talking about?

It must be, because just before he ends the call, he says, "I really did enjoy both of your company."

Fuck. I should have recorded that, but it's too late now. And even if I did record it, I can already hear what the officer would say.

Odd but no true confession to a crime. You have no evidence.

I can't let Robert do this again.

My jumbie and I are on the same page. She smiles, eyes beady.

There's a wolf that will go on to ravage more people if it isn't put down.

Put it down, Laine. You failed your sister once. Twice. Don't fail her a third time.

Put it down.

I get into the SUV, body on autopilot as I speed down the road. I won't fail my sister again.

When the barn comes into view, I linger for a bit, watching to see if there's any movement, but the building and surrounding area is as still as death itself. Ah, that's right. There's a horse-showing event today. Ana must not be back yet.

Quickly, I slide through the old half doors of the barn, which allow the animals a view of the yard. A few of the horses let out whinnies and stomp their hooves, but I ignore them, walking to the storeroom. Dad always said Ana was a bit naive when it came to trusting people. I never really agreed until now, my hands reaching for the rifle she has in an old cabinet below a rack of saddles.

She keeps it in case wolves linger too close to the barn. But right now, in my hands, it's for one thing—one person.

My jumbie won't have it any other way. The sooner I put an end to him, the better. But the hospital is on the same route to his house, and before my jumbie can intervene, I pull into the hospital parking lot. I need to see my sister.

Actually, this can work. How about you go take one last good look at Alyssa? See how she ended up because of you . . .

I navigate the halls with a hand over my nose to block the smell of bleach. Visiting hours ended at six p.m., but the guard must be on a break, because I don't see him. All I see is a glimpse of Eric—who apparently likes to frequent the ward despite being an ER physician. His eyes flicker to me even though he's talking to a nurse, but before either of them can say anything, I slip into Alyssa's room and close the door.

God must be looking down on me, giving me this much-needed moment between me and my sister. Because Eric is paged over the speaker by one of the nursing aides.

Certain he won't rush in here to tell me I must leave, at least for another five minutes, I crawl into my sister's bed and wrap my arms around her.

Since her stroke, she's already gotten a UTI. According to the doctors, she's likely to get more of them, maybe pneumonia, too. And a UTI or pneumonia, as they tried to explain to me, can lead to sepsis. In other words, I need to prepare myself for the day that my sister's condition starts to deteriorate.

But the doctors don't know Alyssa. She's a fighter. Strongest girl I know, before the accident and now. "We'll show them all," I whisper.

Alyssa jumps a bit at my touch, her eyes flickering open and shut. She lets out a groan, but I hold on to her tighter, nuzzling my face into her back.

Did the stress of everything that happened at Lake Forest cause her stroke in the first place? Or was it a culmination of everything before and after?

My sobs vibrate against her back. "I'm sorry for failing you. For failing Mom and Dad. But I'll fix it, Alyssa. I'll fix it."

It's at this moment I imagine that I, Laine Highland, have become something scarier than evil itself. Because my jumbie, the one egging me on, cowers on my shoulder.

Wait, do you really think this is a good idea? Who's going to take care of her, Laine?

I roll my eyes. She won't get me to change my mind now. I've already made a mental note to text Marcella once I'm done with Robert, ask her to make sure Alyssa finds a decent home.

I give my sister one last squeeze and slip out of her room.

CHAPTER
28

ALYSSA

I'm awoken by the sound of scuffling in my chambers, the doors creaking.

I almost jump when my eyes settle on my elder sister, her hair tousled and face bone dry.

What's wrong? I want to ask. But only a groan escapes my lips as she crawls into my bed. She pulls the fur sheets over me and wraps her arms tight around me, her breaths mirroring my own, her tears wetting my gown, her skin like ice. How could the guards let her leave the castle in such a state? What happened?

"Would you allow me to stay here, just for a little while longer?" she asks.

The question is strange. Never before has Laine asked permission for anything. Even before the attack, she was quite stubborn, hardheaded, as Mother liked to say. But right now she seems delicate, like she just might break. Not to mention there's also an air of a ferocity inside her, one that might consume us both. It scares me.

She holds on to me as if I'm the sanity she's desperately searching for, like I'm the only thing holding her together. "Do you remember when you first fell off Sprinkler?"

I remember when Mother and Father and Laine and I were all together, at the stables.

Laine had just mastered jumps several feet high. According to Father, she had a natural grace and was a kindred soul with her mount. Surely, she'd be able to master dragon riding as well. And she did within the next few months, traveling the kingdom with Father to partake in dragon races and the balls that came along with it.

"I told you you were too small after you fell off Sprinkler. But you got back on and flew over the trees. Two years younger than me, and you bested your elder sister. And you went on to best me in so much more, didn't you? You were bright, Alyssa. And because of me, because of what I let happen to you, your brightness has faded."

She's wrong! I was only ever a light because of Laine. It was watching her triumph over those who cursed our names that made me even decide to mount a horse, to mount a dragon. It was her I aspired to be.

She pulls me closer to her, and I feel my heart breaking. I want to tell her what she means to me. I want to tell her it's going to be alright. But I—I can't.

"I'll make sure to fix this, Alyssa. We might not have the backing of the blue robes or the army. But I will fix this. I'll make sure the dark prince pays."

What is she saying? What does she mean by make him pay? But I already know, and it makes my stomach churn. Facing the dark prince alone will mean certain death. She can't do it! I won't let her do it!

But how can I stop her? How can I—

The sweet smell of decaying plant matter starts to fill my nostrils, and suddenly I'm assaulted with a stabbing pain that starts at the crown of my head and shoots through the soles of my feet.

The walls of the chamber start to fade out of view, and what fades in makes my heart drum loudly. I see the plane, the fairies on the ground, sprawled out over dead flowers.

Nerra's long mane is stringy, her ribs poking through her flesh. She collapses to the ground beside Emerald, a ghost of the fairy she once was.

But the images are murky, Laine's figure, walking out of my chambers, coming back into view. She's going to do something that might cost her her life. I'm not sure what's happening in the other plane. And here I am, unable to move or speak. Unable to do anything to help anyone.

I have no other options aside from calling out to Terra, to the moko jumbie, so I do so in my head, begging for help. And I feel it—a blessing from Terra that causes sweat to bead on my skin, my heart to race in my chest, my breaths to rumble.

One of the orbs near my bed begins to glow, the sound of bells cutting the air.

Within seconds, White Robe Jeon is in my chambers, staring at me with wide eyes. He glances at the orb while unraveling the silver cord around his neck. He looks around the chambers, searching for something or, maybe, someone.

I wait until the end of his silver cord is pressed against my chest and the other end—it splits into two—is planted inside his ears. I unleash a thought, and this time, pain doesn't threaten to fracture me in two.

"The first princess plans to attack the dark prince. She must be stopped."

I repeat those words silently like a mantra until finally, the white robe removes his silver instrument. He stares at me with eyes that hint at an uncanny awareness, then runs out of the chambers.

I exhale loudly. Hopefully, he reaches her in time. Hopefully, he saves my elder sister.

LAINE

I'm just starting to pull my SUV out of the lot when I hear a loud bang.

What the hell?

BANG! BANG! BANG!

The noise continues, moving around the side of the vehicle until I'm staring at Eric, banging against the window on the passenger's side.

"Can I come in?" he asks.

Of all times, why now? "Uh...I'm kinda busy."

"I have an emergency," he says. "Please. You have to help me. It's a matter of life or death."

Life or death—it's such a basic answer, but my mind is playing catch-up with my body. Before I can pick apart Eric's words, I unlock the door.

Eric doesn't waste a minute, jumping in the car and pulling the seat belt across his chest. "Drive."

Almost as if his words are law, my foot presses down on the gas pedal. "Where are we going?" I ask.

"You'll see," he says, voice curt.

Staring straight ahead, only half-aware of what's really in front of me, I drive down the freeway, turning off on the exit when Eric directs me. Sweat beads on his brow, and he constantly glances at his phone. But he doesn't call anyone to ask for an update, doesn't call 911 or the ambulance.

Just what is his emergency?

Off the exit, I make a few right turns, cruising at the speed limit until I get to a hole-in-the-wall convenience store. The glare of its neon lights stab into the darkness.

I put the SUV in park. "What kind of emergency is this?"

"I'll be right back," Eric tells me as he hops out of the vehicle.

Part of me wants me to go immediately, to get done what I need to do and finish my plan. But another part is dredging up every reason I shouldn't leave him.

It's dark here. How will he get back to the hospital?

What if he needs help with something?

What if he's in danger?

What if. What if. What if. The goddamn what-ifs!

I'm still asking them when Eric hops back into the passenger seat, a large plastic bag in his hand.

He hands me something wrapped in foil. "For you."

My fingers flinch at the warmth seeping through the foil, my stomach grumbling at the smell of something fried. But I don't let myself be fooled. "What is this?"

"Take it." Eric's tone doesn't leave room for backchat.

Hoping to get whatever this is over with, I unwrap the foil, finding a sandwich. It's filled with layers of crisp bacon and lettuce and tomato. Cheese oozes from the sides along with a copious amount of mayonnaise. "This is the emergency?"

Eric nods, taking a bite of his sandwich. "Yes. I'm on my dinner break."

Anger bubbles up inside me like a witch's cauldron. "What the hell? I thought something was actually wrong! That you needed help!"

"I do need help, Laine. If I don't eat, I can't take very good care of my patients. And if I don't make it back to the hospital in time, I might lose my job." He twists his body so I'm looking at more than just his profile. "You said before that I should work hard to become an attending...a good one. So, if it isn't too much to ask, I'm hoping you'd drop me back at the hospital once we're done?" He smiles. "Dr. Thomas isn't exactly the friendliest boss."

Not friendly is an understatement. When Alyssa was first admitted to the hospital, I was happy to get rid of Dr. Thomas. Unlike Eric and the internists, he insinuated that maybe I put my sister in her current predicament. That I'm a shit sister.

I mean, technically Dr. Thomas is right. But it still rubbed me the wrong way. It still— It doesn't matter. I should be well on my way to Robert's house.

"Come on, just eat with me. Food tastes better when you eat with friends," Eric says as a piece of lettuce falls out of his mouth.

It pulls me up short...the silliness, yes, but mostly this use of the word *friends*. I mean, are we friends?

I run a hand over my face, thinking about what Caroline called a *Notebook* moment—him holding me in the rain, calming me down. I don't know if I subconsciously thought of him as a friend back then, but I know in that moment I consciously thought of him as a savior.

Maybe that's why I bite into my sandwich, glancing out the

window at the neon sign. It flickers every few seconds, the bright lime green turning a dull mossy color.

Eric smiles. "There we go!"

"Don't get too excited. As soon as we're done, I'm taking you back."

That part doesn't seem to register. He says barely a beat later, "Tell me about yourself."

I'm about to suggest we kill all the talk and stick to just eating. However, he's staring at me intently, no hint of letting it go.

I sigh. "I grew up in Serca, went to Virginia Tech for two years before dropping out to take care of my sister. When I'm not working at the coffee shop, I give riding lessons on a horse ranch a few miles out of town."

"So you're an equestrian?" Eric's brows shoot up.

"Is it that surprising?"

He takes a bite of his sandwich. "Not really, actually. I can definitely see you having better communication skills with horses than customers."

I laugh at the jab.

Wait, why am I laughing? And why does this sandwich taste so good? Like a first meal right out of the gutter? The gutter I didn't even go to?

The rifle flashes across my mind, and I stop eating. "I really have something to do, Eric."

Eric ignores the smudge of mayo on the side of his face, grabbing the key before I can start the vehicle. "Let's just finish eating. I promise I'll let you go once you're done."

"What's your endgame, huh?"

He hands me a bottle of water. "I just want to get to know you. I think you're interesting."

I slam my hand against the wheel. His words aren't funny this time, but they make me think of *him*. *He* wanted to get to know me, too. *He* thought I was interesting, too. "For what? So you can just screw me over in the end? So you can hurt my sister? So you can take her from me? So you can punish me for what I did?"

Eric drops his sandwich and grabs my hands, squeezing.

I pull them out of his grasp. "I know I fucked up. I know I'm horrible. But I'm sorry. I..."

"Laine, you don't have to—"

"If I just came home last year, Alyssa wouldn't be in this mess She'd be fine." The words are stirring inside of me, and I need to get them out before I combust. "She would have never gone to Lake Forest. She'd never be where she is now."

And with those words, tears burst forth like water breaching a dam. Eric takes my hands back into his once more, this time refusing to let go. He doesn't say anything. He doesn't ask for clarification on what I mean. He just holds my hands, staring out the passenger window until my sobs have ebbed and my wails aren't our personal soundtrack.

"Thank you," I mutter. "For just now...and for before at the pharmacy."

"No problem, for just now, for at the pharmacy, for any other times that might come..."

I gotta say he's a bit cheeky, but I don't complain, looking at the time. It's been at least an hour since we arrived here. "You know Dr. Thomas is going to have your head."

Eric sighs, leaning back in the seat. "I have a confession."

"And what's that?"

"I'm off my shift."

"What?!" I shriek.

"Trust me, it was an emergency. I was starving and needed to get some grub. Also, I know you saw that I saw you sneaking into Alyssa's room. Your sister...she's strong. A lot of people don't survive her brain injuries, but she's fighting. For the both of you."

The idea of the rifle in the trunk now makes me recoil. What was I thinking?

"Marcella came to see your sister today," he goes on. "We ran into each other in the lobby. She told me about being unable to take over as your sister's guardian. I hope you don't mind."

My face remains as static as my heart. I've cried all my tears for the night. "It's fine. But I'm open to some ideas if you have any. I'm not sure who could serve as one in the interim."

I can almost see the gears in Eric's mind turning. "Any relatives? Someone who has the financial stability and is willing to give you some level of interaction with your sister while things settle down?"

I rest my head against the wheel. "My family unit's small. There's no..."

Wait. That's not true, is it, Laine?

"It looks like someone just came to mind." Eric looks almost ecstatic at the prospect, but I'm not excited.

"Someone did," I say.

"Who?" Eric asks.

I practically hiss the words. "My uncle."

CHAPTER
30

ALYSSA

The calculated steps of white robes making their rounds is like liquid tonic, a monotony that can do nothing but put one to sleep.

I would think myself immune, as I'm a ball of nerves. How can I not be when Laine came this evening to let me know she's to meet with Uncle? How will their meeting go? Will they draw swords on one another? Will Uncle help, or trick her?

Such unrelenting questions swirl around my mind until the questions themselves make little sense. And yet, I find myself leaning more and more into the arms of sleep, ever anxious to steal me away.

That is until a knock sounds on the door.

My eyes flicker open, but my body is still heavy, and everything around me is still hazy.

Nevertheless, I expect to make out a white robe and their silver instrument. However, I see a hooded figure instead. I can't make out the person's face, but their frame is imperially slim, their hands pale.

Their feet barely kiss the ground as they make their way toward me.

"I can't stay for very long," the person says, their voice too muffled to be natural. Either this is all part of a dream, or the person has masked their voice with a spell.

"But I owe it to you," they continue. "To acknowledge what I did and tell you how I got involved in all this."

I want to hear the person's story. But before I can even learn who they are, slumber embraces me with its sweet, unrelenting grip.

CHAPTER
31

LAINE

Sweating bullets, at 11:58 a.m., I click on the Zoom link in the email. I've made sure to wear a decent enough top, something Freidmore might find "professional," if only to appear more in line with him. He lets me into the meeting room exactly on time, and cue the staring competition.

Unlike me, whose eye bags have grown in the past year, he looks just like he did when he came to my parents' funeral, if not for a few more wrinkles. His business suit is as crisp as his blue eyes, his gray hair almost a silver color. He slides his hands across some papers on his table before saying, "Good day to you, Niece."

The fact that he addresses me by our blood relation instead of my actual name should make me feel a little more at ease, considering he's almost always refused to acknowledge it. But his pinched voice makes *niece so*und like a weapon of sorts.

"Good day to you, too, Uncle," I say, matching his tone.

His lips curl upward with a smile, although nothing that remotely travels to his eyes. "Well, let's not drag this out. You said it was imperative we have a call to discuss the future of the house. I take it you've finally agreed to my terms?" He glances at the papers in front of him. "I've gone ahead and sent—"

"Before you continue, I don't want money in exchange for the house. Well, I do, but there's something else. Something you must agree to before I sign any contract."

"You know I don't even have to give you money, right? I can just wait for them to take the house, then buy it."

I know my uncle. His words insinuate he's performing an act of kindness, but kindness and Freidmore don't exist in the same universe. "Then why don't you?"

There's a reason he doesn't. One he won't say but I already know. A man as rich as Freidmore came scoping out our home a few months after the funeral, asking if it was for sale. My guess is that he has just as much money and connections as my uncle. Buying the house from me before it goes up on the market would be much easier, less of a hassle.

Freidmore rests his hands flat on the desk. "So then what are your terms? Just come right out and say it. I'm a busy man."

"I want you to come to Serca and serve as Alyssa's legal guardian. During this time, she and I will be staying in the house. With you," I say.

He huffs; it's a fair reaction. "The sum I'm offering is more than enough for a downtown apartment large enough for you and your sister. In some places, enough for a down payment on a small home. So why in God's name would I serve as her guardian, much less let you two stay in *my* house?"

I look at my notepad, where I've outlined some ways to go about responding to this exact question. "I was deemed unfit to care for Alyssa. That means I have two options. Find a suitable relative willing to be her guardian, or allow the state to make all decisions regarding her care. A few zeroes added to the sum in my bank account and new apartment? It would help, but I'd still have to petition to get the guardianship back."

"And that could take up to a year," he finishes. As expected of a lawyer, he catches on quickly.

He leans back in his chair and folds his arms. "Did you ever stop to think that maybe it'd be better for the state to send her to a residential facility? A group home where she'd have round-the-clock care? This insistence that you two stay in the house even after I pay you for it?" Freidmore's laugh sounds archaic, like how I'd imagine Julius Caesar to laugh. "I might as well take my chances bidding against that weasel from South Carolina who wanted the house. Clearly this is some kind of scam."

"Not a scam," I snap. "Desperation. Alyssa...she was raped by someone at her adult day center. And before you start with 'not all day centers and group homes are bad,' I already know. I—I just can't stomach the idea of her being cared for by people she doesn't know. Not after what happened."

Since Freidmore has always been so cold to us, I don't expect much of a reaction aside from him expressing how the situation is unfortunate. However, he clasps his hands so tightly his knuckles turn white. "What do you mean she was *raped*?"

"I mean what I said. She was assaulted by the director of Lake Forest's adult day center."

"Has this person been arrested? A court date been set? What about Alyssa? Where is she now? How did this come to light? Is there..."

Massaging my temples, I wait for the barrage of questions to stop before finally rehashing the details of what led us to this very moment. As I do, I hope that look in Freidmore's eyes, a look that hints at concern, is genuine.

"Charges have been brought against someone else who worked at the facility, but not the person who did this," I say.

"Why would they bring charges against the wrong person?" Freidmore asks, gaze dissecting me like I'm on the stand.

I scoff. "Because unfortunately, Uncle, the person who did this has the last name Remson."

There's a long pause in which Freidmore says nothing, and I swallow hard. The fact that Freidmore, top gun that he is, actually looks startled? Clearly, the Remson name has weight.

Thankfully, I don't need to provide any more specifics on just how fucked the situation is. Exhaling loudly, Freidmore sees fit to refocus on my current concern. "With regard to Alyssa's guardianship, I'm assuming there's a social worker managing the case?"

"There is. And if you agree to my terms, you'd be required, at least to keep up appearances, to come to Serca and meet with her and Alyssa. You'd also have to be present for a walk-through of your—our—living arrangements. Of course, that won't matter if you plan to just ship Alyssa off to a residential home, but the whole point of this call, as I said, is to avoid that." I hold up my notepad and point to a timeline I drafted. "You'll declare the house as your permanent residence, Alyssa your charge. Given your busy schedule, I'm sure the social worker will expect you to hire some form of help to assist you in caring for Alyssa. I will assist and oversee that person while also continuing to work. Once everything blows over, we can apply for guardianship to be handed back over to me. Alyssa and I will move into our own apartment." I put down the notepad and interlace my fingers. "So, do we have a deal?"

Even with all my carefully constructed arguments, I still wouldn't be surprised to get a rejection. My best-case scenario is a begrudging acceptance. Freidmore has barely spoken two words to Alyssa and me before now, yet I want him to tolerate living with us? It's insane. However, Freidmore placidly accepts the deal and notes he'll make arrangements. Then he ends the call.

I remain at the table, staring at the Zoom logo. I wish I could say that relief washes over me...kills some of that tension that makes it hard to breathe. But this is in no way any real victory. It can't be, not until the person who hurt Alyssa is behind bars.

CHAPTER
32

ALYSSA

Was the cloaked visitor I had just a dream? Or did my mind conjure the images because it was ravenous for sleep? It's the one thought I have as faces, definitely real, linger in my chambers.

"With your return to Mirendal, I am sure the white robes and elders will feel more at peace. Have your chambers been prepared? I assume you are staying at the castle," says an officious woman. She's an auxiliator we've met with before, not long after the accident, when the kingdom's affairs came into question.

Laine's eyes dart toward our uncle, who stares at me like I'm some puzzle he can't seem to understand, one he might want to piece together. "Uncle will sleep in the king and queen's chambers," she says, but the words come out of her mouth like venom.

I imagine she's wondering the same thing I am. Does Uncle feel good? Getting to sleep in the castle he's been vying for since our parents were kidnapped? If he does, he shows little sign of it.

To be quite honest, I'm shocked he's even here at all.

The auxiliator hands Laine several parchments. "I know this is hard, but I assure you it is for the better, Princess. Your uncle is a beacon in this trying time."

Laine scoffs for the both of us. The woman might think otherwise, but Uncle is only helping us because Laine promised him something. What that is isn't hard to imagine, but I refuse to get wrapped up in thoughts of how she's giving everything up to save our parents...to save me.

Laine clears her throat, glancing at Uncle. "Now that the three of us have met, is it necessary for you to come to the castle tomorrow to perform your inquest?"

"Of course. A simple meeting doesn't absolve you from the rest of the steps, First Princess. I'll arrive by carriage, mostly likely before sunset. Every member of the royal family, with the exception of the second princess, must be present." The auxiliator gestures to the parchments, still in Laine's hand. "Now, if you will be so kind to provide your seal..."

"Here is the seal. Now, please, I'd like to be alone with my sister. I'm also sure you two would like to discuss a few other things privately."

Uncle narrows his eyes, as does the auxiliator, but neither says anything. Tight-lipped, they step out of my chambers while Laine sits in the chair beside my bed.

She looks at the sunlight trickling in through the window above. "I'm sorry you had to witness that, Alyssa. They're vicious...the lot of them. But let's not speak of such matters anymore, huh? Rather, are you excited for the special day?"

Special day? It's not Mother and Father's anniversary. It's not the day of the attack.

"I'm not sure what we're going to do for your nineteenth, but I'll be certain to make it special, Alyssa. Even if you're stuck here."

Oh, that's right! One week from now will mark the day Terra brought me into this world, the day I took my first breath.

My annual celebrations of life have always been simple, usually spending time with family in the castle. But this year, that isn't possible, and nothing Laine can do will compare, will it? Because I'm stuck in the healing temple, and Father and Mother aren't here.

Besides, more important than my birthday celebration is finding out what is plaguing the fairies. I need to find a way to get back to the other plane. I try not to think about it, just like I've been trying not to think about Wren and anything else aside from my sister and the battle she's—we're—about to fight. But I still feel I have responsibilities to them.

Laine rests her head on my lap. "May I just stay here a minute? I'm quite tired and could use a nap."

Soon after, Laine's light snoring fills my chambers. She stays there, pressed against me, sleeping. And strangely enough, I'm at peace.

Breaking that peace is White Robe Jeon. He knocks lightly on the wooden doors, but Laine does not stir. He opens the door, stepping inside quietly, much like a cat desperate to remain hidden. "How are you, Alyssa? I decided to make a quick visit, if that's alright with you," he whispers.

I smile, or at least I do so in my head.

White Robe Jeon hasn't been a part of my care for the past couple of weeks, but his effort rivals that of those who are. He's visited me every few days since they moved me to the temple's west wing. Apparently, it's where changels requiring middle-tier care stay.

Today, a spark lights up his face. And I have a feeling that spark has a lot to do with Laine. He watches her, reaching out a hand as if to touch her face. But he ultimately withdraws, staring at his hand as if it moved on its own.

Laine's eyes open just as White Robe Jeon turns on his heels to leave. "Eric," she calls.

He spins around, blushing. Does Laine notice?

She must not. "What are you doing here?" she asks.

"I just came to visit the second princess. See how she's faring. The white robes, regents, and vorns do seem to be treating her well, though. So I shall take my leave."

Wiping the spittle off her chin, Laine sits up in her chair. She muffles a yawn. "How—how are you?"

"I'm good," White Robe Jeon says, but the words come out unsure. "Actually, would you like to accompany me for a bit?"

Laine glances at me, then back at White Robe Jeon. "Sure," she says. "I should also be on my way back to the castle. I have to prepare for my uncle's stay."

Promising to return soon, Laine kisses my forehead. But her kiss is hot, her touch like fire.

I swallow hard, but my saliva feels like shards of glass in my throat, and the walls of my chambers have begun to close in on me.

I close my eyes, letting out a piercing scream that threatens to rip me apart.

It just might have.

Because when I open my eyes, I find myself standing upright,

THE PRINCESS OF THORNWOOD DRIVE

my dress the color of dead leaves. The sun overhead is no longer a sun, but a star that seems to let off dusty smog in waves.

Perched on a log eaten by black flies twice her size is Emerald.

I run toward her. "Emerald, what's going on?"

She lifts her head, staring at me like I've become a stranger in the past several weeks. Maybe I have.

"It's me, Alyssa," I say.

And even though it takes a while, Emerald's eyes glint awareness that can't be denied.

"What's happening?"

She nestles her head against my finger, giving a weak tug before pointing west.

I start to walk, Emerald perched in my hands. Her wings have lost their shine and have shrunk in size. I follow her directions through the dying fields of flowers until we come to a stop.

My breath rumbles in my chest as I back away slowly from the edge of the Dark Forest where she's led me. Wren told me entering the Dark Forest in this plane is certain death. And now it has begun to encroach upon the fields of flowers, much like a slow-moving wave desperate to ravage whatever is in its path.

From it, black smoke rises to cast dark-rimmed clouds in the sky.

My breath hitches. "The realm is dying, isn't it? The Dark Forest is swallowing it whole."

Emerald nods, confirming my fears.

"What do I do to stop this? How can I—I save you?"

"Your sister will soon wage a secret attack on the dark prince. Ensure she wins, and you shall save us all." The voice comes from within the darkness, hitting me like a single beam of light that warms my skin, makes my senses tingle despite the thick air rife with death.

"Mother," I call out, but there's no answer.

And before I know it, I'm back at the healing temple.

CHAPTER
33

LAINE

I wasn't exactly expecting the social worker's visit to the house to be peaches and roses, but every other minute she has some offhanded comment on the state of the house, things that I can't afford to buy that will revolutionize Alyssa's care. Of course, there is some truth to it. I can't buy a better mechanical bed or renovate the bathroom more than I already have to suit Alyssa's needs. Still, as the walk-through continues and Freidmore jots notes, it starts to feel like it's not a matter that I can't afford those things despite all the hard work. Rather, I'm simply not trying hard enough.

I walk a few steps behind Freidmore and the social worker, telling myself it's almost over, to keep it together. But then comes a comment from the social worker that has me charging past her and Freidmore.

"I must say I'm glad Alyssa has an uncle willing to step up. From the beginning, I had concerns about Laine's mental state, especially with regard to caring for her sister."

I mean, how dare she? Sure, I had a little rough patch right after the accident, but I've done everything in my power since then to make sure Alyssa is cared for.

Freidmore chases after me. "You can't just storm out."

"Watch me!" I snap, and I burst through the doors and into the backyard, certain I'm about to have a panic attack if my uncle utters another word.

My legs feel wobbly as I plant my butt on a bench in the garden. The bench is in desperate need of a paint job, the white paint now yellowed and worn away completely in several spots to reveal the brown wood beneath.

I haven't had time since the accident to do much house maintenance. But it's not like it matters now. It'll be Freidmore's problem soon enough.

"I'm trying to put my best foot forward. The least you can do is put yours, Laine." Freidmore blocks out the rays of the setting sun like the asshole he is.

A sharp retort should be easy given how angry I am, but panic has begun to stir in my stomach.

"I'm trying," I mutter, tears welling in my eyes, making them burn.

"If snapping at me in front of the social worker is what you call trying, then you're hopeless," Freidmore says, and bingo—I'm a hot mess in an instant, my hands shaking. Thoughts that aren't even relevant begin to rise to the forefront of my mind, dizzying me. "I know I'm hopeless. I—I killed them, after all, you know?"

Freidmore's brows shoot up, and again he looks so much like Dad. Honestly, that was the hardest part of this whole inspection. Every time the social worker made some snide remark about my shortcomings, Freidmore would stare at me, and I'd see my father looking at me with eyes that shone with disappointment.

"Excuse me?" Freidmore takes a step away from me. It's a smart move. I'm bad luck.

"They're dead because of me." The words are soft, but somehow they drown out the sounds of the garden insects, the birds, the social worker shuffling about the back porch.

"If I just came home for my birthday, if I didn't pretend I was sick, they—they wouldn't have come to visit. They'd be alive. Alyssa wouldn't be..."

Freidmore closes the distance between us, his movements jerky. "Laine," he starts, but I've begun to breathe quickly. If I don't calm down, I'm gonna pass out.

"Do you want me to call the paramedics?" the social worker asks, but Freidmore shakes his head.

It makes sense he'd tell her not to. He wants me dead. If I die, he can just absolve our agreement...let Alyssa go to some government home, and take the house.

Does he really want you dead, though? my jumbie asks. Her tone is soft, too soft for the inner voice I've learned to hate. She's been nice to me lately, rarely popping up, whispering kind words when she does. Does she fear I'll off myself? To say I didn't think about it when I snuck back into the barn to return Ana's gun would be a lie.

Maybe that's why she's been so nice to me. If she pushes too much and I decide to take my life, she'll die, too. So she's switched gears.

"I'm...a murderer," I stammer, spittle trailing down my chin, eyes blinking so much it's like I'm watching Freidmore through the shutter of a camera.

His hands dig deep into my shoulders as he shakes me. "Laine, breathe!"

I can't breathe. My rampaging thoughts fight to be spoken. I happily oblige them, rambling words that don't allow me to catch my breath.

Instead of sitting beside me on the bench, Freidmore kneels in front of me, and I think, for a sliver of a second, of Eric. The way he managed to calm me down. There's no way my uncle can manage to do the same. However, him, in his perfectly ironed khaki pants, on his knees, slows the cogwheel of thoughts.

He presses his arms against the bench, locking me in place, holding my gaze. "You didn't kill your parents, Laine."

A hitched laugh escapes from the pit of my stomach. "You don't know that."

"But I do," Freidmore snaps, and when I look at him, really look at him, his blue eyes are like the underbelly of a brewing storm. He looks angry. Sad. Regretful. Why?

"Gerald called me a day before the accident. Our conversation was brief, as you might imagine. We've never seen eye to eye. But…"

"But what?" I shift in that invisible square he's boxed me into with his arms.

"But he mentioned you. He always did the few times we spoke. Said how you're very much like me. Sneaking off from family events to hang out with friends." Freidmore digs his fingers into the chipped wood of the bench, and I'm almost certain I see tears forming in his eyes. It doesn't slow the cogwheel but puts a whole damn wrench in it.

"He was coming to Virginia to surprise you, inasmuch as he was coming to see me. I was to be there for a business trip.

He wanted to discuss something. In hindsight, the business deal that went sour."

His words shatter me into a million pieces. They also piece back together. It hurts. "What—what are you saying?"

"I'm saying your father knew you weren't sick. And if him coming to visit you for your birthday makes you a murderer, so am I."

I'm not sure I process Freidmore's words very much after that. What I do process is that the social worker is standing beside us with a glass of water.

I gulp it down.

And I sit there with Freidmore.

I should thank him for telling me the accident is not my fault. But there's a lot of other stuff that makes *thank you* warble in my throat. Like his letters. The fact that he wants the house. That he refused to acknowledge my father's relationship with my mother.

He must sense my line of thinking. Because when I say, "This does not make us friends," he simply gets up to see the social worker out.

Not eager for any more interactions with either of them, I head to my room and message Caroline.

Prob going to the hospital to see Alyssa in the next few minutes. Is it alright with you if I swing by on my way to grab the stuff?

Her message comes back in almost the same instant I sent mine. *Of course. Anything to help. That said, you sure about this?*

I let my fingers linger over the screen. I might have changed my course of action with regard to confronting Robert with a rifle, but that doesn't mean I haven't thought about other ways to bring him down.

One working theory that I quickly scrapped was making a TikTok or Facebook video talking about the situation. I thought if I have enough public support, the police would have no choice but to do their jobs. But chances are high it might turn into a "she said, he said" situation. Not to mention, there'd be no way to fight the defamation lawsuit I'd be sure to get slammed with. That left one remaining option—gathering concrete evidence against Robert. Something so irrefutable they'd have no choice but to put him away.

I type *YES* in all caps. The fact that Robert kept Alyssa's charm in that box of items I'm almost certain don't belong to him means he's the kind of person to keep mementos of his crimes. Maybe there might be evidence to pin him to a crime. Whether or not there is, though, there's only one way to find out. Breaking into Robert's apartment tomorrow morning while he's at work.

The only good thing about Robert still being able to work is that I have a pretty good idea that he isn't home when I park my SUV a few blocks down Fontaine Avenue.

I readjust the sun hat on my head so the blond wig doesn't shift too much, and I continue down the street.

In my periphery, I see a man walking a dog, a couple pushing a stroller. It's a picture-perfect day in Serca, which is all the more reason I couldn't come in my regular attire. Baseball cap, jeans, beat-up Converse? People would notice me. Especially if they think to check the cameras later.

Head tilted downward so my face isn't visible, I enter the building at the end of the street. The lobby attendant is a young woman, setting out packages by different mailboxes to my right.

I whip out my phone just as her gaze settles on me. "Hey, I'm coming up right now. Sixth floor, right? Also, do you have a pair of sneakers I can use? My feet are killing me..."

I press the elevator button, exhaling a big breath as the lobby attendant's attention shifts back to the boxes.

Bypassing the lobby attendant—check.

I'm sure someone once said it in a spy movie, or maybe I just pulled it from my ass, but it's always best to feed into your fake identity as much as possible...divert any attention from your real goal.

Whatever business I—my cover—has, it has nothing to do with Robert whatsoever. However, once the elevator spits me out, I escape into the stairwell. I take a moment to orient myself, noting there's a camera at every level cemented in the top-right corner. I do my best to stay in the blind spots while making my way to the fourth floor, where Robert lives. If a camera does manage to pick me up, my gaudy hat and blond wig obscure most of my face.

I poke my head out of the staircase, watching and listening for movement. When I'm certain no one is going to be strolling out of their apartment anytime soon, I hustle over to Robert's.

On TV, people use hairpins to pick locks, but after watching a dozen YouTube videos last night, I still couldn't wrap my head around it. This credit card trick is my best bet. Just like I saw my father do when I was younger to pop open the bathroom door after I locked it from the inside, I slide the card to the side of the door, right by the handle. I hold on to the knob, forcing the card into the space between the jamb and the lock. It takes some effort, and for a second I think the card is completely stuck, but it dislodges just enough for me to slide it up and down.

Click. The door opens and with it a flood of new anxieties. I'm breaking and entering. If I get caught, there's no way I'm ever going to be able to regain guardianship of Alyssa.

I close the door behind me. There's no time to tear myself up over what might happen. I need to move.

Robert's bedroom looks even more painfully pristine in the daylight. I set my bag on the bed and sink to my knees.

Please. Let it be here. Let it be here. Let it be here.

I repress a string of profanities. The only things under the bed are a couple of boxes of brand-name shoes, a sleeping bag, and a suitcase that turns out to have nothing but clothes and more shoes.

I get up and take a deep breath to ground myself. Maybe he's hidden stuff in the other room. However, a quick check reveals it's empty, as if he never figured out what he wanted to do with the space.

Mind abuzz, I return to the bedroom and sift through the clothes in his drawers, the closet, and the smaller wardrobe wedged next to the side of the bed. But there's no hidden drawers like Caroline told me to look out for, no lockboxes hidden under piles of clothes.

I sit on the edge of the bed, chest tightening as the likely scenarios begin to play out in my head. He could have destroyed any form of evidence after getting questioned by the police. Or he could have another place somewhere...somewhere no one would even think to look.

No. I'd found those charms under his bed. That meant he wanted quick access to those items. So if the evidence is here, and I have a strong feeling it is, it's somewhere close. Somewhere like...

On the wardrobe is a vintage figurine of a Siamese cat. I walk up to it slowly. The rest of Robert's apartment has a minimalist aesthetic. There's nothing unnecessary. No extra lamps, no wall art aside from a large print in the living room. But here, on the wardrobe that has nothing but a few bottles of cologne and deodorant, is an odd cat figurine.

Measuring about the size of two fists, it's heavier than I'd think. I turn it over, only half shocked that the porcelain is hollow.

I stick my pointer and middle finger inside the space, dislodging a small stack of Polaroids bound by a rubber band. It tumbles to the ground, and I bend to pick it up, freezing at the sound of jangling keys and the front door unlocking.

Shit.

CHAPTER
34

ALYSSA

"Niece."

Uncle sits in my chambers with one leg crossed over the other, parchment detailing recent events in our kingdom tucked under his arm. He has golden hair with silver threads and a sharp gaze that pins me in place.

He shifts in his chair, seemingly unable to get comfortable. "I know what you're thinking. Why am I here, right?"

Why he's here is obvious. Whatever bargain Laine made with him mandates he come to the healing temple to satisfy the white robes and the auxiliator. However, I do not understand why he asks the regent for updates on my progress when she enters. His voice carries a hint of concern. I can't tell if it's real.

"I see. Well then, thank you for all you've done," Uncle says once she's done relaying my progress. He directs his gaze back to me as she exits. "Hopefully, once you're better, you can return to the castle. However, until then I will also do my best to ensure you are comfortable. How does that sound?"

He knows I cannot answer, yet he stares at me much like he did the last time he came, almost expectant.

Nothing but the sound of the white robes' instruments and his breathing resounding through the room, after a minute or two, he swipes at his face.

"I'm sorry." He opens up the parchments, obscuring the top half of him from view. "For not being here sooner. I'm . . . sorry."

No. I won't forgive him. He might not have orchestrated the attack on Mother and Father, but he has always made his disdain of my family clear. His feelings right now . . . they're simply a matter of guilt. Still, as Uncle reads what's happening in the kingdom to me, I can't help but feel a sense of peace.

Wherever Laine is at the moment, I hope she feels a sense of peace, too.

CHAPTER
35

LAINE

Hiding isn't an option in a two-bedroom apartment where the only places to hide are under the bed or in the closet. So I make up my mind as I pull the curtain to the side and look down at the fire escape. That's my only out.

I force open the window as quietly and quickly as possible and scramble out, praying the fire escape will hold my weight. I move down the rungs as fast as I can, bag slung over my shoulder, but all too soon I'm out of ladder. And the ground still looks awfully far away.

Shit.

I reach for the wall with my right foot in an attempt to slide my way down, but before I know it, I'm falling. My descent is slowed momentarily as my leg snags on something jutting from the brick walls, but I don't stop to inspect the damage.

Pure adrenaline piloting my body, I run to Main Street, slowing my gait when I meet eyes with a few passersby. However, as soon as I round the corner, I'm running to my SUV.

Heaving for breath, I climb inside and pull my dress up, gasping at the shredded flesh I can see beneath a rip in my tights. I've seen enough *Grey's Anatomy* to know this is going to need stitches.

I bang my fists against the wheel and groan. If I go to the hospital, it will lead to questions about how I was injured, and questions will lead to flimsy explanations that might raise a few brows. I can't afford that, not when there are already eyes on me.

I rest my pounding head against the wheel. There is one person who might be able to help and do so without judging, but to get him involved...

Screw it. When he gave me his number a couple of days ago, he told me don't ever hesitate to call. It's worth a try.

Hands trembling, I fish in my bag for my phone and call Eric. The phone rings once, twice, a third time.

I tighten my grip on the phone as the fourth ring starts. I didn't think that he might be working a shift. Might be busy with his mom. Might be—

A bit of static comes first, then an enthusiastic, "Wow, well look who called? Gotta say I'm surprised."

"I—I need help," I say, skipping over greetings. "Do you think you can help me?"

The enthusiasm in Eric's voice peels way to leave nothing but urgency. "What do you mean? Where are you?"

Pain shooting up my leg, I ask him if he's willing to take a look at a very bad "cut."

He sends his location in almost the same instant, and after taking one final moment to steel my nerves, I turn on the ignition and make the three-mile drive to his apartment complex.

He's waiting for me in the parking lot, thank God. My leg is on fire.

He opens the door to the SUV, eyes widening as soon as they land on the "cut" in question. "That's less a cut and more a gash! We should go to the hospital. Get it sutured."

"No," I snap, but I calm myself quickly. He's my only hope right now. "Stitch it up here. Please."

It could be the tears in my eyes or the shrillness of my voice, but he helps me out of the SUV. As he slings my arm around his shoulder, he shifts his body to close the door, but I stop him, reaching into the vehicle to grab my bag.

He doesn't question it, silently helping me hobble from the parking lot to the couch in his studio apartment. Straight-faced, he lays me flat on my back and uses throw pillows to prop up my right leg. He doesn't flinch as the blue cotton gets blood-stained.

"I have a suture kit I used in medical school to practice for my surgery rotation." He winces. "No numbing medication, though. Are you sure—"

"It's fine," I say. "I'll put up with it. Please, just get it to stop bleeding and make sure it doesn't get infected."

Nodding, Eric leaves and returns with a glass of water, a bottle of iodine, cotton balls, and the suture kit.

He stares at me pleadingly one last time, but I grab one of his cushions and squeeze with all my might. "Do it."

Eric begrudgingly obliges. What follows is five minutes of bottled screams, tears, and more tears. A two-minute break. More screaming and tears. Another break, this one lasting five minutes. One final set of tears and screams as Eric puts in the last of thirteen stitches.

Eric coats the wound with a handful of bacitracin before bandaging it.

I stare up at the ceiling, sweat trickling into my eyes as the last of my tears dry. "Finally."

Eric breathes into his hands as he sits in the chair beside the couch. "Finally is right. You owe me big-time, you hear?"

He's not wrong, but there's just one problem with his statement. "I don't have anything to give you, unless treating you to lunch works."

He smiles at that, a surprising painkiller that helps reorient my thoughts on what landed me here in the first place. Propping myself up, I grab my bag off the ground and pull out the small stack of photos bound by a rubber band.

Eric leans forward. "What is it?"

"Hopefully, proof to put Alyssa's real abuser away."

The disgust that flares in his eyes is palpable, but he doesn't get up or look away. He remains seated, as if ready to help me shoulder whatever it is I'm about to see.

Bracing myself, I flip through the pictures, bile creeping up my throat by the time I'm looking at the fifth photo of her. Reena. Possibly late teens. In compromising positions.

It could be mistaken for some crazy BDSM fantasy, only her eyes are like that of roadkill, completely still. Dead. And in the last photo, her nose is bleeding.

Eric shields his eyes, even though he's already looking away. "You should take that shit to the police."

I shove the photos back in my bag. "I can't. Robert isn't in any of them, and if you haven't guessed it already, I didn't just stumble upon these. Worst of all, Reena's relationship with Robert...it's complicated."

Eric gets up and leans against the wall, skin already pale but going paper white. "I have something to tell you."

His tone of voice reminds me of when he told me of Alyssa's diagnosis. I brace myself. "What?"

He avoids eye contact. "Can't be sure, since she had longer hair and seemed some years older, but the woman in the photos?" There's nothing but his heavy breathing before he lets it out. "I think I saw her in Alyssa's room when I ran up to the wards the other day."

My adrenaline stores must be empty because I'm too tired to yell for an explanation. I just stare at him, waiting.

"I didn't say anything, since I had just assumed she was a friend of yours."

The word *friend* spikes into my brain like an icepick. I ignore the pain. "Why the hell would think you that?"

Eric looks up at me, face twisted with a guilt it wasn't my intention to incite, and says something that echoes in my head long after he's said it. "She actually seemed concerned about your sister."

ALYSSA

Laine delivers the news while dressed in light armor. She holds on to me, explaining that to win the battle against the prince, we must wield a special magic that only one person can use. And that person is none other than Reena.

"If I fail to convince her...if we fail...the kingdom will be lost." Her body begins to rack with sobs. But before I even dream of holding her, I'm ripped back to the other plane—dim and reeking of death.

"I need to go back," I scream. "I need to go back to my sister!"

"And you will, soon enough. But save your strength, dear child," a voice demands.

"No. I must...I must...go..."

Each limb grows heavy as slumber takes me into a choke hold. "Who...are you?"

"That, right now, does not matter. Only that you rest, child. For the battle—your battle—is near."

I try to stay awake, but this magic is too powerful. Unable to fight it, I sink to the ground and sleep.

CHAPTER
37

LAINE

I pull the hood of my rain jacket over my head. When I explained to Eric how I had no idea where Reena was, he made a simple suggestion—why not just call her?

I had stared at him like he was stupid. I mean, I did have Reena's number. She gave it to me the day before one of the outings on which Alyssa had supposedly lost her bracelet charm. It was so I wouldn't send the phone straight to voicemail in the event of an emergency.

I didn't expect her to answer. I also didn't expect her to agree to meet me.

On the count of three, I step out of the vehicle. The rain has picked up, but there are no mind-whirling thoughts of car accidents to provoke panic attacks today.

Touching the Polaroids in my pocket to confirm they're there, I dart up the stairs of a crummy motel, struggling not to slip.

I find the room number Reena gave me and, as instructed, knock on the door three times, wait, then knock three more times.

The door creaks open, revealing a cold blue eye.

"I'm alone. Are you gonna let me in or what?" I ask.

The door closes and opens again, this time fully. Reena pokes her head outside and glances left and then right before dragging me inside.

I retreat to the far end of the room, teetering at the edge of one of the twin beds. There's a table with empty bags of what must have been takeout. I can still smell the lingering scent of sesame.

She holds out her hand, voice higher pitched than I've ever heard it. "Did you bring it?"

I hesitate for a moment. These photos are the closest thing I have to evidence, but they're photos of *her*. Holding them hostage? It makes my stomach churn.

I take the pictures from my pocket, and she snatches them from me, immediately covering her mouth as she glimpses the first in the set. "Where—where did you find them?"

I sit at the edge of the bed, inspecting every detail—the tears welling in her eyes, the ruffled shirt, the trembling hands. She doesn't look like someone who'll report me if I tell her the truth. But then again, looks can be deceiving. "You know the Siamese cat figurine on Robert's wardrobe? Found it inside."

She tucks the photos somewhere under her shirt and hunches over. "I've never been inside Robert's apartment. At least, not his new one."

"Really? I thought you two were..." I pause. Before I considered them friends, but those photos...a friend wouldn't do that.

A smile dances on the edge of her lips, and a grimace tries to take back control. "He has rules for me. He can come to my place, but I can't go to his. He can date...I can't. It's been like that since we were kids. As for the cat"—she closes her eyes and keeps them shut—"I found a stray when I was younger. Robert's father was strict with him, but when it came to me...I could get away with things. I wasn't his child, after all. So he told me I could keep the cat as long as I kept it in the section of the house he'd set aside for me and my mother. I fed her over the next few weeks, but one day I came home and she was gone. Robert...he gave her away."

"So he was a cruel piece of shit since he was a kid. All the more reason to tell the world what kind of a person he is. Let's go to the police station."

Reena shakes her head aggressively, stuttering, "No. I—I have no intention of turning him in."

It takes a moment for me to process those words, but Reena waits patiently for my response. "I don't get it. Then why did you agree to meet me?"

She flashes me the photos before tucking them back under her shirt. "If anyone should have these, it's me. That's it."

"Bullshit! Why did you visit Alyssa in the hospital then?"

Reena presses up against the wardrobe next to a decrepit-looking bathroom, arms wrapped tightly around herself. "I've been doing my own form of reparations...saving people who have the unlucky fate of meeting him. Some might call it warped, but in my own way, I've been trying to lessen his impact on people. Ensuring they don't suffer too much when they come face-to-face with him...that side of him." She looks at her feet. "But...but there are good sides to him, too. Kind...caring—"

In less than three seconds, I've boxed Reena in place with both of my arms. "Listen to me, he's manipulating you! Get a hold of yourself. Let's go to the station. Make a report. Bring him down!"

She runs a hand through her hair, her fingers catching knots she pulls right through without a squeal of pain. "You're the youngest girl he actually took an interest in, you know that? For a minute there, I thought you might also be the one to see through his ruse. But you were so clueless. You still are. Otherwise, you'd realize there's no bringing him down. Just look at what happened to Bennett!"

"Don't tell me..."

She shoves me back. "Not in the way you might think, but yes. Robert...he has a way with words. And Bennett was always struggling mentally. My guess is whatever he told Bennett sent him over the edge. Which is why I can't help you!" She grabs my arm and pulls me to the door. "I've seen too many women speak out against rich men who aren't even half as crafty as Robert, and lose. I won't put myself through that. So, please leave! Now!"

"Wait, Reena. Please! You have to—"

The door slams shut, and panic begins like a cluster of sparks, exploding in my chest.

Breathing becoming more rapid and shallow, I hold on to the railing to steady myself.

100. It's okay, Laine.
99. It's not.
98. You need to calm down.

97. How the fuck can you calm down?
96. Just breathe.
95. You'll figure shit out.
94. Judging by what Reena said, that's not likely.
93. Breathe, Laine! Fucking breathe!
92. . . .

I climb into the SUV and rest my head against the wheel, panic whirring and whirring until suddenly there's silence and something much worse than panic sets deep in my bones. Something I'm unable to shake even when I return home. Resignation.

CHAPTER
38

ALYSSA

Marcella arrives to my chambers first, followed by a fair-haired woman named Caroline. Laine and Uncle arrive next, followed by White Robe Jeon shortly after.

Caroline holds up a covered dish and a satchel with wooden cups. "I brought warm tea and sweets."

"Thank you. I can't tell you how much I appreciate your presence," Laine says. She glances at Uncle, staring from across my chambers with arms crossed. "Caroline, you two are not acquainted, but that is my uncle. Uncle, this is a dear friend."

Introductions complete as the two exchange nods, Laine and White Robe Jeon situate themselves at the side of my bed. Together, they help me get into a dragon chair much larger than the one I have at the castle.

"How can we be sure the second princess's health won't fail once she leaves her chambers? Is the head white robe even allowing this?" Uncle asks.

White Robe Jeon points to engravings on the chair's arms, and the headrest that juts out from the chair's back. "It's been spelled with magic to alert us of any issues. As for the white robes seeing about the second princess...most have agreed, but we must move quick. It's uncommon to move changels in Alyssa's state to and fro. Only reason they're making an exception is that it's the eve of her nineteenth year."

Tethered by invisible threads, we huddle together as we leave my chambers. When we get to a clearing in the temple from where moonlight leaks through the roof, Uncle pauses. "Are we sure about this?"

Laine sighs. "You have the option of waiting in her chambers, Uncle. You do know that, don't you?"

Uncle responds by way of an elevatus spell. Bodies collectively afloat, the magic dissipates once we're on the roof of the temple, wind stealing our breaths.

Laine gathers everyone in a circle as fire emits from her fingertips. She passes that fire to the others—little balls of flame that manifest in their hands.

I don't feel insulted that I'm not gifted with a little piece of her. My magic is too weak in this realm to control the flame she shares with the others.

Fire cupped in their hands, everyone, even Uncle, begins to sing an ode to my life, their voices pleasant despite the slightly disjointed rhythm. It makes me feel warm inside but not as warm as I feel when Laine takes a deep breath, calling upon all of her magic.

Caroline and Marcella continue to sing, but much like White Robe Jeon and Uncle, I watch, stunned, as Laine's flames transform the air around her into hot ribbons of light. Those ribbons whisk upward with the air, flickering in tune to the rhythm

Caroline and Marcella sing. It shines with glory, restrained yet wild, pained yet happy. And Laine is its master, calling to not only it but all those gifted with flame, to the creatures birthed from the flame itself.

Dragons.

Only one appears tonight, wild and true as its silver scales catch the glimmer of the moon. It doesn't look back at us, but it has sensed Laine's magic. And it lets out a raw cry that could only have reverberated through Laine to reveal hidden truths. For when the fire dissipates from her fingertips, she stands in front of me, arms pulled closer to her core.

"I'm—I'm sorry, Alyssa, but I failed," she mutters.

I understand immediately that Reena must have refused to help us take down the prince. But it's worse. Much worse.

A man wearing fine blue garments greets us upon our return to my chamber, staff in right hand. Everyone, White Robe Jeon included, watches curiously as he asks my sister to speak in privacy.

Laine stares at me with that forlorn expression, but there's a sliver of urgency... of fear.

I swallow hard. Even if she wants to, denying the blue robe's request is uncouth. They ensure Terra's divine will be carried out, and the ruling family isn't excluded. However, nothing about this feels right.

"What is this about?" Uncle asks.

"A Mirendalian villager trespassed into a neighboring kingdom, and I am obligated to see whether or not the first princess here is aware of the situation."

No. They'll take her from me. Imprison her if they see fit.

However, before I can see it come to pass, I'm torn from my plane and sent careening to the other.

"I need to go back," I scream. "I need to go back!"

"And you will, soon enough. But for now, you must help her from here," the voice says.

I look down at the few daisies left alive in a field of death. A few feet ahead is the Dark Forest. Soon enough, it'll be by the lake, poisoning it with rottenness.

"Mother? Is that you?" I call.

Her voice comes like disjointed whispers, much like when Omniscius's leaves spoke a message to me.

If Wren's warning didn't echo in my mind, I'd risk darting into the Dark Forest. Fighting whatever creatures lurk in its murky depths waiting to prey on the weak. But I need to help Laine.

A squeal comes from somewhere below me, and I look down to find Emerald on the ground, her breaths slow and painful. Her skin has become so thin I can see the blood pulsing beneath.

She says something to me, but her voice, once sweet like honey, is now a screech.

"It's okay. Rest," I tell her, but I imagine she has no other option. If I don't help Laine win this battle, the creatures in this plane who did so much to help me will also die.

I glance at Emerald, then back at the Dark Forest. My parents' voices no longer echo on the wind.

Laine's efforts might not have worked, but there has to be some way. What if I could reach Reena somehow? She is the key to saving us all.

But to share a thought with her would weaken me, no?

I shake my head, as if I can shake out self-doubt. Wren risked his life to protect me. So did Freah. So did Emerald. Who would I be if I didn't try?

Wren's voice, his kiss, him calling me a princess, come to mind with the answer. I wouldn't be Alyssa Highland, second princess of Mirendal. Daughter of Gerald and Maya Highland.

So, fighting back tears, and thoughts of Wren and love, I channel all my energy to connect with Reena, just as I did Laine. As the spell spills from my lips, the skies begin to change, and in it, I see Reena, cloaked and maneuvering into a healing temple.

My cloaked visitor—it was she.

The revelation serving as motivation, I concentrate as the sky ignites with images of Reena in the present, sitting in a dark room.

Her love for the prince envelops me as our connection grows, but so does her bitterness…her hate…her regret. And I can feel it—she's always wanted to absolve herself of the evil. Laine brought her to the cusp of taking that path, but Reena needs one final push.

A push from me.

Closing my eyes, I pray to Terra that what I'm about to say will bind the pieces of her the prince has shattered. "I'm with you, and we are not alone."

Reena choruses my thoughts with sobs that echo through the plane. Yet eventually she rises and pulls curtains aside for light to trickle into her chambers.

I drop to my knees as sweet relief floods my veins. The tide of this battle is about to change, and I'm ready to witness every moment of it by way of the skies. Comfort, however, is a fleeting thing.

My parents' voices ring out from the Dark Forest, its darkness growling to devour Emerald and me whole. "Prepare yourself, Alyssa."

I force myself to my feet and scoop Emerald into my arms, screaming through pain threatening to wrench me in two. "Prepare for what?!"

My parents say it in unison, and everything stills. "The prince. He's coming."

LAINE

My heart is still racing well after Freidmore and I return home. I wonder if his is racing, too? It must be. After all, we just committed a crime.

He heads straight to Mom and Dad's room as soon as we're inside. I don't bother to shower or brush my teeth, just climb right into bed.

When the police officer showed up at the hospital, I walked toward him as best I could without limping and asked him what he wanted.

He said it deadpan, as if he was waiting for a confession as opposed to an alibi. "Robert Remson reported a break-in two days ago. Where were you between the hours of ten a.m. and two p.m.?"

I couldn't find the energy to conjure a believable lie. So I opened my mouth ready to speak the truth.

But just before I could get the words out, Freidmore was at my side, arms crossed. "Lawyered up already, did you?" the officer asked snidely.

Before I could tell the officer otherwise, Freidmore turned what was supposed to be an interrogation of me into an interrogation of the officer's sleuthing skills. He also made it very clear he deemed the police showing up at the hospital on such a special day as nothing less than harassment.

Unable to sleep or think straight, I head downstairs to the living room. Before the accident, on birthdays, we'd usually gather as a family to watch old home movies. Keeping up tradition, and eager for a distraction, I fire up the tablet Dad kept with all the videos and pair it with the TV, starting a playlist that begins with Alyssa's first riding lesson. The next is her first riding event. It's followed up with a mini-competition we had among ourselves at Ana's stables.

I sit up, feeling the anticipation all over again even though I already know the outcome of our race. All that anticipation swings back to anxiety as someone sits beside me, and I jump off the couch.

"Wow, do I look like that much of an old gremlin?" Freidmore asks with a cocked brow.

He doesn't look so much a gremlin as a bit of a wax figure—too clean-cut and straight-faced even when his voice seems rather flippant. Honestly, I'm surprised he even came to Alyssa's birthday party at the hospital earlier. He doesn't seem to enjoy such events. Especially *our* events.

I slide back onto the couch slowly. Be that as it may, I would be sitting in jail right now if it weren't for him. "You lied to the officer for me. Why?"

He whips his head toward me. "Now, now, I didn't lie. I simply told the officer that you're my niece. And not a blond, after he showed me that picture of the person caught on camera."

Aside from the hat and wig, the snapshots were too grainy to make out any true distinguishing facial features. And as for the skin tone? Well, per Freidmore, looked like a blonde with a heavy tan.

I thought the officer would never buy that shit. No way. However, he apologized to me—or rather to Freidmore—for wasting our time.

Perks of being a white man, I guess. And rich.

"But you could have said nothing. Let him haul my ass away. Why didn't you?"

Freidmore rests his hands on his lap and stares at the television. "Quite frankly, I'm not one hundred percent certain, but if I had to say something, it'd be because you're my niece. Alyssa, too. And while you haven't been *kind* enough to share all the pieces of what's going on, I got the feeling that whatever you did…" He smiles as TV me does a victory dance for the camera. "I have the feeling why you did it negates however wrong I might think it is."

Tongue rooted to the base of my mouth, I just sit there, watching…watching…watching. Until all those bottled-up frustrations begin to spill out one by one, and soon Freidmore is offering input.

"Since you've been honest with me, I'll be honest with you. I looked into the Remson boy after our Zoom call, and you were right to assume you need hard evidence. I don't want to say it, but unless Reena brings an accusation, the police won't get involved. And even if they were and this was to go to court, their complicated relationship…"

"She's been manipulated by him since they were kids. Surely, that'd count for something?"

He frowns, and I squeeze the sides of my head as I hunch over. "He's gonna get away with it, isn't he?"

Freidmore doesn't attempt to rub my back or anything. I have a feeling that might be too quick too soon. However, there is a pressure that I can read in his eyes. Distanced from Alyssa and me as he might be, he cares about what's happening, and that makes me feel a bit better.

He gets up. "We should get some rest. Tomorrow is a new day."

I swipe my fingers along the tablet. "I'm gonna stay. Watch a few more."

"Okay," he says, pausing as his phone begins to ring.

He stares at the number.

"Work?" I ask.

"Something like that," he says, and he answers all the while staring at me.

"This better be good. What…Are you certain? When?" He continues looking at me, that pressure from earlier deflating, that edge to his voice dulling.

He leaves the living room and returns with his laptop. "Laine, take a look at this."

I keep my hands on the tablet, gaze trained on him. "What is it?"

"Just do it," he snaps, and like a child getting scolded, I walk over to the laptop he's placed on top of the piano. My body stills as I see the online headline.

Son of Remson Industries Founder Charged with Multiple Counts of Rape

Below it is a subheading, noting that he was rushed to the hospital after being found by arresting officers to have taken a bottle of pills. Before I can read any more details, my own phone rings. I recognize the number immediately and spare us both any greetings. "Why?"

Reena's breaths are strangely audible, as if she's breathing for the first time. "It's gonna sound strange, but I guess... I just had the energy to do it? I tried doing it a few times before but could never follow through. This time, I don't know. I... just did it."

"But what about not wanting to go to court? Him getting away with it?"

"Robert had me so wrapped up in his delusions, I didn't think the pictures would make a difference, but Robert has more photos. Not just of me but others. Some, like your sister, not capable of consent."

"I searched his entire apartment. I didn't find any other pictures," I say, preparing myself for this bit of hope to come crashing down, just like everything else has.

Reena sighs. "Of course you wouldn't have. He kept the majority somewhere he could have even easier access—his office. Place looks pretty typical, but there's a hollow book on his shelf. He didn't think I knew about it, but when you've been in love with someone for so long, you notice all the little things they're trying to hide. But you know what? He... he can't hide anymore. That's why..." The breaths stall, and there's something resembling a cry. "You might hate me for saying this, but I hope he lives."

"I hope he lives, too," I say, because I don't want him taking the easy way out. He deserves to be tried... to suffer. That said,

I won't say more than I need to. After all, I'd be silly to think this is easy for Reena, that part of her isn't torn up over everything. So I silently hope she finds comfort with my agreeing with her before telling her thank you.

"No. Thank your sister," she says, and with that she hangs up.

Hands in the air in exaltation, I prance around the living room. Freidmore joins by way of affirming head nods. The world knows now what kind of person Robert is. This is our celebration.

However, it isn't meant to last. Freidmore gets one more call. From the hospital.

CHAPTER
40

ALYSSA

The fault line splits the earth in two as I follow it, my feet taking me forward despite the pain assaulting me with each step. Emerald digs her tiny nails into my palms, and somehow that helps me remember I'm alive. I'm not dead.

The path we're following narrows until we come to the lake.

Standing on the surface, in the middle of mermaids desperately trying to sink back into the watery depths, is the dark prince. His head tilts to the side as we make eye contact, and Emerald squeezes my finger, pointing in the direction of the Dark Forest, now just a few yards away.

She doesn't need to say anything for me to understand she's giving me a warning. Because I can feel the dark prince's thoughts.

He wants to stay in the Dark Forest. There, he'll be able to escape punishment from Terra. Ensure we'll never find the king and queen.

The dark prince lets out a laugh, but it sounds more like an empty scream in my ears, the pain of a monster who knows their options have dwindled and the only option left for them is a wicked death.

Still dressed in his armor from the battlefield, he takes a few steps toward me, each movement calculated. "To think Reena would betray me in battle. That whore!"

"She saw the error in her ways, and saw you for what you are," I bark.

The dark prince's eyes widen as he looks me up and down, my body threatening to drift with the thick air that settles over us. "You're the one who convinced her to give up my position to your sister, aren't you?"

My body wants to collapse, but I force myself to stand tall. "I am. I'm also the one who will stop you from going to the Dark Forest. You don't belong in this plane."

"Unfortunately for you, I've taken so much of a sleeping potion that I'm bound to be here eternally. Ample time to make it to the Dark Forest." The dark prince huffs. "But I don't think I need much time. Soon this entire realm will be the Dark Forest, and I shall sleep in forever night, untouched by your sister. Untouched by Terra's justice."

It's strange. Despite the dark prince's beautiful skin, I see the rancid hide of his decaying flesh, the evil that bubbles up to the surface.

"You must send him back," says a familiar voice, and my eyes find Freah, beached up on the shores of the spelled lake.

I glance over my shoulder. The Dark Forest is quickly approaching. Within minutes it'll be here.

"Do you think she can best me with magic, mermaid?" The dark prince scoffs. "There's nothing left in her."

He's right. I can't beat him in magic. I never finished my

spell-caster classes. I never—I shake my head. I won't doom myself to failure before I begin. Not when my sister is in the other plane, fighting for us.

I stand in the dark prince's path. "Why?"

"Why what?"

"Why do the things you did? Were you born shrouded in darkness?"

The dark prince looks up at the hazy sky as if it holds all the answers. "Does it matter? Maybe I was born steeped in darkness. Or maybe I acquired it after I was born due to the cold indifference of my father."

He glances at the sigil—the letter *R*—on his armor. "I debated it once, you know? Killing the man who made me. But alas, it would have been too messy. Too much work to pick up the pieces. Besides, I'm not very keen on handling kingdom affairs."

"So what?"

"So I went on doing as told, speaking when spoken to. But I honed my magic as I did, observed all the wrongdoings people in power got away with, things that I could get away with. Truly, it's an art form, learning how I can manipulate commoners, changels, and the rich. I was certain I'd be able to control everyone one day." An angry snarl escapes the dark prince's lips. "But to think you and your sister would force me out of my own plane, make me face persecution!"

"You made a mistake the moment you trapped our parents in the Dark Forest. Tell me where they are!"

"I'll take that information with me into the darkness." Laughing, the prince begins running toward the Dark Forest, which kills everything it touches. It approaches us like a shadow, and I can feel myself sinking to the ground, my legs wobbling beneath me.

But then I hear my parents, calling to me. No, not just them. Their voices are joined by the voices of the merpeople, the fairies who are still alive. I'm almost certain I can hear Glior as well, the whinny of Nerra. And pulling on the strength they lend me, pulling on the last bit coursing through my veins, I extend my hands toward the dark prince. "Reditus."

Despite the pain that rips me apart as the word leaves my lips, I smile. Making the dark prince return to the other plane is impossible if I try to do it alone. But all of us, dying as we are, can do so if we stand together.

We can—we will—we do beat him.

Letting out a wild scream, the dark prince starts to walk toward me, but his figure has begun to dissipate.

Bits of his body morph into steam that begins to flutter away with the wind. But his hand makes it around my throat, squeezing.

I don't fight for air because I trust in the strength everyone has lent me. I trust in the strength of my sister. And sure enough, the dark prince's hand evaporates along with his face, rife with anger.

I collapse to my knees once he's gone, each nerve feeling singed, each sound making my ears bleed. Each breath making me want to rip out my lungs. Each second making me scream out.

Until a hand is on my shoulder. No, two hands.

I look up.

"Rise, my child."

I do as told, the movement, much to my surprise, fluid. The pain, much to my dismay, gone.

I spin around. "Father?"

Indeed it's him, and beside him is Mother. They're dressed in the gowns they wore one year ago when we left the castle, their gazes bright, their smiles warm. Behind them is the Dark Forest, but something about it is different. The gloom that clouded the forest line has begun to lift, much like the haze blocking out the sun. Blues and yellows fight for attention in the sky, while greens and whites fight below it.

"What's happening?" I ask as the ground begins to shake and the fairies rise from it.

A single tear streams down Mother's face, but her smile doesn't fade. "It's time."

CHAPTER
41

LAINE

When Freidmore and I get to the hospital, Eric is standing outside Alyssa's room. Several nurses shuffle in and out, and Alyssa's monitor is beeping so loud that I can hear it even when the door is closed.

"What's going on?" I ask, but he doesn't need to say anything. He *shouldn't* say anything.

He already told me over the phone, on my way over, that Alyssa started having trouble breathing. A chest X-ray showed pneumonia, a bad case of it, and that's more than enough information to process.

Eric must not sense the mood, though.

"Her blood pressure is dangerously low. They've started a PICC line, but..." His voice fades out, his implication making my head spin. And his eyes, the way they're glazing over with a despondent look—all of it chips away at the idea I set in stone from the moment all this began.

Alyssa will get better.

"I'm sure there's another option," Freidmore says. "I know of a doctor in New York."

I bite back a bitter chuckle. The thought that money can save Alyssa? It makes my blood curdle and my anger skyrocket. But I hold my tongue. In his own way, Freidmore's trying to help, and if anything, it's a sliver of light—this vague tenderness I'd never have expected from him when it comes to us.

Thankfully, Eric doesn't take offense at my uncle's words about Serca Grace Hospital. He steps closer to me, face flushed. "You should go see your sister."

God knows I want to, but I can't bring my feet to move. I know he's telling me to say goodbye. I dig my nails into my palms. Stepping inside the room and talking to Alyssa is admitting that I don't have hope she'll pull through this.

"Laine, you should...see her," Freidmore says, voice low.

No. Not him, too. We agreed just a few hours ago that Alyssa's strong. That she'll be able to pull through anything. So why the hell is there a sheen to his eyes?

One of the nurses exits the room and plants herself next to Eric. "She's fading in and out. I'm not sure for how much longer." If it's her intention for me not to hear, she's failed.

"Laine," Eric says, "You should—"

I hold up a hand, silencing him. Silencing everyone there. I know what I should do. But I don't want to do it.

I don't want to go in there and watch my sister die.

My jumbie hasn't reared her head in the past several days, but she appears today, out of nowhere. And this time, she isn't scowling.

You'll regret not saying goodbye. You should go.

The jumbie that has taunted me since the accident, the me that has hated myself, issues the command cloaked as a suggestion.

Reluctantly, my feet move toward the room, where the smell of chemicals is rivaled by one thing—the smell of death.

A nurse stands in the corner of the room, tinkering with a portable monitor, while another one watches Alyssa's vitals. She gives me a half-smile, the kind that says she's sorry, before gesturing to a seat next to the bed.

I stare at it for several seconds, feeling my knees creak when I finally sink into it.

My hand finds Alyssa's. Her curls are stuck to her forehead with sweat, the veins beneath her skin visible. Her lips are too dry, and her eyes focus on nothing in particular.

Her breaths come slow, almost as if they don't want to come at all, and I squeeze her hand, resting my head against it.

"Reena went public about Robert," I hear myself saying. "The evidence she provided? We should be able to get justice."

Well, I'm not so sure what will be the outcome. But right now, in front of her, I'll be hopeful. Being hopeful might get her to improve. Hopeful might— Her hand gives mine a light squeeze, and I lift my head, glancing at the nurses. They don't seem to have noticed it. Was it in my head?

No. I refuse to believe it was imagined. I continue to talk to my sister, words warbling in my throat as I fight back tears. "Do you remember when we snuck out of the house to camp in the garden at midnight? Mom and Dad practically shit themselves."

I let out a cross between a laugh and a sob, recounting at least a dozen more memories we had together. Finally, recounting *that* memory as my laugh-cry becomes a straight-up sob.

"I didn't mean for you to get hurt. For Mom and Dad to die. If I could go back and change things, I would. But…"

Another squeeze, this one harder.

I look at the nurses with what must be hellish eyes. "She squeezed my hand! That's a good sign."

"A lot of things happen as…"

I turn to Alyssa, already reasoning what the nurses are going to say. No. Alyssa squeezed my hand. She's—she's pulling through. And she—she understands me.

I scoot closer to her, bombarding her with more memories. More events of our childhood. And even if I'm going crazy, I promise I can see a focus rapidly materializing in her eyes. I can see a sliver of the girl I knew before the accident. I can see my sister.

ALYSSA

Laine stares at me with teary eyes, her silver crown shimmering atop her head like a beacon, one that shines to my left. I look at it—at her—before looking back at my parents, standing in front of the Dark Forest, which is no longer so dark.

"Can she hear us?" I ask.

"No, but she can feel your presence. She knows that you hear her," Mother says.

Her words are like a match, igniting an explosion of sobs. I squeeze Laine's hand, asking what I already know the answer to. "What if she came here? What—what if I stay?"

My father forces a smile, the kind that lets me know I've exhausted all my options. "It is no fault of your own that you cannot stay, Alyssa."

The muscles in my face tighten. Laine and I were strong. We were a force to be reckoned with. We were victorious. And yet this is what we get? Separation? "You two said we'd be together again," I tell my parents. "All of us!"

Their hands press deeper into my shoulders as tears fall from their eyes. Even then, they remain steadfast. "We shall be together again, Alyssa. The day shall come. But today is not that day."

I'm about to protest again, but my parents echo a chant in unison. Emerald, now perched on my shoulder and full of life, echoes it along with all the other creatures present. "One more must die for all to live. When such comes to pass, you shall be reunited with the king and queen."

It takes a minute for me to remember how Omniscius's leaves whispered those words several fortnights ago, how I wondered what they could mean.

My grip on Laine tightens as the swaths of clouds seemingly begin to battle, whisking around one another until they all dissipate at once to reveal him.

Wren. His green eyes materialize in the sky. Where is he? A chamber? My heart gallops as he watches the sea in the distance from a window, listening to the waves crash against the rocks.

"Wren," I call out, desperate to have him see me, hear me.

Terra must bless us because his head snaps to the left, his eyes scouring his chambers. "Alyssa?"

"Can you hear me? I defeated the dark prince!" I say, but Wren continues calling my name.

It's hard—not keeling over with the desperation to hold him. And it takes every ounce of my being to remain steadfast and hope he feels one thing—my love that will surpass any boundary between the planes.

I take in every feature of his face and watch as a tear rolls down his cheek. Does that mean he really can feel me, my heart?

His face twists, and he's breathing so hard I fear for him. But then he forces his lips into a smile, his eyes softening until finally he mutters, "In the next life . . . Alyssa."

Those words piece me together as much as they break me apart. I shudder, and the forest's trees begin heaving collectively, the ground beneath me pulsing in rhythm as it begs—yearns—to embrace me.

Wren isn't the only one I'd be leaving, though.

I grip Laine's hand even tighter while Emerald and the other fairies chant the riddle louder. A world without Laine by my side and a world without me by her side still make little to no sense. However, my fate is sealed, and to be brave is not to outrun it but embrace it. So I brace myself.

LAINE

A character in a movie I can't remember once said that the worst part about dying is knowing you're leaving people behind. I never really paid much attention to it back then, but as the minutes pass, it's the one thing that keeps popping up in my head.

So, steeling myself with strength and courage that go beyond me, I tell Alyssa all about how she no doubt helped protect all the residents at Lake Forest from further abuse. I also tell her about Reena, a victim in all this as much as any other. "I'm sure there are others, and they all wanted to thank you themselves, but"—I clear my throat—"this time is just yours and mine."

I kiss her hands.

ALYSSA

I welcome her kiss to my hand, watching our parents as their golden crowns begin to turn from gold to bronze. And that's when I look back to my precious older sister, the silver crown atop her head also morphing before my very eyes.

LAINE

"I will always love you," I tell her.

ALYSSA

I will always love her.

Drawing on my last bit of energy tethering me to her realm, I speak words I hope she can hear and understand. Words that must resound in her plane, pristinely clear, as her silver crown turns gold.

"Rule well, Queen Laine."

CHAPTER
42

LAINE

They say funerals never get easier, but it's a lie. My parents' funeral was a shit show. I pretty much cried the entire time. When I wasn't crying, I drank; when I wasn't drinking, I was having a panic attack; and when I wasn't having a panic attack, I was tending to guests.

But while tears do come today, I'm not reaching for my bottle of vodka. My Xanax is still in the picture, though, working its way through my system.

I'm holding on to Marcella and Caroline, watching how everyone's heads are down, if not staring at the coffin at the front of the church.

It's dark mahogany, polished, and I wonder if Alyssa finds it comfortable. Father's and Mother's caskets weren't as nice, but then again, Freidmore didn't cover the cost of those.

I hold Marcella's shaky hand as she wipes tears onto her sleeve, helping her sit down when the priest starts to deliver his sermon on death and life. I'm not listening.

I'm just thinking whether or not there's anything after death.

I tell myself there must be, because that makes this entire thing a little less sad.

Once the priest is done, he welcomes me up to give the eulogy.

My feet stall several times as I make my way up to the podium, and I mentally give myself a pat on the back because I feel crushed. I don't want to be here. I want to be at home, with my sister who is never coming back.

I clear my throat as I smooth out the single sheet of paper that was crumpled in my pocket. My voice cracks as I start, and I take a moment to steel my voice. Eric, sitting behind Caroline and Marcella, nods. When I told him how I was struggling to write the eulogy, he suggested instead of writing about the past, write about the future that would let Alyssa know we're doing okay. And as I start to read all the things I hope to do, all the things I know she'd want me to, I can only pray she's holding me in her heart from above, just like I'm holding her in mine.

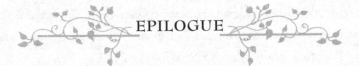

EPILOGUE

Three Years Later

"I hope popping champagne at the cemetery counts as trying new things," I say.

Caroline chuckles. "Oh, I'm sure it does. Hence my insistence we do a toast!"

I stand between her and Eric. Since Alyssa died, I've always come to visit her and my parents every couple of months. But today? It's particularly special. I graduated from college.

Eric keeps a hand nestled on the small of my back, and when I look at him, he wipes away a tear that trickles down my right cheek. I smile. In the two years since we've started dating, there have been many of these interactions in which we somehow get each other without so much as having to speak. I'm grateful for it . . . for him.

"Thank you," I mouth.

"Anytime," he says, barely audible.

"Think you can pour an old fella a cup?" says a crisp voice.

I look over my shoulder at Freidmore, sauntering up to us in a button-down shirt and jeans, something I never would have imagined him wearing three years ago.

But then again, a lot has changed since then. For starters, he never actually took the house from me, although he does visit every couple of months to check in on me.

It was awkward at first. I mean, sure, he was around for Alyssa's final days, but that didn't change a lot of the problematic shit he said before it. However, a few months after Robert was sentenced to life in prison, he gave me a picture of him and Dad with Mom in the middle. Not only did they appear to be in their early twenties, they were all smiles, arms slung around each other. And even though we've yet to discuss it, he uttered four words then: *I loved her first.*

I look up at the clear noon sky, wondering now just like I wondered back then. How would Alyssa have reacted to that photo?

I imagine she'd have asked Freidmore outright what was up. Make him lay out the details of why he distanced himself. In this way, she was different from me, and I tell myself one day I'll work up the courage to discuss it. I imagine Freidmore's waiting on me to do so. But today is not that day.

"Where is Marcella?" Freidmore asks.

"Back at the house. She wanted to prepare some food for when we get back," Caroline says.

Not only that, visiting graves of loved ones is something she finds traumatic. She would rather remember a loved one in the company of the living, and that is quite alright. Alyssa touched many people, and it's important we all honor her in our own way.

Everyone else finally gathered, though, I pull out a letter from my pocket and begin to read aloud.

Dear Alyssa,

It's me. Again. But this day, as I told the others, is a little special. You see, when I spoke at your funeral three years ago, promising to live out a hopeful and bright future, I didn't mean a single word of it. I mean, how could I move on without you? Without Mom and Dad? But there's some truth to the saying time heals all wounds. Although, I don't think it's time per se but the people that come with it . . . the interactions and outpouring of love. Because while I haven't stopped struggling completely, each day that has passed since your death, I've struggled a little less with the help of everyone around me. Pushed myself a little more to see things in a positive light. And finally, I could say it's paid off. I got my bachelor's degree in animal science and a job offer from a fancy stable a few miles outside of Serca as a chief nutritionist and trainer to boot!

I nudge Eric in his side. *"Although, I'm not sure I'm gonna take it. Eric thinks I can go even further . . . should chase after that dream I had growing up. You remember it, don't you? Vet school?"* He runs his hand up my back and squeezes my shoulder gently. *"I guess that's what happens when your boyfriend is a doctor."*

Eyes welling with more tears, I glance at Caroline—the girl who's become my ride or die. She stares at me with brows arched high above puffy eyes. *"Also, I'm proud to say we finally succeeded in making Caroline a horse girl. She joined her college's riding club last month. I imagine she'll do them proud. And before you ask about Marcella, she sends her love, which I'm sure you already knew."*

I tighten my grip on the letter as my gaze settles on Freidmore, his head arched downward. *"As for our dear uncle? Well, and make sure to tell Dad, last month I finally bested him in a race down the old trail behind Ana's stables. He all but asked to go again ten times, but I refused. Better to end on a high note."*

Freidmore rolls his eyes, although his smile doesn't waver. And we both let out something that's a cross between a laugh and a sob. I take a deep breath. *"Three years have passed, baby sis. And as I said three years ago, every visit since then, you'll be forever in my heart . . . forever and always. So."* I take the fifth cup of champagne, knocking it against everyone else's cups, and pour it over Alyssa's grave. *"Cheers to us. And till next time. Yours truly, Laine."*

ACKNOWLEDGMENTS

Firstly, I'd like to thank my cousin June. I know you are happier above.

I would also like to thank the Forever Team: my editor, Leah; assistant editor, Sabrina; publicists Nicole and Estelle; Daniela, for the gorgeous cover; Luria, for shepherding through all the stages of production; and everyone else who has had a hand in bringing this book into the world. I would also like to thank my agent, Lucienne Diver, for seeing my potential and joining me on this journey.

To Isabelle Felix, who read at least three versions of the novel, thank you for all your hard work. It wouldn't be possible without you pushing me to do better not just for myself but for my readers. I also want to thank Elaine Buckner for always telling me what works and what doesn't without pulling punches. Beta and sensitivity reader Kayla and beta reader Jessica Curlock also deserve shout-outs. To my dear friends Daniel Justus, Kimberly Llanos, and Chane Cilliers, I want to thank you not only for reading and providing me with feedback but also for your kind words. Too often, I thought about giving up on this story, but you guys motivated me to keep writing. Joyce Opara, Khristian Brooks, Caroline Paltoo, Gech Nwosu Hickman, Miatta Elvina, Jaeda Stoute, Alexander Johnny, and Davonte Elmore, you also kept the motivation coming; I'm grateful for that.

To my parents, Fay Moreau and Shane Barrett, none of this would be possible without you. Literally (lol). Also, the insight you two provided will always be invaluable. Thank you. To my brother, Ronnie Brown, you have always been in my corner, cheering me on. I want you to know those cheers mean the world. To all my aunts and uncles, especially Claire and Alice, thank you for your prayers. They were heard. And lastly, I want to thank my loving husband, Kendell Padarath. The late-night phone calls in which I debated giving up on more than this story are too numerous to count, but you helped me keep the faith and pushed me to be better. Thank you for being my rock.

AUTHOR'S NOTE

In 2018, a cousin of mine fell into a persistent vegetative state. No longer was she able to talk, walk, or interact with us the way she used to. While hope remained dim, my family continued to rally around her, telling her about our day and asking about hers. I was in my first semester of medical school at the time, and based on everything I was being taught, I should have been well aware that my family's actions wouldn't make a difference. Wouldn't offer her any actual comfort. While that might have been true, I held on to a bit of hope that the spirit hears and knows. And from this, *The Princess of Thornwood Drive* was born.

Writing the novel while juggling medical school rotations wasn't easy, but my school experiences were pivotal in shaping the story. During my clinical rotations and time working as a medical scribe, I saw things that made me proud to be in the medical field. I also saw things that made me question the process… things that made me want to change the system, especially when it comes to persons who are unable to advocate for themselves. Given that I was also grappling with anxiety, depression, and an assortment of symptoms that would later be diagnosed as fibromyalgia, I found myself on an uncertain path.

For a while, I didn't see any light at the end of the tunnel, falling into a mundane cycle of sleeping, waking up, going to school, and repeat. However, as I continued to interact with people from various walks of life, people who often simply needed a listening ear and a touch of kindness, I felt inspired to keep writing. Truly, in the end, writing *The Princess of Thornwood Drive* not only gave me peace, but also the courage to continue pursuing my goal of becoming a doctor.

My undergrad years in Charlottesville, Virginia, provided inspiration for Serca. However, I've always been a fan of small towns, especially those with good coffee shops! Incorporating horses was also a must. Growing up, I had always loved horses and begged for my aunt and mom to put me in horseback riding lessons. Even though they were quite expensive, my family organized for me to take them at a stable a few miles away from our home. My experiences there were some of the highlights of my childhood, with Dirty Dancer, a retired racehorse, becoming a dear member of my family. That said, I had one too many experiences in which my interest in riding was met with confusion. There aren't many black equestrians, after all. As such, it felt important to me to have Laine and Alyssa not just be riders, but great ones at that. Admittedly, riders better than I was (lol).

To delve deeper into the setting and background of the characters, it was important to me to incorporate some elements of Trinidadian folklore. I was born in the US to a Trinidadian mother, although unlike Laine and Alyssa, I moved to Trinidad when I was nine before returning to the US for my last two years of high school and college. To say the transition was easy would be a lie. Upon my return to the US, I experienced several things that made me feel like an outsider, and in my undergraduate years at the University of Virginia, I found myself trying to fit into the mold rather than being proud of my background. Of course, this would be something I overcame with time. Nevertheless, it felt necessary to touch upon the struggles of identity, especially in someone who might feel even more separated from their island culture.

But the folklore represented in this novel is in no way exhaustive. Trinidadian culture is extremely diverse, and while this novel only incorporates some elements, I one day hope to publish a novel that is completely steeped in the culture, with descriptions of foods like cou-cou and roti, trips to Surrey River, and lingo like *back back* (to reverse).

All in all, I hope this story does for readers what it did for me—inspire hope.

DISCUSSION QUESTIONS

1. Given Alyssa's brain injury, one can't help but speculate whether everything that's happening in her fantasy narrative is simply a warped version of the real world. But when Alyssa breaks the dark prince's spell and returns from the realm in the novel's second act, she uses magic to send a mental message to Laine. We see Laine receive this message in her POV via her thinking of Alyssa and experiencing a sudden bout of sickness. Given this, do you think that magic actually exists? Is Alyssa's fantasy narrative completely made up?

2. Eric and Laine butt heads in several of their earlier encounters but become lovers by the end of the novel. Have you ever experienced a love-hate relationship? Have you ever been in a relationship with someone you initially were at odds with?

3. Laine mentions Lake Forest Day Center playing the Tinkerbell movies during one of her visits. She also notes in chapter 1 that Alyssa was a die-hard fan of Harry Potter.

Do you think these influenced Alyssa's narrative in any way? What about the setting, and characters like Wren and Emerald?

4. Laine not only blames herself for the fatal car accident that occurs prior to the story's start, but also drops out of college to make ends meet. She works multiple jobs and does her best to bottle most of her emotions, often letting no one in. However, she later finds a friend in Caroline, Glenn's niece. Why do you think the girls hit it off?

5. Laine and Alyssa's mother is Afro-Trinidadian, and their father is white American. In Alyssa's POV, we see her struggle to merge her cultural identities, especially when she travels from one realm to the next with the help of Glior. What do you think of Alyssa's experience in these other realms? Do you think it helped her to come to terms with the racism and prejudice she felt growing up in Mirendal as a child?

6. The Dark Forest in the other realm is guarded by what someone fears most. For Alyssa, it is the douens—children in Trinidadian folklore with no faces and their feet turned backward. However, Wren notes he sees a woman who lives in a chicken house, rides a mortar, and screams that she's hungry. Based on the woman's description and Wren's last name, do you have any ideas about Wren's possible background? What is your biggest fear?

7. Laine experiences great emotional turmoil when it comes to riding again, as she feels guilty about being able to do something Alyssa is no longer able to. What do you think Alyssa would tell Laine about this? Have you ever been afraid or found yourself no longer able to do something you love?

8. A harmful stereotype in fiction regarding characters with disabilities is that they have to be cured in order to find happiness. Wren, paralyzed in a dragon-riding accident, notes this is precisely why he comes to the next realm—to be as he was before. However, by the end of the second act, we see a shift in Wren's perspective on his injury. We also meet changels like Sam and Veranda who are happy as they are and refuse pity. Were you happy to see this change in Wren? What do you think Alyssa's stance is on the matter?

9. Laine and Alyssa's uncle Freidmore comes to stay with them in the novel's third act, and in the epilogue we learn that he and Laine have grown closer. Why do you think he initially pulled away from his nieces? Do you think Laine should have stayed mad at him?

10. Robert and Reena have a peculiar relationship. Can you think of any factors that may have caused Robert to become the person he did? What do you think of his hold on Reena? Why do you think Reena finally decided to help put an end to Robert's crimes?

11. What would you have done in Laine's place with the knowledge about Robert harming her sister? Was she justified in breaking into his apartment?

12. What did you think of the ending? Would you have preferred an ending in which Alyssa didn't die?

ABOUT THE AUTHOR

Khalia Moreau is a Brooklyn-based doctor and aspiring forensic pathologist who loves writing twists and turns. When she's not in the hospital or doing something book related, you can find her watching anime or K-dramas while snuggling up with her cats.

Find out more at:
    Twitter @kmoreau11
    Instagram @kmoreau11225